Published by I
www.inkub

CW01500588

Copyright © 202‹

Steve Sheffield has asserted his right to be identified as the author of this work.

ISBN (eBook): 978-1-83756-446-0
ISBN (Paperback): 978-1-83756-447-7
ISBN (Hardback): 978-1-83756-448-4

ZERO HOUR is a work of fiction. People, places, events, and situations are the product of the author's imagination. Any resemblance to actual persons, living or dead is entirely coincidental.

ZERO HOUR

AN EDDIE VIRGO THRILLER

STEVE SHEFFIELD

INKUBATOR
BOOKS

CHAPTER 1
TEN MONTHS AGO.
GUERRERO STATE, MEXICO

Where the fuck are they?

Globs of sweat dripped from Eddie Virgo's stubble onto the collar of his lucky shirt. It was the vintage, silk Hawaiian, covered in little, blue sea turtles with matching blue coconut-shell buttons, which came out of the closet every time he had to get personally involved in a ransom drop. Maximum three or four times a year. Never let him down, but there was something different about this case. It made him nervous. He tucked the Glock 19 into his belt and shouldered the Nike duffel that had been carefully stuffed with one-hundred-dollar bills.

Come on, forget it, Virgo. This is what you do…

It was dusk. The abandoned mining town was a single, dust-bowl street of ramshackle buildings, frozen in time. Looked the kind of place Clint Eastwood might ride in on a mule any minute, were it not for signs everywhere of modern blight: graffiti, plastic bags, candy wrappers and .50-caliber cartridges strewn in the undergrowth by the cartels.

He stood in the doorway of the old church and scanned the hills. Nothing moved. No sign yet of the shitbags who'd kidnapped Isabella Alvarez, a forty-six-year-old nurse, then cut off five of her fingers, one for each day they'd waited on their money. Tough guys. Husband Martin Alvarez was a surgeon at a private clinic in Beverly Hills. Even so, it still took time to liquidate assets and get cash. Virgo had brokered the deal down from one million dollars to eighty grand, but that was still way above the going rate in this part of the world, where life was cheap. Not his best work. Maybe it really was time to quit.

Shouts and laughter came from a derelict store across the street. Seemed the officers of the Mexican state police had forgotten they were supposed to be hidden away, and Virgo cursed under his breath. Same old story. As an FBI international negotiator, it was always harder to manage local law enforcement than the actual law-breakers. He pulled out his phone and called Comandante Huesca.

'Tell your men to be quiet.'

'Don't panic.' There was an undercurrent of amusement in Huesca's voice. 'These are amateur narcos we're dealing with tonight.'

'Just remember. Nothing happens until the hostage is recovered safe and well.'

'I remember. Take it easy.' Call ended.

Virgo felt a strange tightness in his chest. He double-checked the handle on the Nike duffel to make sure the stitching looked exactly as it should. The bag had a micro GPS tag sewn into the seam of the handle, which was being monitored at the FBI's Crisis Negotiation Unit in Quantico. Some gangs might suspect a tracker and dump the bag at the first opportunity, but others might not. It was worth a try, as long as it didn't endanger the life of Isabella Alvarez. The Mexican authorities would be informed of the bag's location once the hostage had been released safe and well. It was the usual plan. Tried and tested.

A hot, desert breeze brought the sound of engines down the valley. Virgo ducked back into the church, and a flash of color caught his eye: one of the niches in the stone wall had a wreath of fake flowers pinned on a faded photograph – a makeshift shrine to a loved one. It was less than a year since he lost his own wife, Crystal, and the emptiness in his soul was a constant and all-consuming source of pain. They say time's a healer, but it leaves scars. Maybe they're worse if you don't want to move on.

Hey, come on, there's work to do. Focus…

The only window had a view onto a square, where the village market had once been. He saw the headlights. Two pickups snaked down through the silver birch and scrubland, roared into the main street, and slewed to a stop. Four men climbed out: cowboy boots, Ralph Lauren polos and baseball caps. The shitbags. One cradled a heavy semiautomatic rifle, another held a stainless-steel handgun, like a Dan Wesson Razorback. They stood and looked around for any signs of a setup.

Virgo waited. He needed proof of life. He watched another vehicle coming into town on the same route. It stopped a hundred yards back up the track, lights on, motor ticking over. Just biding its time. More sweat dripped onto the little, blue sea turtles, and some rolled down his back for good measure. Not knowing if a hostage was still alive was the worst part, but there was nothing he could do about it. He slowed his breathing.

Okay, be patient. You know they want the money…

It looked like the guy with the Razorback was the boss. He motioned to two men, and they dragged a figure from the back of a truck. When they removed the pillowcase from her head, Virgo saw that it was Isabella Alvarez. Her eyes and lips were swollen. Both hands wrapped in bloodstained bandages, and she could barely stand. It was just a week since she'd taken a trip from LA to visit her elderly parents in Guerrero, but now she was a different person. At least she was alive.

The phone in Virgo's pocket vibrated. He saw it was an incoming call from Martin Alvarez and declined it. Now was not a good time. He gently slid the phone back into his pocket, and that's when it all happened. *BANG*. A crack of gunshot. *What the fuck...* Then a burst of nine or ten, coming from inside the derelict store: Huesco's men. The narco with the semiautomatic rifle was hit and went down. The others took cover behind the trucks.

Virgo ran out into the street. 'STOP SHOOTING.'

Isabella Alvarez turned his way. She looked drained and beyond fear. With what strength she had left, she tried to run towards him. He saw the boss-man lift the barrel of the Razorback, 'PLEASE. LET HER GO. I'VE GOT THE MONEY.' No use. Three bullets tore into the back of Isabella Alvarez and exited her chest. She collapsed forward, and her face hit the dirt.

No, no, please God, no...

Virgo dived behind a low wall as the Razorback muzzle-flashed his way. *Thunk, thunk, thunk,* then silence. He saw the boss drop his empty gun, run away and cut down a gap between two buildings. The other three narcos were dead. A few state police started to emerge from their positions, but none showed any inclination to chase after the main man. They slung their rifles on their backs and lit cigarettes. Job done.

Outside of town, the headlights were still waiting, and Virgo knew who for. He dropped the bag of cash beside the body of Isabella Alvarez and ran down the street. Skirted the hood of a bullet-hole-ridden pickup, and turned up the alley where the gang leader had gone. It was dark. There was a smell of puke, sweet and sour, mixed with smoke. The ground beneath his feet became damp, and he slowed to a jog. Picked his way through the shadows and the blankets where addicts had been rough-sleeping.

Towards the back end of the alley, the light improved. He made his legs shift up through the gears, and bowled out into an open area on the edge of the scrubland. Nothing. Just the skeletal remains of a burnt-out truck. He wheeled left. The only way his man could have gone if he was heading for the waiting vehicle. Fifty yards farther on stood a roofless warehouse that marked the edge of town. The thought of the killer getting away propelled him towards it through the thick night air. He rounded the last corner. And stopped.

Up ahead, Comandante Huesca and two of his men had already got the gang leader. They stood shouting. Virgo started to walk towards them. Why hadn't they cuffed the bastard or made him lie down with rifles pointing at his head? An alarm bell screeched in his brain. He quickened his pace, breathing heavy. They saw him coming, and stopped shouting. Then with a casual air, the man who'd shot Isabella Alvarez walked off on a trail into the chaparral, and nobody tried to stop him.

Virgo was stunned. 'What the hell's happening?'

Huesca shrugged. 'He's the son of a very important man.'

'I don't care who the fuck he is. He just killed a US citizen.'

'That's not how things work here.'

'Outta my way.' Virgo barged past Huesca and set off on the trail.

Up ahead through the twilight, he saw a silhouette going cross-country towards the main track. Running. No baseball cap. Knowing he was being followed, and not so casual now. Virgo reckoned he had two minutes to make good the ground between them before the waiting pickup came into play. No need to panic, and waste energy. It had been ten years since he left the Army, but he'd maintained his fitness levels.

The figure in front disappeared over the brow of a bush-lined hill, and Virgo felt the fires erupt in his quad muscles as he pushed on up the incline. It was as he crested the summit that instinct told him what was going to happen next. Combat profiling had honed his natural intuition, so he fully expected the blade that flashed out from behind a stunted oak and shot towards his throat. He feinted right, dropped his shoulder left, and the knife sailed wide of its target.

Now Virgo stood face-to-face with the leader of the cartel who'd kidnapped and killed Isabella Alvarez, and saw he was no more than twenty years old. Just a kid, but with a life-time's hatred in his eyes. A sneer on his top lip that said he was untouchable because he was the son of an even bigger drug-dealing shitbag, who had the local cops in his pocket.

The weapon was a folding, tactical knife with a serrated blade. Maybe it was the one used to encourage speedy payment by severing the fingers of innocent women. The kid was quick. Before Virgo could grab his Glock 19, the knife barreled towards his chest. He parried it, but the blade caught his shoulder. The thing about a full-on lunge attack is that it needs to be a finisher. This wasn't. The assailant was now off balance. Virgo gripped his wrist, used the kid's momentum to twist-swing him around, then dropped him to the ground, and deployed a knee to snap his elbow clean in two. Game over.

It was a while before the screaming stopped. Virgo stood gun in hand, blood running down his arm, and waited for the state police. Where were the useless rabble? Helping them-selves to the ransom money? Probably. He felt the phone vibrate in his pocket, and knew it was Martin Alvarez ringing again for an update. How many more Isabellas would this kid kill if the local cops refused to lock him up? He closed his eyes and smelled aniseed in the night air. He knew it was time to quit, but what would he do with his life? A fresh wave of grief took him by surprise.

The sound of voices. Comandante Huesca and his two sidekicks appeared. Virgo looked into their faces for any sign they'd been seized by a renewed passion for justice, but saw only cynicism and fear. Decision time. Did he want to risk the rest of his life in a Mexican jail, or did he want to walk away and let this kid take more innocent lives? Who would it be next time? Another nurse? A teacher? A mother or even a child?

He felt his finger squeeze the trigger. A look of shock contorted the face of the kid who'd murdered Isabella Alvarez, and then a bullet took away the back of his head.

CHAPTER 2
LOS ANGELES

CLUB-GOERS ARE FICKLE. The hottest spot soon cools, to be superseded by the latest must-go venue, where lines of selfie addicts snake up to the front door. La Souris was different. It had a secret entrance and was a constant haven of class in a sea of fads and reinvention: upmarket without being elitist. Stacy Donovan really wanted to like it, but for the third week running, she sat at a table on her own and wished she'd tried a college party instead. How hard was it to get laid in this city?

Pushing midnight, and the place was full. She scanned the dance floor until she saw her friends Joey and Beth, hands all over each other, singing every word to 'Baby Don't Hurt Me.' Stacy relaxed. One day, she'd be brave enough to come here on her own, but right now she was happy to play gooseberry. She poured herself a glass of chardonnay, leant back, and hoped she didn't look desperate.

Strobe lights pulsed to the beat, and blue lasers darted around the ceiling. There was a lot of exposed pipework and iron rails with rust bleeding through the paint - anything to evoke an industrial ambience and twentieth-century antiquity, apart from the price of drinks. Stacy knew deep down she was lucky to be a Donovan and afford $500 for a bottle of wine, but it came with a caveat. Her life wasn't her own. She loved them, but one day, she was going to have to escape her family and taste real freedom.

The DJ switched to hip-hop. Stacy knew Joey and Beth hated that music, and looked for them coming back, but couldn't spot them. That's when she noticed the guy stood at the bar, staring at her. He was huge and stocky, wearing a black suit, with a red baseball cap. At first she thought he might be a bouncer or a cop, and started to worry about the solitary gram of cocaine concealed in her bag, but there was something awkward about him, like he'd never been in a nightclub before. Then he smiled. *Shit, he's going to come over.* She looked away and pretended to scroll on her phone. *Leave me alone. Pleeease…* Maybe she could make a dash for the restroom? She glanced back.

Too late, he was right there in front of her at the table. Mid-thirties, pasty complexion and an underbite that made his oblong chin stand out like an open dresser drawer.

He smiled again. 'I think you should know, I'm not a man to take no for an answer.'

'Then don't ask me a question.' Stacy manufactured a thin smile in return.

'Come on, just one dance.' He held out a hand to escort her.

She recoiled. 'No thanks, I'm waiting for my friends.'

The music was loud. He bent down towards her ear, and his hand went onto her shoulder. 'Let me show you a good time.'

Stacy felt uncomfortable. He was the size of a dump truck and creepy. 'Look, even if I were straight, you're really not my type, so I'd be grateful if you'd get out of my space and try someone else.'

He didn't blink. 'You forgot already? I don't take no for an answer.'

There was a personal safety alarm on a keychain in Stacy's bag, and she thought about going for it, when there was a flash of bright red nail varnish, and a hand grabbed the dump truck by his ear.

'Didn't you hear what the lady said?' The manicured fingers belonged to a blonde woman half his size. She yanked his head around and bawled into his face, 'Piss off and leave her alone.'

The guy looked shocked. His mouth opened, but nothing came out. Within a second, the last vestige of arrogance had drained from his face, and he slunk off into the crowd.

'What a dick.' The woman watched him go. 'I've been keeping an eye on him since he hit on my friend.'

'Thanks.' Stacy took a deep breath. 'Please sit down and have a drink.'

The woman hesitated. 'No, it's okay.'

Stacy's eyes did a quick appraisal of her guardian angel: mid-twenties, scarlet lipstick, oversized hoop earrings, fish-nets, shorts, pink Doc Martens, denim jacket with only a bra underneath. 'I insist. It's the least I can do.' She took the wine from its cooler and hovered over a fresh glass.

'Just one.' The angel sat down. 'I'm Kayla. Where's your boyfriend?'

Stacy peered across to the mass of gyrating bodies. Still no sign of Joey and Beth. No doubt they were outside in the smoke zone and would come back stinking of weed. 'I've not got a boyfriend.'

'Me neither.' Kayla smiled.

Stacy smiled back. Maybe it wasn't just another wasted night. Now she felt hot and knew that the red rash that always showed up with her social anxiety was clawing its way up from her chest to her cheeks. She tried to drown it with a mouthful of Chardonnay, but it didn't work, and the blush blossomed some more. It wasn't supposed to be like this. She'd imagined this scenario so many times, and the conversation always flowed, interspersed with amusing anecdotes and knowing glances. *Say something. Anything.* 'You look like you should be in the movies.'

'I am.'

'Really?'

Kayla laughed. 'Not the sort you'd want to watch with your parents.'

Stacy did her best to laugh along. *Great. First girl I get a chance to pull, and she's a porn star.* Is that good or bad? No, terrifying. *Come on. Say something else.* 'I guess it pays the bills.' *What? Is that the best you can do?*

'Don't worry, it's okay.' Kayla put a hand on the back of Stacy's and fixed her with big mascara eyes. 'Tell me a little bit about you.'

Stacy didn't know where to start, because it was one of her rules to try and be honest. No way she could create a false persona and casually lie. She was only a month into her sophomore year at UCLA Med School and wouldn't be in the club were it not for her fake ID, but of course lying about your age to buy alcohol is not strictly an honesty issue. That's just life. Nevertheless, she didn't think her new friend would be impressed to know she was just a college student. What about sharing some of her upbringing in Oklahoma? Maybe not – politics and religion are both divisive issues. So it had to be hobbies and interests? Wait, no way - everything she liked was so uncool. *Come on, say something interesting. Think, think, think...* The problem was, she was having difficulty trying to think. Every time she had an idea, it slipped out the bottom of her mind, like sand through an hourglass. A numbness filled the vacuum.

And without warning, the world changed. She was blind.

Panicked. Her limbs wouldn't react or move. She was weighed down by a ton of molasses, locked inside her own body, and next she was spinning out of control. Nauseous. Tired. Scared. Voices in her subconscious screamed she was a fool. Somebody had taken hold of her. She hugged the floor, and it vibrated. Movement. More voices. A bomb exploded nearby. Then the ground tremors started again, and a pain that started as a pinprick in her neck ballooned up and filled her head. In the end, she smelled the imagined scent of anesthetic produced by the brain just before it shuts itself down. Then nothing.

CHAPTER 3
FEDERAL CORRECTIONAL INSTITUTION EAGLE VALLEY, CALIFORNIA

4:45 A.M. Virgo lay in his prison bunk and focused his mind once more on the day ahead: roll call, breakfast, work assignment, lunch, roll call, educational program, dinner, final roll call, then lockdown and lights out. It didn't require a lot of mental power, but it took his mind off the high-pitched whistle in his left ear. Eleven years ago, in Syria, he'd been in the rear of a Special Operations Vehicle when it hit an IED, and the audible souvenir was a constant presence. Silence was now his enemy, and nighttime the hardest part of being incarcerated.

Bang on 5:30 a.m., the wake-up buzzer filled the cell and brought relief. Metallic clunks of locks and doors opening welcomed him from outside in the corridor. He pulled on the beige, elastic-waist trousers and matching button-up shirt, and joined the line for the toilets. Less than a month since he'd been repatriated from Mexico into the US federal prison system, but he'd already fallen into the routine. It wasn't too different to the time he'd spent in custody south of the border. Just a different set of petty rules and regulations.

Before heading off to breakfast, he made up his bunk. The

other three cellmates were still asleep in their coffins, because breakfast wasn't compulsory, and they were lazy kids, all doing time for drugs. Virgo didn't mind. They were no trouble and treated him with respect because he was one of the select few in there for murder. Eagle Valley was a medium-security establishment, and he guessed his FBI background had scored him some good-boy points. No doubt saved him from shuffling around a maximum-security joint in ankle chains. Small mercies.

The line for breakfast stretched down one side of the chow hall. He filtered in and joined the end. He saw the tables were half-full, with the usual segregation of whites, blacks, Chicanos and a few smaller groups. Nobody was allowed to be an individual. He hated the way gangs used race to control inmates and run the prison, but that's how it was. Groundhog day. Just another 2,758 of them to go if his calculations were correct, and if he kept himself out of trouble.

He held out his tray and got cereal, powdered eggs and toast. The usual. Found a seat in no-man's land and ate as slow as possible. No point rushing what was now one of life's only pleasures. Everything is relative. It was as he tried to spread an over-refrigerated rectangle of butter onto an under-cooked triangle of toast that his radar picked up the first signal that something might be wrong. The noise level. It wasn't as loud in the chow hall as it usually was at this particular time in the morning. Why? The same numbers were in there as every other day.

That morning in Syria when his team set out to recon a target, they knew something wasn't right, and should have turned back. There were no kids playing at the side of the road. The first rule of sensing danger is to know what the normal situation should be, and to recognize when there is any subtle change or deviation. It's taught in military academies across the world, but comes from the brain's limbic system, and is the result of thousands of years of natural development in the wild.

All done, he went to one of the trolleys, where used trays and utensils were deposited. Here he noticed the second anomaly. Some tables at the back of the hall were more populated than they usually were at this stage of proceedings. Were these inmates taking more time to eat their breakfast, or were they hanging around longer for another reason? The number of heads glancing around in expectation gave him the answer.

Virgo still didn't know what was going down, or if it involved him, but he was prepared. Instead of throwing his spork into the receptacle on the trolley, he palmed it. The plastic was flimsy, but when he broke it in half, the jagged point might be useful. It was when he walked down the window side of the room to take the exit for his block that he identified the three guys who were going to give him trouble.

After the Army, it was training to be a crisis negotiator when he first came across the 7-38-55 rule, established by psychology professor Albert Mehrabian. It states that less than half of human communication is achieved by words or tone, and that 55% is actually down to pure body language. That's why the three stood out. They were big guys, but even so, they were puffing themselves up, trying to look even bigger, and spread out to signal they owned the space. They were also shaved-head no-necks covered in tattoos, so maybe you didn't need to be familiar with Professor Mehrabian's work to know they were trouble.

The thing about animals that inflate themselves to ward off rivals or predators is that they really don't want to fight. They want to trick their potential adversary into thinking they are faced by overwhelming size and strength, to the extent the adversary will be submissive or fly away. Virgo wasn't inclined to do either. He put a skip in his step and headed for the exit.

Before he got there, one of the no-necks blocked his way. Virgo had seen him in the gym and knew he was an Aryan Brotherhood member called Briggs, who controlled half the drugs and gambling in the prison.

'I know you were a cop.' Briggs jabbed a finger.

'Who told you that?' Virgo always liked to kick off any negotiation with a question. It put pressure straight back on the other guy.

'Never mind who fucking told me.'

'Never mind who fucking told you?' Virgo smiled. Mirroring was the technical term for it, but it was simply repeating what somebody said. Guaranteed to confuse or annoy.

'I just said that.' Briggs bulged his eyes.

'Why did you say it?' Another question. Virgo kept his voice polite and his smile wide.

'What?' Briggs was momentarily bemused. 'Look, just fucking listen, cop.' Now he'd lost it. More finger-jabbing. 'This is our yard. We fucking own you.'

Virgo spotted movement. The other two no-necks had reached into their pockets, where no doubt they'd stashed improvised weapons. A sharpened biro or a razor blade. It looked like Briggs didn't like to get his own hands dirty, and his pals were the ones going to try to teach him a lesson. Virgo readied himself. At least he'd attempted to be reasonable. Now it was time for controlled aggression.

No point in waiting. Briggs stood face-on, legs wide apart to emphasize his authority. Big mistake. Should have been side-on in a fighting stance, on the balls of his feet. Virgo pivoted, whacked a lightning-fast roundhouse kick into Briggs's right knee, and felt the joint give way. Before he hit the ground, Virgo was already past his body and driving the broken spork into the throat of shaved-head number two. Not a clean strike, but good enough. Finished him off with a fist to the side of his jaw.

That left number three. Big guy with a shiv in his hand, but Virgo could see his heart wasn't in it. There was fear in his eyes. He was slow and cumbersome. Virgo snap-kicked the arm with the blade, spun round in one movement, and smashed an elbow into the bridge of the guy's nose. It made a dull, squidgy sound. Three down and it had taken less than five seconds.

An alarm sounded, and inmates started to back away and leave the chow hall.

Briggs writhed around on the floor and shouted, 'You're a fucking dead man.'

Virgo bent down and patted the side of his face. 'Just to clarify, I wasn't a cop. I was a federal agent. And before that, I was US Army, Task Force Orange. Happy now?'

First guard to arrive was Ruthenberg. Virgo put his hands behind his back and turned around for the cuffs to go on. No point pleading innocence at this stage, when there were three casualties on the ground with major damage, and fifty witnesses who'd probably swear he started it. There would be a hearing, and until then he'd be in the hole, the shoe, the box or whatever they called solitary confinement in PCI Eagle Valley. Time to catch up on some reading.

Ruthenberg and another guard escorted Virgo to his cell to collect his property. On the way, Ruthenberg sucked on his teeth and said, 'Do you know whose leg you just broke?'

'A shitbag called Briggs.'

'Leader of the council of the Brotherhood.'

'Yeah, he's a real hero.'

'Let me give you some advice: put an application in for PC as soon as you can.'

Virgo shook his head. 'I don't want to serve my time

surrounded by chemos and bent cops.' He'd been given the option to go straight into protective custody when he arrived at the prison, and turned it down. He wasn't changing now.

Fifteen minutes later, he was in the SHU block. A different set of guards made him strip and bend over to check there wasn't an AK-47 or a kilo of smack in the crack of his butt cheeks. He pulled on a loose-fitting orange jumpsuit and was shown into his new living space. A windowless box, maybe big enough to park a Honda Civic, with a bunk, seatless toilet and an overpowering stink of cleaning fluid. Perfect spot to spend twenty-three hours a day. *BANG.* The door slammed shut, and he lay down on the bed, wondering what he was going to think about now to distract his brain from the dog whistle in his left ear.

Since Crystal died, he didn't really have dreams about the future any more. Que será será. He had no intention of meeting somebody else and settling down, or of getting a new job and trying to make himself a fortune. But one thing he did know: if he survived in prison until the end of his sentence, then the day he got released, he was going to buy an RV. Nothing flash or expensive. Just something big enough for him to live in full time, which he could drive up and down the coast without attracting attention, and park up every night near the ocean. Fall asleep listening to the waves, and wake up to the sound of the sea. Sound therapy for the soul. Maybe then he could have dreams about the life he could have spent with Crystal and not feel bitter.

He ran through the latest favorites: Airstream Interstate, Winnebago Paseo, Jayco Swift...*BANG.* The door hatch slammed down, and a voice shouted, 'Get up. You're going to the visits hall.'

'What?' Virgo's forehead creased. Nobody had been to see him since his arrest in Mexico. Not even those work colleagues he classed as good friends. There was something else that puzzled him. 'I thought inmates in solitary were not allowed visits.'

The guard opened the door. 'They're not, but legal is an exception.'

'I've not got an attorney.'

'You have now. She's in reception.'

Virgo turned and put his hands behind his back for them to be cuffed. He didn't like surprises, and he didn't like lawyers. It was fair to say his day hadn't got off to the best of starts.

CHAPTER 4

STACY LAY face down on something hard and cold. Drowsy. She drifted away again from the edge of consciousness and back into the recesses of her mind, where incoherent thoughts surfaced and then dissolved. Gradually, something in the brain's engine room started to do its job and bring her round, and that's when the most terrible bolt of panic shot through her body. She screamed. The nightmare flooded back: the club, the weird man, the girl who must have spiked her drink. Being carried…

Her heart banged so hard in her chest, she thought it might break. She opened her eyes, but couldn't see. Was she blind, or was it pitch black? No noise. The ground felt like solid rock, with a thin covering of dirt. Was she outside in the countryside somewhere? It didn't feel like nature. There was no fresh air or scintilla of light. Slowly, she tried to calm herself down, and think her heartrate back to a safe level. Then she pushed herself up onto one knee and raised herself with care in case there was something above her head. There wasn't. She stood up and yelped in pain as her spine straightened out. How long had she been unconscious in a fetal curl? What had they done to her?

Her leather trousers felt wet around the crotch, and she knew it was urine. The indignity made her angry. Didn't they know who she was? Somebody was going to pay for this. There was an ache that gripped the inside of her head like a vise, as her body reeled with the effects of dehydration. It needed water. She stretched her arms out in front as a shield and set off walking, still unsteady on her feet. Three small strides, and her hands hit something solid. She felt the texture. It was rock, the same as the floor. She turned right and felt her way along it, hoping to find something familiar: a door, a window, a gap or a chink of light. Anything to establish a sense of where she was, and which direction to set out for help.

Within three yards, she hit another stone face. Turned right again and edged her way inch by inch. Four, maybe five yards on, it was the same story: she hit another corner of the rock wall and could only go ninety degrees to the right. She carried on, feeling her way. It took a few circuits around the edge, but finally Stacy had orientation and started to realize her predicament. She was in a square space the size of a bedroom, except it wasn't a room. There were no apertures or vents, and the walls were carved out of solid, coarse-grained rock, like granite. Where was she? Some kind of pit or tomb?

The panic came back in stages. Had she been raped or abused on video for some sick, internet website? Had she been dumped here to die? Think. If there was no door in any of the walls, then the only way she could have got there was from above. She reached up. Nothing. She stood on tiptoes, and now she felt it. A metal roof. She jumped and pounded it with her fists until her knuckles bled. It was solid. She moved across the floor to try somewhere else, and immediately tripped over something soft. It sent her crashing down, and a hard point jagged deep into her left ribcage.

Adrenaline numbed the pain. She scrabbled around with her hands and found the point that had dug into her side was the corner of a box. She stepped up onto it and now had a good feel of the metal roof that was her only way out. It was heavy and thick. Maybe cast iron, like manholes and storm grates are made from. She pushed up with all her strength, but it didn't even seem like it would move even a fraction. There must be a hatch or portal. She scratched and tore at the surface until half the nails had been ripped from her fingers. No tangible sign of a handle or hinge, but she had to keep trying.

'Help.' The word came out strange at first. A strangled squeak. She cleared her throat and filled her lungs. 'Help. Help me…' This time loud and clear. She had a feeling there were people above the iron ceiling, but no idea who. Of course, it might be those responsible for drugging and performing whatever else they'd done to her, but it could also be ordinary citizens going about their daily business. 'Please help me.' She screamed until she was hoarse, and her chest was on fire. Carried on until no sounds came out.

When she stepped back down, she stumbled again over whatever soft object was in the middle of the pit floor. This time she steadied herself and didn't fall. She knelt down and used her hands to identify what it was. Material, buttons, sticky wet cloth. She couldn't picture what it was. Then the tips of her fingers touched something her mind recognized instantly. Human flesh. A shudder racked her body, and she retched. The flesh was cold. She felt a neck, a face, hair. Male or female, she had no idea and no desire to find out.

Dead bodies didn't bother her. She was a second-year medical student, and although forensic pathology was later in the course, she'd already attended autopsies as an observer.

But the shock, the proximity and the darkness combined to destabilize her defenses and ignite her imagination. Who was it? How had they died? What suffering had they endured, and why had she been incarcerated in the same tomb?

Stacy backed away into a corner and pulled her knees up under her chin. She started to cry, but when the first tear ran down her cheek, she stopped and wiped her eyes. This was what they wanted. What if they were watching her? Nothing she did from now on would give them the satisfaction of thinking she was scared or submissive. The more she thought about it, the more clarity she had about what had happened at the club, and was certain the ugly giant was part of the set up.

She stood and tilted her head back. 'FUCK YOU.'

CHAPTER 5

VIRGO WAS ESCORTED through the main visiting hall and into one of the bijou side rooms reserved for legal consultation. Two guards unfastened the cuffs from behind his back, threaded them through a heavy-duty D ring, and refastened them at the front. Now he was chained to an anchor that was bolted to the table, which in turn was bolted to the floor. Overkill? Maybe not for some of the more excitable inmates, who would rip the head off their own defense lawyer given half a chance. Chain-duties done, the guards retreated, but didn't leave the room.

After twenty minutes, the door opened. A woman in a tweed business suit walked in and sat down opposite. She was followed by two men in black sports jackets, who took up positions like Roman statues behind her on either side, and Virgo knew straight away they were federal agents from the cut of their cloth. Of course, the shoulder holsters would be empty, because not even the FBI or Homeland Security are allowed weapons in prison. Rules are rules.

The woman didn't smile. No *good mornings* or *how's it*

going? If anything, her face was iced with a frown of irritation. She simply pointed to her photo ID on a lanyard and said, 'I'm Marion Cutts, senior attorney with the Department of Justice, and I'm here today to secure your release from custody.'

'Very funny.' Virgo sat and waited.

'I'm glad you find it amusing.' Marion Cutts hauled a briefcase up onto the table. 'Personally, I think convicted murderers should serve their full sentence, without exception.'

'For your information, I was found guilty of involuntary manslaughter not murder.'

'A Mexican judge ruled that your mental capacity was impacted by the death of your wife, even though it was several months earlier. Personally, I don't think a US court would have been so generous.'

'Then why are you here?'

'Because I do what the attorney general tells me to, even if I disagree. That's my job.' She opened the briefcase and took a sheet of paper from the top of a pile. 'Here, sign this. It's a copy of the order from the AG that I've just served on the governor of this institution. You're a free man. Congratulations.' The last word stuck in her throat.

Virgo scanned the paper. It looked legitimate. The DOJ crest at the top, followed by paragraphs of convoluted language only lawyers use. Something towards the end caught his eye.

Release is conditional on Edward McKinley Virgo reporting directly to the Federal Bureau of Investigation, where he shall operate under their direction and control for a period of seven days, commencing from the time…

'What's this all about?' He pointed to the clause.

'I don't know.' Marion Cutts had a look of irritation.

'Then you'd better find out, or I'm not signing it.'

'Are you serious? You'd rather spend eight years in here than a week working for your old employer?'

'Doing what exactly? Where?'

'Please yourself. Stay here and enjoy the company.' Marion Cutts pulled a humorless smile. 'I heard there was a fight at breakfast.'

'It wasn't a fight. A threat was neutralized.'

'Play with words if you want, Mr Virgo, but the Aryan Brotherhood have a presence in every federal prison in California, and believe me, one day they will get you. Of course, you could apply to go into protective custody with the child molesters, but I get the impression that's not your style.'

Virgo said nothing. Some elements within the FBI are devious enough to have engineered that morning's confrontation with Briggs to give him added incentive. Try to make him desperate to get out. But why would they do that? He wasn't sure. It depended on what they had lined up for him, and he couldn't begin to imagine what it was. If something seems too good to be true, it's always because it is.

Marion Cutts signaled to the prison guards and they stepped forward and removed the hand restraints. She pushed a pen across the table. 'You signing or not?'

'Not.' Virgo pushed it back. 'Not until you answer my question. Why?'

'I already told you, I don't know.' She picked up the paper and threatened to put it back in the briefcase. 'Last chance. I've got a plane to catch.'

Virgo spotted the bluff in her face. No way she wanted to return to Washington and tell the attorney general that she'd failed to accomplish such a simple, straightforward task. What kind of idiot couldn't persuade a convict that freedom was a better choice than life behind bars? He smiled. 'Have a nice flight.'

Marion Cutts looked ready to explode. Her face went a shade of burgundy, that matched the silk scarf round her neck nicely. She threw up her arms and turned to the two statues over her shoulder. 'For God's sake, help me out here. You guys are from the bureau.'

The two agents looked at each other; then one of them said, 'All we know is that our orders are to escort Mr. Virgo immediately to meet Deputy Unit Chief Hartman.'

Silence. Virgo leaned back and rubbed his wrists, where the shackles had been. Nick Hartman was the man who'd taught him everything he knew about crisis negotiation, and if there was anyone left in the unit whom he still trusted, it was him. Virgo relaxed. What was the worst they could make him do? Go back to the Middle East or Africa? Not places he'd choose to visit, but whatever fate lay ahead, it was only temporary. Then he could get holed up in his RV behind the dunes, somewhere off the Pacific Coast Highway, and in a better place for his brain to heal.

He leaned forward. 'Okay, give me the pen.'

Everything signed and sealed, they were taken through a succession of gates to the reception block, where Cutts and the agents were shown one way, but Virgo was directed into a holding room and told to wait on a bench. The door locked behind him. Ten minutes later, there was the sound of keys, and a senior guard called Borovsky came in with a bag of clothes. He said, 'You're catching the chain.'

Virgo was unsure. 'Catching the chain?'

'Prison slang – you're getting released.' Borovsky shook his head. 'Never met such a lucky son of a bitch before, and I've worked here twenty years.'

Virgo stepped out of the orange boiler suit and pulled on the pants he'd last worn in a Mexican courtroom. It wasn't time to get too excited about his change of fortunes. There was a reason someone high up the food chain had pulled some strings to get him out, and ten minutes' thinking time had given him an inkling what it might be. The bureau needed a job doing that nobody else would touch, or it was a job they wanted to distance themselves from if it went tits up. Either way, he was the sacrificial lamb. When he was dressed, checked out on a computer, and escorted to the main doors, Borovsky undid the locks and waved goodbye, still shaking his head.

Outside, the day was already hot. The early mist that sat in the valley most mornings had burned away, and the sky spread out over him in a kind of artificial blue only seen in holiday-brochure swimming pools. The air was fresh, and felt good. He was ushered into the rear of a waiting black SUV, with something about his newfound liberty bothering him.

'So, have I got a pardon from the President?'

'No.' Marion Cutts's voice was definite. 'The DOJ can only issue pardons on behalf of the President if you committed a federal crime within the United States.'

'What about an official commutation of my sentence, then?'

'Can't be done. You weren't sentenced by a court in the US.'

Virgo stared out the SUV window as it exited through the barriers of the correctional facility and out onto the service road. 'So I could be sent back to serve the rest of my sentence?'

'Yes, if you breach the conditions of your release, but there's one more thing you should know.' Marion Cutts turned back from the front passenger seat with a smug look on her face. She was enjoying herself now. 'If the FBI decide that you've breached your conditions, then you'll be deported to Mexico to serve out the remainder of your sentence.'

'Thanks.' Virgo deadpanned. He wasn't going to give her the satisfaction of an emotional response.

'You're welcome. I hope you're good at kissing ass.' Marion Cutts pointed to her briefcase. 'But I've read your file, and I don't think you are.' Then she laughed and turned back to face the front.

CHAPTER 6

DOWN ON THE San Diego Freeway, traffic shuffled like a dying sloth. Virgo stared out at the fumes and haze from inside the air conditioned SUV and wondered what he was still doing there in Los Angeles. Not for the first time that day, events didn't seem to be unfolding in a logical fashion, and that concerned him. He'd been expecting to be put on a flight to Washington, then shunted down to Quantico, but when Marion Cutts and the two agents had been dropped at LAX departures, he was told to sit tight. Now what?

A mile south of the airport, the car peeled off the inter-state, crossed a junction, and drove straight into the parking lot of a Walmart Supercenter. It pulled up outside the in-store burger joint, and the driver said, 'This is where you get out, sir.'

Virgo stepped into the sticky heat of an LA afternoon and watched his ride spin round and roar off, leaving two smears of rubber on the tarmac. What was he supposed to do now? Stand and sweat until another car came and shipped him somewhere else? Then he saw the answer. The acting head of the FBI's prestigious Crisis Negotiation Unit sat at a table in the window of the fast-food place, wearing a beat-up, straw trilby, and shoveling fries into his mouth.

Virgo went inside, sat down opposite. 'Too embarrassed to meet a convicted felon on FBI premises?'

'It's not like that.' Nick Hartman dropped his lower jaw, and half a quarter-pounder disappeared.

Virgo studied the old friend and mentor he'd not set eyes on for a year, and saw no change. The same straggles of greasy hair down to his shoulders. The same oversized, pinstripe jacket to cover a beach-ball belly, and a cheap hat to hide the fact that beneath it was a scalp as bald as a Trappist monk. The same overall demeanor best characterized as grubby. It was hard to imagine this man had been, without doubt, the greatest negotiator the bureau had ever seen.

Virgo said, 'Come on. Why am I here?'

'What can I say? We all felt bad about what happened south of the border.' Ketchup leaked from the quarter-pounder and dribbled onto Hartman's tie. It joined some flecks of mustard from a previous gourmet-dining experience. 'As soon as I knew you were back in the US, I called in some favors and got your liberty back.'

'Wait! Don't take another bite of that burger.' Virgo reached over and stayed Hartman's arm. 'It'll get covered in the bullshit that just came out of your mouth.'

Hartman laughed. 'Okay, I got a job for you.' He pushed the last of the burger into his mouth and chewed as he spoke. 'I needed some reason to convince the DOJ to release you, and one just came along. Don't worry, it's nothing difficult or dangerous.' He nodded towards the counter. 'Get a coffee and some food, and I'll fill you in.'

Virgo glanced across at the kid serving. He looked like a one-toothed crack addict, with a lazy eye. 'Just give it to me straight. What's this steaming pile of crap nobody else wants to touch?'

'Cynicism isn't a good trait in a negotiator.'

'I'm all out of trust and empathy.'

'Relax.' Hartman wiped his mouth, then his hands, and produced a foolscap, buff folder seemingly from nowhere, like a magician. 'Yesterday, two miles up the road from here, the daughter of a US senator was kidnapped. No demand as yet, but they're a wealthy family.'

Virgo stared at the folder and fought the urge to grab it. For a moment, he was back in the saddle at his old office, and the adrenalin switch flicked on at the arrival of a fresh case. Strange how someone else's torment and misery can arouse professional instincts in that way. He took a deep breath. 'There's a dozen agents in your office can handle this as good, if not better than me.'

'Maybe, but it was the opportunity I needed to get you out of that prison.'

'You were a great teacher, Nick.' Virgo steepled his fingers and smiled over the top of them. 'I still remember that full week we did on my initial course, just on kinesics and biometrics, the reading nonverbal communication stuff – it was outstanding.'

'Thanks.' Hartman only managed to return half a smile.

'That's why I know you're lying. Do you want me to list the signals I've identified since I walked into this room?'

'No need. You got me.' Hartman dropped his voice and leaned across the table. 'We've got a problem in the Operational Support Branch.'

'What kind of problem?'

'The worst kind. Think Robert Hanssen.'

'You sure?' Virgo's shock was genuine. The Branch were part of the bureau's Critical Incident Response Group, established to make sure fuck-ups like Waco and Ruby Ridge never occurred again. It was a big team, and not everyone was perfect, but there'd never been so much as a whiff of corruption. 'What happened?'

'Last three cases leaked to the press within the first twenty-four hours.'

'Shit.'

'I've no idea who, and I can't risk being compromised on this one.' Hartman shoved the buff folder across the table. 'Senator Donovan has power and influence.'

Virgo hesitated, then picked it up. 'Do I get my badge back?'

'Very funny. Do you think the FBI's commitment to a diverse and inclusive workforce extends to the employment of convicted killers?' Hartman reached down and produced a rolled-up shopping bag. 'You got a phone, a bank card with a daily limit of a thousand dollars, and the usual USBs and recording devices. Be grateful.'

'I suppose it beats being banged up.' Virgo tried to sound grudging and reluctant. He unrolled the bag and peeked inside. He knew there were still things he wasn't being told, but filed it away at the back of his mind. Secret information is shared on a need-to-know basis, and maybe it wasn't essential for the role he was about the play, but there was one thing he definitely needed.

'There's no gun.'

Hartman laughed. 'Of course there isn't. You're not on the books.'

'How can I protect the senator? What if the kidnappers make a direct approach?'

Hartman hesitated. 'It's unlikely.'

'Then it's also unlikely I'll be taking the job.' Virgo pushed the shopping bag across the table. 'No one in their right mind would do it unarmed, and you would never ask them to.'

'Fuck, have it your own way.' Hartman reached inside his jacket and slid his own pistol into the shopping bag. 'Now, start by buying some new clothes. You smell like toilet cleaner.'

'Thanks.' Virgo tucked the bank card in his pocket and rolled the bag up. 'I'll need a number two, plus intelligence and investigation resources.'

'No chance. I can't risk it.'

'You're going to have to. We can't cover all the bases without ops support.'

'And whose ass is going to get a rocket shoved up it when tomorrow's news websites tell the whole world what's happened, and then the bad guys get spooked and put a nine millimeter into the back of a young girl's head? Mmnnn? Answer me that.'

'Find me someone you trust.'

'Okay, okay, you got it.' Hartman started to unwrap another quarter-pounder with cheese. 'Just go babysit the senator, and tell him how to respond when the demands come in.'

'I remember how to do the job.' Virgo wasn't convinced by his old boss's promise of extra resources. The capitulation had been too glib.

'Everything by the book.' Hartman licked a trail of mayo from the base of his thumb. 'Make sure you do everything by the book.'

Virgo thought there was an unspoken *or else*, but maybe he imagined it. Any slip-ups and he was on a flight to Mexico, is that how it was? A threat? Nick Hartman was a good guy, but there were people above him more ruthless. Not that it mattered, because ex-members of Task Force Orange did not feel intimidated by threats.

CHAPTER 7

Stacy couldn't understand why she was so cold. The ends of her fingers were numb, and her toes hurt, even though she was stood up, flexing them, and stamping her feet. Maybe it was the effects of the drugs they'd pumped into her. The stuff they'd put in her drink was probably gamma-hydroxybutyrate, known to partygoers as GHB or liquid ecstasy, but first developed as an anesthetic. A few drops can shut the brain and nervous system down for up to four hours.

But she was sure they'd given her something else. One of the nightmare flashbacks was of a needle being stuck into the side of her neck, and the jugular below her left ear felt tender. That could have been the injection site. Probably a more stable opioid-based anesthetic, or a barbiturate. That meant she could have been under for a significant length of time and transported a long way from the club.

Then another thought struck her. What if this subterranean cell was deliberately cold to make sure the corpse didn't decompose? Maybe they wanted to keep it fresh and presentable for some reason? Stacy had recovered from the initial revulsion and was now interested in who the dead body was. If she knew *whom* she was sharing her incarceration with, she might know *why*.

She was debating whether it was worth using her sense of touch when everything turned blue. She squinted. It took her eyes a few seconds to adjust. Slowly, she raised her head to the source of the light and saw it was a tiny LED in the top corner of the pit. She stepped onto the box and went to touch it, but her hand hit thick glass or Perspex. A camera. They were watching her. She raised a middle finger. 'Think you'll get away with this, moron?'

Then she remembered the dead body on the floor. The blue light was just a tiny LED, but it was enough to bathe the whole underground cave in its cobalt glow. Even before she got off the box to take a closer look, Stacy could see it was a young man. Around the same age as herself. She knelt to get a better view of his face: clean-shaven, good cheekbones, eyes open but clouded, staring into the abyss of eternity. There was something familiar about him, but she was pretty sure she'd never seen him before. Definitely, didn't know him.

The red-black blood on the chest of his shirt indicated where he had been shot or stabbed. For a moment, Stacy had an instinctive urge to unbutton the shirt and clarify the exact cause of death for her own medical interests, but she shook it off and settled for searching the pockets for ID or maybe something that could be used as a weapon. Nothing. Both empty.

Looking around, she noted that the box that she'd used to reach the roof was a twelve-pack of bottled water, and nearby on the ground was a smaller box of protein bars. She tore at the packaging of the water first, but it took an age for her fingers to get inside the cardboard and pull it open. The seals on the plastic bottle tops looked unbroken. She twisted one off and smelled the contents. Then poured a splash onto the end of her tongue. Satisfied it was water, she drank the full bottle, then went through the same careful process with the protein bars. She needed strength. When the time came for whatever it was they had planned, she was going to fight.

No sooner had she finished the protein bar, her stomach cramped up. She needed to empty her bowels. No. Not while they were watching. She looked around the pit for any nook that might not be covered by the camera, but there was nothing. Stone walls and a solid rock floor. They'd left a supply of food and water, but no privacy screen or toilet. Not even a bucket. Stacy knew they wanted to keep her alive, but beyond that, they had no consideration for her comfort or dignity. The pain in her intestines grew worse. She fought it, and the wave of agony subsided. How long before the cramps came back and she had to defecate?

Stacy felt something run down her forehead, and realized it was sweat. For a period of time, the fear and panic receded. She closed her eyes and imagined she was back in her childhood bedroom, surrounded by toys and books. It was Sunday, and she was getting ready for church, in a pastel-green dress with bouncy ruffles. Then *SHIT*, she was back in the present, and the enormity of her situation hit her in the solar plexus like a battering ram. What had she done to deserve this? What? What sin could be so bad?

She looked up at the blue dot, and that's when a voice filled the pit.

'Smile for the camera, Stacy Donovan. It's your big moment.'

For a second, shock paralyzed Stacy's limbs. It was the big freak from the club, and he knew her name. She forced her muscles to move. To turn away from the light and curl up into a ball. She shouted, 'Go fuck yourself.'

Whoever had done this, and whatever they wanted, she wasn't going to make it easy.

CHAPTER 8

Virgo bought a small, soft-side carry-on case and wheeled it out of Walmart, full of clothes, toiletries and a spare pair of camel-colored desert boots. He took a cab and skimmed through the file Hartman had given him. Just a couple of photographs, a copy of an article from the *New York Times*, and a summary report knocked together by Hartman himself. It wasn't the comprehensive briefing package that usually accompanied a case like this, but maybe that was to be expected in the circumstances.

Daniel Donovan was a senator from Oklahoma. The *NYT* bio described him as coming from old money, but with a new vision for America. He wanted to end divisive politics and bring people together into one community. Three books to his name. Active within Congress, and widely tipped as a future presidential candidate if the stars aligned and he won over some of the major hawks within his own party. The article signed off with a prophesy: *The next JFK will be a Republican.*

The next JFK was staying at the Ritz-Carlton in downtown. Virgo rode the elevator to the twenty-third floor, where two security guys stood outside the door to an executive suite. They weren't Secret Service, but had a military bearing. Private contractors? Probably part of the major glut since the withdrawal from Afghanistan.

'FBI — Senator Donovan is expecting me.' Virgo presented himself for inspection, but they didn't ask for ID or pat him down. Sloppy. One of them knocked on the door and poked his head inside.

When the door opened, Virgo heard the sound of raised voices. Two men, who went quiet when their argument was interrupted. People react to stress in different ways, so it wasn't unusual to find anger and frustration in these situations. He was shown in and recognized Daniel Donovan from his photograph in the *Times.*

'My name's Eddie, and I'm here to help get your daughter back.' Virgo had opened with the line many times, but for him it held the same weight as the first time he'd used it. Direct and honest.

'It's good of you to come. Thank you.' Donovan had the politician's hundred-watt smile, which could be flipped on and off. It flickered, then shone. He looked younger than his forty-six years and was groomed to perfection, like a French poodle at the Westminster Kennel Club show. Tight blond curls framed a shiny, smooth face, and his big eyes coordinated nicely with the pale blue linen jacket and tie.

Virgo shook his hand. 'Has there been any contact yet from whoever took Stacy?'

Donovan said, 'No, nothing. It's driving me mad.'

The hesitation was barely perceptible, but Virgo saw it. The senator was not giving him the truth. It happens. The first threat hostage-takers often make to a family is identical – if you involve the cops, we kill your kid. Virgo said, 'Good. It means I can help you control the narrative from the first time they get in touch.'

At that point, a man standing by the window coughed to

clear his throat, and came over. 'I'm Duncan Donovan. We've decided that we can deal with this situation on our own.'

Situation? Like someone had stolen the family pet. Virgo had seen it all. He noticed Duncan walked with the aid of a silver-topped cane, and he also had the hereditary ringlet hair, but on him it was salt and pepper and over his collar. 'Pleased to meet you, sir. Are you also the senator's legal advisor?'

'I'm his chief of staff, unpaid secretary, counselor, confidant and older brother.' Duncan tapped his cane on the floor in time to every epithet. A rhythm that implied agitation or impatience. 'Like I said, we will handle it.'

It wasn't the time or place to recount stories about other families who flew solo and got the remains of their loved ones back in a box. Virgo ignored Duncan and addressed Stacy's father. 'It's not *either-or*, sir. We'll work together, and you personally will always have the right to ignore my advice and make the final call.'

Daniel chewed on his bottom lip and didn't say anything. There were tears in his eyes.

Virgo waited, but nothing came. 'Where's Stacy's mother?'

'Fiona is at home, being comforted by friends.' It was Duncan who spoke. Seemed he didn't appreciate being side-lined, and did the tapping thing again with his cane to emphasize his words. 'Just...leave...us...be...and...'

Daniel Donovan glared at his brother, then raised a hand. 'Just stop.' He turned to Virgo. 'What do the bureau normally do in a case like this?'

'The overriding priority is the safe return of your daughter. I stay by your side twenty-four hours a day to help you with any communication, and I act as your link with the investigation back in the office.'

'I thought I made myself clear to your boss.' Duncan again. The cane waving about now. 'There is to be no investigation that might jeopardize the life of my niece. We have funds, and if necessary, we are willing to pay the bastards what they want.'

Virgo said, 'It's not that simple.'

'Isn't it?' said Duncan. 'In my experience, money uncomplicates things.'

Virgo wanted to say that paying a ransom doesn't mean someone isn't killed. The mission of a kidnapper is twofold: getting paid, and getting away with it. Live witnesses are a threat to the second part of that mission. That's why there should always be an investigation concurrent to the negotiation, in case a rescue becomes the best chance of saving a hostage's life. He didn't want to cause the senator more distress than necessary, but he'd had enough of his brother's interventions.

'Okay, let's wargame this.' Virgo squared up to Duncan. 'The phone rings now. A man wants five million in cash by ten o'clock tonight. What are you going to do?'

'This is ridiculous.'

'Have you got it in a bag in the bedroom?'

'Of course not.'

'Then what are you going to say?'

'Tell him to be reasonable.'

'Ten o'clock or he kills your niece. Come on, quick. Time's ticking.'

'I'd withdraw what cash we could, and make arrangements for the rest.'

'It's a ransom, not a finance agreement on a new car.'

'I don't think he'd say *no* to fifty thousand dollars.'

'Who? Who are you giving this fifty grand to? The janitor?'

'What?'

'How do you know this man has your niece? It could be some chancer who's found out she's missing.'

'Stop! That's enough.' Daniel Donovan stepped in between them. He had his head in his hands. Slowly, he lowered them and took a deep breath. 'Thank you, Agent Virgo, my family will be very grateful for your advice and support. However, given my position, it isn't possible for you to remain with me at all times. If you let me have your number, I'll give you a call as soon as I receive any contact from whoever has taken my daughter.'

Virgo gave a shrug of acceptance. He was now convinced the two Donovan brothers had already received contact from the kidnappers, but there was no point forcing the issue. They would deny it. He'd often wondered what he would have done himself if he and Crystal had been blessed with a child who'd been abducted. Would he have reported it or dealt with it himself? The FBI is like any other organization: there are many good, professional people, and there's a sprinkling of lame, useless fuck-ups. Do you want to risk one of the fuck-ups working your case? Would you jeopardize the life of your son or daughter, or would you rely on every piece of your own spirit and resolve to save them? He always came up with the same answer.

CHAPTER 9

Virgo took a room at a budget hotel a few blocks down the street. Not the Ritz-Carlton, but a step up from where he'd been staying of late. It didn't do room service, but there was a flyer for Uber Eats, and he ordered takeout from a Chinese place that specialized in dim sum. He lay on the bed and waited. The room was quiet for a downtown locale, and soon his brain was distracted by the ever-present whine in his left ear, like feedback in a Hendrix solo. He picked up his phone to put some music on, and as he scrolled, it rang. The screen said *Hartman*.

'You've reached the STD clinic. How may I help?'

'I'm guessing you're not seated next to the senator?' Hartman sounded out of breath.

'I think they've already been in touch with him. He's frightened, and he's got big brother acting as his offensive line. I'm not even in the same building as them.'

'We've got intercepts on his email, mobile and landlines, and there's been nothing.'

'Contact could have been via an app, and we'd never know.'

'Or in person, although that's unlikely.' Hartman puffed. In the background, a Tannoy voice announced it was the final call to Gate 32. 'Look, he's under no legal obligation to have you hold his hand. Just sit tight.'

'Where's the intel and investigation team?'

'I'm working on it. Give me time.'

'Come on, Nick. It's me you're talking to, not some kid wanting ten bucks for a bag of dope. Has the senator's brother bent your ear? Is that it? Threatened to ruin your chances of getting head of Unit? I've met his kind before, and know how they operate.'

'You've not heard? I'm retiring next month.'

'Why go now, when the top job's up for grabs?'

'I won't get it. None of the old management team will get it because of what happened in Mexico.'

'That was all down to me. No one else.'

'It's not how the Office of Professional Responsibility see it. Their internal review team said someone should have recognized that Isabella Alvarez was a nurse the same as Crystal, and substituted another negotiator instead of you.' Hartman's laugh was heavy with sarcasm. 'Davison surprised us all by falling on his sword and resigning – the only decent thing he ever did – but none of us will get promoted to his desk. We're all tainted.'

'I'm sorry, Nick. I didn't know.' Virgo was sure it was true. The bureau would bring in new blood. Someone with the right image. They might not be good at critical incident response, but they wouldn't wear dinner down the front of their shirt or have rat-tail hair.

'There's something else you should know,' Hartman huffed. 'The leak in our office I told you about – it got one of our undercover agents killed. Be careful.'

'So, what shall I do now?'

'Do nothing.'

'Get me the staff.'

'Sure thing.' Hartman was clean out of breath. He wheezed. 'Got to go. Plane boarding.'

Virgo had an uneasy feeling, like something monumental was going to happen. He downloaded a TV app and paid for a subscription using the bureau's bank card, which gave him access to dozens of channels. He dipped in and out of some of the live streams from the major broadcasters, but there was nothing unusual making headlines. The world still turned on its axis, and people carried on as normal, even though a young woman's life hung by a thread.

Twenty minutes later, there was a knock at the door, and a sweaty guy in motorcycle gear thanked him for the tip. Virgo lined up the open foil trays, then flooded them with soy sauce. He used his fingers and bit into the first dumpling. It was pork and ginger, and fizzed in his mouth. The taste should have been exquisite, but the problem was it made him think what food Stacy Donovan was enjoying right now, if any. Hartman was on a five-hour flight to Washington, which meant investigators would not be assigned until tomorrow. Assuming he was satisfied there were no bad apples amongst them.

In the Army, Virgo had been a soldier in a secret special forces' unit, and then in the bureau, he had specialized in crisis negotiation, so he had never been an investigator. But he'd worked alongside a few, and he knew one thing: the first twenty-four hours following an incident are the most important. So, what was he going to do? Sit on his ass in a hotel room, or try and find out what had happened to an innocent kid?

The report Hartman had given him was classified *secret*, which meant he couldn't risk leaving it unattended, so he photographed the relevant information, then tore it up into a million tiny pieces and flushed it in batches down the can. Tom Cruise would have had an automatic, self-exploding briefcase, but he had a porcelain bowl and the LA sewage system. The glamorous life of working for the FBI. It was what he'd missed most.

CHAPTER 10

BOUTIQUES, bars, stalls selling handmade ephemera, the mandatory Charlie Chaplin street performer, and a homeless man, spiced out of his brain, held up only by a shopping cart. Virgo was five blocks east of the beach in Santa Monica, stood next to a fountain in a pedestrianized square. Somewhere over the vast, purple Pacific, the sun had half-set and ushered in a twilight glow that hung heavy. It was shaping up to be a hot Friday night in the city of angels.

La Souris was on the corner of the square, and Hartman's report said a witness had seen a girl matching Stacy's description being helped out of the club by a man and a woman and lifted into the back of a waiting van. The usual assumption: drunk. The witness didn't want to give a statement or get involved, and the cops didn't push it at the time.

The club was open, with just one guy on the door. No line. The DJs and banging music would be later, but right now it was okay for cocktails. Virgo checked his phone one more time to make sure he'd not missed a message or call from Daniel Donovan, and paid the $40 early-bird entry fee with his new bank card. Normally, he would have badged his way in, but Hartman had said a return to FBI agent status, even temporarily, was out of the question. So here he was: Mr. Joe Public.

At the top of a dark flight of stairs, he found the main area, bought a beer, and leant on the bar. The place was empty apart from a dozen crew getting the club ready for later, and a bachelorette party playing some kind of drinking game with penis straws. Every now and then, there were whoops and shouts of *down in one*. Some things never change.

He paid attention to the movement of the staff. The CCTV hard drive and monitors would be in the manager's office or a separate room close by. One door, marked *private*, looked like it was used mainly by the bar workers, restocking shelves and fetching glasses, and was constantly swinging on its hinges. Another had a sign, *Strictly No Admittance*, and saw little activity. He guessed this was the one he needed. Naturally, it was locked. When an employee needed access, they produced a proximity card on a lanyard and held it up to the reader.

Virgo ignored one of the bachelorette party who was smiling at him, and walked over to be nearer the door. The woman followed him. Eight-inch heels and a baby-doll dress, with dirty-blonde hair piled up in a beehive.

She moved in close and said, 'Hey, I know you. Let me buy you a drink.'

'No, thank you, ma'am. I think you're mistaken.'

'You're the crazy guy who shot that kid in Mexico. I saw you on NBC news.'

Virgo laughed: *the crazy guy*. Fame at last. Maybe he could start selling autographed T-shirts and cutting the ribbon at new shopping malls. Roll up, roll up, see the freak.

She put a hand on his arm. 'Sorry, I don't mean you *are* crazy, but they said you'd had some kind of breakdown.'

'It's okay. I'm fine.'

'My name's Bobby, short for Roberta. All of us think you did the right thing.' She pointed the beehive in the direction of the party.

'*All* of you? Does everyone in LA pay such close attention to the news?'

'We all work in the same hospital as Isabella Alvarez did. None of us knew her personally, but that's not the point. Come on over; let's get you another beer.'

Virgo glanced across at the rest of the bachelorette party, who were now smiling and waving back at him. He felt uncomfortable. They should be castigating him for not saving their work colleague, not wanting to buy him a drink. At that moment, the strictly-no-admittance door swung open and a bald, middle-aged man came out into the club. Virgo threw out an arm and grabbed the handle before it closed and the magnetic lock kicked in. The bald man looked back over his shoulder as though he might say something, but appeared to think better of it and just walked off. 'Maybe later, Bobby,' Virgo said, and shot off into the staff-only corridor. As soon as the door plipped shut behind him, he checked his phone to see if there'd been any contact from Daniel Donovan. Negative.

The plaque on the first door said *Food and Beverage Director*, so he skipped past to the next, which said *General Manager*. He knocked and went in, but it was empty. Just a single workstation with an antique desktop PC from the Middle Ages. He ducked back out into the corridor and tried the third room. Bingo. There was a bank of six monitors, displaying internal and external views of the premises. There was also a kid sat at a big square table in the middle of the room, eating sandwiches from a Tupperware container. Seemed the CCTV suite was also the staff mess room. There was an overstuffed, leather Chesterfield down one wall, and a coffee machine and water cooler on the other.

'I'm from the FBI.' Virgo smiled at the kid. 'The manager said you'd download some video footage for me from last night.'

'Did she?' The kid wore a crumpled black suit with a name badge: *Tyler*. He arched one eyebrow. 'It's not really my job. I'm accounts.'

'Do you know how to?'

'I've done it before, but I'm on my meal break.'

'It's kind of important.' Virgo bent down and narrowed his eyes. 'That's why I'm not asking, I'm ordering you to do it. NOW.'

Tyler scuttled over to the CCTV station and went through a log-in protocol. Then he opened a new window and pulled up some folders. Double-clicked and scrolled. Five minutes went by, and he was still going. Every now and then, he went *urgh?* and arched the same left eyebrow.

'Come on. I need it today.' Virgo was worried about the bald man. Maybe he'd seen him sneaking in the staff corridor.

'I can't find it.'

'What do you mean, you can't find it?'

'It's not there, or someone's blocked my access to it.'

'How?'

'I don't know. I told you – I'm accounts.'

The door burst open, and the crevice-faced doorman bowled in and shouted, 'What the fuck do you think you're doing?'

Virgo held out open palms. Universal sign of peace, guaranteed to defuse any situation. 'It's okay. Tyler is just doing a little job for me.'

Tyler jumped up. 'He made me do it, Mike.'

Virgo shook his head with disappointment. *Thanks, pal.*

A second bouncer appeared. His frame filled the entire doorway, and he had to dip his box-shaped head to get into the room.

Mike took a step towards Virgo. 'We can do this the easy way or the hard way.'

'You choose, but if either of them involve you touching me, I'll break both your arms.'

'Hah.' Mike didn't scare easy. Not with a seven-foot box-head behind him. In fact, he seemed to relish the gauntlet being thrown in his direction. 'I don't know who you really are, mister, but it's time someone taught you a lesson.'

Virgo still gave it the open palms. 'Walk away. Stick to bullying teenagers and selling drugs or whatever you do. Go and show your pecs off in front of the girls. Have a bit of fun.'

Mike smiled and pulled some brass knuckles from his jacket. 'Take a walk, Tyler. You don't want to see this.'

Tyler didn't want to see it. He bolted out of the room.

Virgo waited. He'd never choose a confined space to engage in combat, but on this occasion, he wasn't unduly worried. The layout made it difficult for his adversaries to attack him at the same time. They had to stand in line and wait their turn, which made his task a whole lot easier. Like shelling peas.

Mike came at him. Virgo knew, as soon as he'd seen the brass knuckles, that the first attack would be a straight right punch, intended to break his jaw or cheekbone. He held his nerve, and let it come onto him. At the last moment, he turned sideways and swayed back at the hips. The fist shot past the tip of his nose. Mike's arm was now fully extended. Virgo hooked his own right arm around the front of Mike's forearm and used his upper-body weight to push against the back of Mike's bicep. Elbow locked, there was nothing to absorb the pressure. *SNAP.* The arm gave way. Clean breaks to both radius and ulna.

Virgo let him drop to the floor and spun round, ready to block an attack from box-head, but the big fellow hadn't moved. His brain seemed to be having difficulty rationalizing what had just happened. He stood, mouth open. Then he let out a two-hundred-decibel roar and charged head down. Mass times acceleration equals force. Virgo was cornered. He knew he couldn't defy Newton's second law and somehow repel the impact with a blow or a kick. Best chance was to dodge or deflect some of the momentum.

Matadors make it look a piece of cake, but they have space. Virgo didn't. The top of the huge doorman's head made contact with his chest and sent him flying backwards, over the prostrate body of Mike and across the CCTV desk. There was a loud crack as the back of his own skull smashed into one of the big monitors. Tiny shards of glass rained down. His lungs couldn't suck in air, and screamed for help. Virgo knew that kinetic trauma had sent his diaphragm into spasm, and it was temporary, but he didn't have time for recovery. A fist buried itself in his left cheek.

Virgo was dizzy. He tried to roll away, but another fist slammed into his right kidney and fired bolts of agony through his entire body. So much for shelling peas. He knew this was the critical point. Another punch to the right area could finish him off. He was pinned down on the desk with nowhere to go. Quick. He shimmied one way and rolled the other. Sent up an arm to block the attack. It was just enough. The next piledriver missed its target and caught him on the shoulder. Painful, but not the coup de grâce.

It gave him a split second. He used the leverage of the wall to send a roundhouse kick into the bouncer's ribs. Followed it up with an even more powerful one to the exact same spot. Then he sprang up. Lungs finally pumping oxygen. Grabbed a porcelain coffee mug, and introduced it to the bridge of the big guy's nose. There was an eruption of blood. The bouncer swung some wild punches.

Now things were even. Street fights last less than sixty seconds for many reasons, but one is physical fitness.

Boxhead was breathing heavy. Virgo flicked out a left fist to tee him up, then hit him square on the jaw with a Sunday-best right. The big guy blinked. Blood from the split nose splashed all over, but he didn't flinch. Virgo couldn't believe it. Time for some improvisation. He picked up a swivel chair and rammed it wheels-first into the bouncer's face. The big man staggered backwards and went down.

Virgo launched himself and planted a knee on his chest. Never let an advantage slip until your opponent no longer poses a credible threat. He crashed a fist down into the bouncer's mouth. Pulled it back for another, and…

'FREEZE. THAT'S ENOUGH.'

Two uniform cops stood in the doorway. Weapons drawn and pointed firmly in his direction.

CHAPTER 11

THE DISTANT SOUND of a drunk puking his guts, the rancid stench of stale body odor, and a brutal fluorescent light that burned patterns in the back of his eyes. Virgo lay on the bench of an LAPD cell and stared hard at the ceiling. He'd started the day behind bars, and it looked like he was going to finish it on the wrong side of another set. Not bad for someone who'd spent most of his adult life in the law enforcement arena. Maybe he really was the crazy guy.

In another cell down the corridor, a man started singing 'Heartbreak Hotel.' His voice was awful, but he knew all the words. Virgo groaned and slapped the wall in frustration. The discomfort didn't bother him, but the feeling of impotence did; without his phone, there was nothing he could do to contribute towards Stacy Donovan's safety. The senator could be trying to contact him right now.

Time passed. Tone-deaf Elvis ran through his full repertoire. A hundred years later, keys clattered, and a uniform officer escorted him up a flight of steps to an interview room. He was told to sit down and wait. Another hundred years dragged by. LAPD incompetence, or a softening-up tactic?

He'd already told them he didn't want a lawyer, so why the hold-up?

Finally, the door opened, and a couple of plain clothes walked in and sat opposite. Man and a woman.

The woman smiled and said, 'I'm Detective Accardi, and this is Detective Nash. You're Virgo.' It was a statement, not a question.

'I was born June twentieth, so really I'm Gemini.' Virgo smiled back.

Nash wore red suspenders that matched his complexion and held up pinstripe pants. He leant forward and almost spat. 'Don't start with the fancy chat-up lines, asshole. You're in a world of shit.'

Virgo smiled at Accardi. 'Say something nice. I really love the good-cop, bad-cop thing you've got going here. It's beautiful.'

Nash palm-slammed the table. 'Typical fucking federal agent, can't help himself. Got to prove he's the smartest dick in the room.'

'Sometimes it's not much of a challenge.' Virgo folded his arms and leaned back.

Traces of laughter appeared in Accardi's eyes, but she kept her mouth straight. 'Tell us what you were doing at La Souris nightclub.'

Nash jumped in. 'Apart from beating the crap out of their legitimate security personnel.'

'I can't.' Virgo put on his best *trust-me* face. 'It's a secret operation that involves an imminent threat to life. That's why I need my phone back and to get out of here straight away.'

'A secret? How convenient?' Nash's voice was riddled with contempt. 'Why don't you whisper it, and we'll pretend we never heard?' Then he stood up and palm-slammed the table again. 'I'll tell you why you won't, because it's bullshit. Explain this, wiseass: how come someone who got eight years' incarceration is out in under one? You Steve McQueen in the fucking *Great Escape?*'

'No, he got recaptured, I think you'll find.' Virgo tutted at the ill-judged reference to such an iconic movie. 'I got early release. Check with the DOJ.'

Accardi said, 'We will, but their office is nine to five.' She shuffled a few papers until she found the one she was after. 'Apart from the crime of aggravated battery, your other big problem is that you were arrested in possession of a gun.'

'It's just a standard FBI handgun.' Virgo guessed what was coming.

Nash had a look of glee on his crimson face. 'It's unlawful for a convicted felon to own or possess a gun. Stick that one up your smart, ex-FBI ass.'

'Come on, that's a technicality.'

Accardi sighed. 'Look, we can't help you unless you tell us why you wanted that CCTV.'

'I'll give you the number of someone senior who'll vouch for me.'

'Michael Theodore Mouse, care of Disney Studios, Burbank. I'm not going to waste my time.' Nash opened the interview room door. 'Come on, Jenny. The guy's a joke.'

'Don't listen to him, Jenny.' Virgo clasped his hands together in supplication. 'I need to get out of here this minute.'

Accardi followed Nash to the door. 'Sorry, looks like you'll have to take your chances at court in the morning.'

The door was closing, and Virgo had to make a leap of faith. Either that or he'd be banged up for another twelve hours. 'Wait. Let me explain.'

Accardi and Nash both turned on their heels, but Virgo shook his head. 'No, just you on your own, Jenny. I don't want him in the room. Too much negative energy.'

Detective Accardi gave Nash the eyes, and he stomped off. She came and sat back down. 'You've got one chance.'

'Can I trust you?'

'What's your other choice?'

'A girl was abducted, and I'm working the case for the bureau.'

'Why you? You're no longer an agent.'

'If I told you it's because I'm the best in the world at this kind of thing, would you believe me?'

'No.'

'Okay, there's some internal issues in the branch, and they want the case handling by someone on the outside.'

'How can I verify this?'

'Call Nick Hartman. He's head of the Crisis Negotiation Unit. It's his personal handgun I was carrying.'

'We already tried, and he didn't pick up.'

Virgo cursed under his breath. 'His flight doesn't land for another three hours. I can't wait that long.'

'I want to believe you, but you just broke a guy's arm and beat his colleague unconscious.'

Virgo didn't want to say it, but he had no choice. 'Call Senator Daniel Donovan at the Ritz-Carlton. It was his daughter, and I met him this afternoon.'

'Okay, I don't think I need to speak to the senator. Only someone working the case would know Stacy Donovan had been kidnapped.'

'You know about the case?'

'I was the detective who took the initial report from her friends and tracked the witness down at the club. That's why me and Nash are here to interview you.'

Cogs began to turn in Virgo's brain. 'You referred the case to the bureau?'

'Correct.' Accardi nodded and brushed back a strand of black hair. 'They told me to keep it confidential, and an agent would be in touch. I was kind of expecting someone in a suit to visit the office, not an ex-con with bruises and an attitude to turn up in the jail.'

'Yeah, well, it seems I'm the best they've got right now.' The cogs turned again. 'Did you check the CCTV?'

'I got it downloaded to a flash drive.'

Virgo clapped his hands. 'What we waiting for?'

CHAPTER 12

JACOB SAT on the front porch and stared up at the night sky. The location of the farmhouse was perfect. No light pollution to screw up a person's contemplation of celestial bodies. The Seven Sisters was his favorite star cluster, and he located them to the right of a waxing crescent moon. They were some of the closest to Earth, but still 440 light-years away, which meant the light he was looking at this second left their surface around 1570, some fifty years before the Pilgrim Fathers landed at Cape Cod. That's if his calculations were correct, which he was confident they were.

Sometimes, he astonished himself with the infinitesimal detail he could hold in the mental filing cabinets of his head, then pull out at will. He'd spent his time wisely at the Euphemism. He liked to call it that because most people don't know what the word means, and it made him feel superior. Those that did know what he meant had no idea where it was or why he was there. When the sickness first came, he could scarcely remember his own name, Jacob. He still didn't like to say his second name, even in the privacy of his own mind, because of the darkness it carried in its wake. He'd wanted to change it twenty years ago, but they wouldn't let him. When this was over, he was going to change it to something exotic.

The fly-screen door banged open, and Dukes came out carrying a tray with two bowls of pasta in a red sauce. He set it down on the table with a thud. 'There's a fucking Mickey D's twenty miles down the road.'

Jacob said, 'I've told you. We don't show our faces in town.'

Dukes was agitated. 'Why is it me doing the cooking?'

'Because I say so.'

'Tommy Junior's in charge. Not you.'

'Tommy Junior's not here.' Jacob picked up both bowls of pasta, walked to the edge of the porch, and tipped them out onto the dirt. 'Go and fix two more.'

Dukes didn't say anything. The spark of defiance in his eye fizzled out and was replaced by fear and suspicion, like a beaten pack dog. He took the empty bowls and went back inside.

Jacob sat back in his chair and found the Seven Sisters again. They'd almost reached their highest point in the sky. People once believed this was the time when the veil that divides the living from the dead is at its thinnest. Maybe they were right. He checked his phone, but there was no message yet from the Helper. As soon as it arrived, he knew what to do, and a tingle of expectation tickled the nape of his neck and made the hairs on the back of his arms stand to attention.

He looked out across the fields for signs that any stranger might be approaching, but nothing moved. The Helper had made an excellent choice in selecting the farmhouse. It was away from the tourist areas and far enough off the main highways to deter sightseers and hikers. Built mid-nineteenth century by Dutch or German settlers. He especially liked the icehouse, which the farmers had once used to keep their vegetable crop cool throughout the long, hot summers. Perfect these days for storing dead bodies.

A notification pinged on his phone. The Donovan girl must be moving again. He opened the app and selected the camera he'd installed in the roof of the pit. There she was. Walking round and round clockwise like a pet mouse. Moving at a brisk pace, to try and keep the blood pumping because the pit was so cold. The old icehouses were always built near an underground river or spring to take advantage of the naturally low temperatures. Jacob knew he had to make sure she didn't die from hypothermia before the operational objective had been achieved.

As well as watching, the app allowed him to speak to her, and he was tempted to do it now. Should he? Tell her the identity of the man whose body she was busy doing laps around, and savor her reaction. No, patience. That would be a pleasure indeed, but it had to wait. Everything had to be done in accordance with the plan.

Ping. Another notification. This time a WhatsApp from the Helper. Just a couple of little two-letter words:

Do it.

Jacob smiled to nobody but himself, then pocketed the phone and opened the fly-screen door. 'Come on. We've got to go over to the icehouse.'

Dukes came out, dropped a cigarette onto the porch, and ground it out with his heel. 'What the hell for?'

'It's time.' Jacob led the way along the narrow dirt track. It was less than thirty yards from the old farmhouse, through sage scrub and coyote brush.

Inside the icehouse, he'd set up a monitoring station to one side of the giant hatch that covered the pit. It was a table and easy chair, with a MacBook, Wi-Fi extender, assorted electrical equipment and a coffee machine. He perched on the arm of the chair and said, 'Alexa, play my soundtrack.' A synthetic voice said, 'Playing my soundtrack from Amazon Music,' and the iconic intro riff to 'American Idiot' blasted out.

Dukes almost had to shout. 'What the fuck's happening?'

'It's remote here, but we don't want to take chances. Screams can carry distances.'

'Tommy Junior said don't touch her.' Dukes chewed some nail off a finger and spat it out.

'I already told you. Tommy Junior's not here.'

Dukes started to edge backward. 'If you kill her, it's got nothing to do with me.'

'I'm killing you, not her.' Jacob lurched forward, fast for a huge man, and angled a chop between Dukes's head and shoulder. It came down like a drop hammer, and the collar bone snapped instantly. Dukes yelped, and dropped to one knee. Another chop crashed straight down, and the collar bone on the other side gave way just as easy. More yelps.

Jacob took a moment. There was a Sig Sauer and a suppressor in his pocket, but that would be cheating. Most people can point and pull a trigger. Nothing beats the feeling of satisfaction derived from using your own hands or feet to bring death to another living creature. It's hard-wired deep inside all of us from the time we lived in caves and had to hunt to survive.

He dragged Dukes up and pinned him to the wall. Squeezed his throat until his eyes bull-frogged and his knees buckled. 'People dismiss "American Idiot" as just some garbage punk music, but it's a classic rock opera. Jesus of Suburbia escapes small-town boredom to try and find out who he really is, but he can't, because our politics and culture are so fucked up.' Jacob let go, and Dukes dropped to the floor.

'Bet you were more a country boy than Green Day.' Jacob swung a boot and kicked Dukes in the side of the head. Snot and saliva sprayed onto the limewash wall. Dukes groaned. Shallow breaths. Jacob lifted his boot and stamped along to the rhythm of the music, his foot pulping Dukes's head on every fourth beat: *mash, mash, mash*. When the final note of distorted guitar rang out, Jacob stood with a massive grin on his face. It was just like old times.

CHAPTER 13

THE GUY PILOTING the CCTV console looked like James T Kirk on the bridge of the *Enterprise*. He wore a shirt the color of baby shit and had slicked-back hair. A look of mild irritation on a face that had seen too many carbs. 'This is going to take all damn night.'

Detective Accardi stared at the monitor. 'Try the feed from another camera. And earlier.'

Virgo thumbed through the witness statements from the friends Stacy Donovan had gone to the club with: Beth Hudson and Joseph Hagstrom. They'd nipped outside to the smoking area, and when they got back, she'd gone. At first they didn't think anything of it, but after an hour went by, they got worried and tried to call her. He stopped reading. 'Hey. It says here they tried *both* Stacy's numbers.'

Accardi said, 'She had two phones.'

'What sort of kid carries a burner, apart from dealers?'

'Stacy thought her father had put a tracking device on her main phone, so she switched it off when she went out, and used a cheap Samsung.'

'He was concerned for her safety?'

'No. I got the impression he's a controlling dick, who doesn't want his daughter to party his money away at college instead of studying.'

A short time ago, the sergeant in custody had refused to return the Glock to Virgo, but they had given him back his phone. He took it out now and pulled up the photographs of Hartman's report. The bureau had only got one number for Stacy, which was the one her father had supplied. No calls or messages after 5 p.m. yesterday afternoon. He could ask Accardi to check the other number through the LAPD's telecoms bureau, but it would leave a footprint, and, until he knew whom he was dealing with, he preferred to remain incognito. It would have to wait until morning.

'Virgo, look at this.' Accardi called him over to the monitor.

The CCTV footage showed a corridor inside the club and covered the cloakroom. A few people stood in groups chatting, waiting for friends to check bags.

Accardi said, 'Keep watching.'

Stacy Donovan staggered into view. The drunkest woman in the world. She had her arm wrapped around another woman's shoulders, and a tall guy in a Redskins cap was holding her up by the elbow. Her head lolled to one side.

Virgo said, 'They took her out the fire exit.'

Accardi said, 'Play it again, but slow it right down.'

Captain Kirk made a loud tutting noise, as though mundane tasks were a waste of his talents. Maybe he was only a CCTV operator in his spare time, in between saving the populations of faraway planets.

This time the video was snail-paced. Slow enough to see the lack of focus in Stacy Donovan's eyes and the sweat glistening on her top lip. The man supporting her was wide as well as tall and clearly knew he was on film: he had the base-ball cap pulled down, brim angled towards the camera. No view of his face. The woman was bottle-blonde, with bright red lips and lace-up boots.

'I think I've seen her before.' Accardi leaned in close and squinted. 'Yes, definitely. She's on a slab.'

Virgo stared at the screen in puzzlement while the detective joined the dots for him. The woman was called Angie Rogan. Accardi had seen her photograph at evening brief-ing, because her body had been found in a loading bay in Santa Monica. Bullet in the back of her head. Initial hypoth-esis was an unhappy punter or pervert, because Angie Rogan was a self-employed escort who found clients through a sugar-dating app. Like calling a cab. Want a ride? Swipe right.

Accardi rang the mortuary, but the only property that had been brought in with the body was the clothes she wore: no money, no bag, no phone. She hung up. 'Want to try her apartment?'

Virgo checked his own cell, but there was still nothing from the senator. 'Sure, why not?'

'Didn't know whether you high-flying federal agents could bring yourself to do legwork with a lowly police detective.'

'I'm not an agent anymore, so I'm allowed to lower myself to your level.'

Accardi laughed. 'First time I've been partnered up with a convict.'

They headed east on Santa Monica Boulevard, into a night sky tinged yellow by dust from wildfires in Fresno County, and all the way to Silver Lake, where they cut north towards Pasadena. Traffic was light. Accardi drove fast, window down, elbow out, and black hair flapping over her left shoul-der. Nothing wrong with the AC, but the unmarked Dodge had the usual detective-car odor: foot sweat, cigarettes and take-out food.

Angie Rogan's home was a cedar-clad A-frame, snuggled behind hedges of Portuguese laurel, and with a neat, pocket-handkerchief lawn. It was the kind of house you could see Doris Day living in in a 1960s movie, except Doris wouldn't be working the downtown hotels as a hooker and charging five hundred bucks a pop. Extra for the back door.

The place had already been searched by the day shift, and the front door had been blocked by two bands of horizontal yellow tape. A symbolic barrier. Inside, the house was clean with high-end furnishings and adorned with tasteful works of art. It was clear Angie Rogan kept her personal and business lives separate.

Accardi searched the bedroom. Virgo went to work in the kitchen-diner. He wasn't exactly sure what he was looking for. A written plan pinned to the corkboard, outlining how to kidnap a famous senator's daughter, would be nice, but that was unlikely. Angie Rogan had been hired to do a job, and once her role was finished, so was she.

There were a few framed photographs by the window. One looked to be a young Angie playing Tallulah in a school production of *Bugsy Malone*. Another showed a teenage Angie smiling at a beach bar in between an older couple. Mom and dad? Did they know what their daughter did for a living, or just that she left home to become a star to Hollywood? Clichés are sad.

Virgo opened the fridge and was surprised to see it well-stocked. He expected people who lived on their own to have no fresh food in the house, or maybe that was just him since Crystal died. There didn't seem much point in cooking. Next the dishwasher. It looked like Angie Rogan's last meal had been something with broccoli in a cheese sauce, made from scratch. He was starting to feel inadequate.

In the center of the room was a big island with a marble countertop, and four stools. The closest end stool was clearly where she sat on her own most of the time. There were a couple of magazines, and a coaster for her coffee mug. It looked like it was also where she conducted her escort business: there was an iPhone charger still plugged in, a pen, and a pad of lemon Post-it notes, conveniently located to jot down the room numbers of visiting businessmen from Milwaukee.

'Hey, look at this.' Virgo peeled off the top sticky note and waited for Accardi.

There were three words written on the note:

tiger, grape, chariot

He held it out. 'Hell of a shopping list.'

Accardi screwed up her eyes. 'Who buys a tiger?

'Someone who wants to upgrade from a domestic cat?'

'Or a single grape?'

'People on a diet.'

'Chariot?'

'Got me there. I don't know anyone with a chariot.'

'They're just three random words.' Accardi nodded, brushed back a strand of hair from her face, and pulled out her phone. 'Yes, that's it. That must be it.'

'Urgh?'

'What3Words is an app that gives you the most accurate location of anywhere in the world. Ambulance crews use it all the time.'

'Never heard of it.'

'That's because I'm a detective, and you're a dumbass FBI reject.'

'Stop with the flattery.' Virgo folded the Post-it note into his top pocket. 'Just tell me where we can find *tiger, grape, chariot*.'

Accardi used a finger and thumb to zoom in and navigate a map on the phone. Her tongue popped out of her mouth as an aid to concentration and hovered around a while before bidding farewell and retreating home. Job done. 'Okay, don't get excited. It's a parking lot in Westwood Village.'

CHAPTER 14

WESTWOOD VILLAGE WAS a minor detour on the way back to Santa Monica. Accardi took the 405 to Wilshire and left onto Gayley. The app sent her left again at a church, then right at an In-N-Out Burger onto a narrow street, where two hundred yards later, she pulled into a parking lot and said, 'Tiger, grape, chariot.'

Virgo looked around. 'Strange place to meet a client.'

Accardi backed up into a space and killed the engine. 'It's not covered by any cameras, which means it's the perfect place if you don't want to leave evidence.'

'Notice anything else?'

'Like what?'

'The license plates are nearly all from out of town: Wyoming, Nebraska, Illinois…' Virgo pointed some out. The parking lot was half full. Maybe twenty vehicles.

'That's because we're spitting distance from UCLA.'

'Do they look like college students to you?' Virgo nodded towards two men approaching a black Cherokee SUV with Nebraska plates. They were both over six feet, mid-thirties, dressed smart, and carrying sports bags.

'Postgrads?'

'I don't think so.' Virgo stepped out of the car to get a better view of the adjacent buildings. It looked like the parking lot serviced a gym, a sushi bar, a bookstore and a letting agency. All of the places were closed apart from the gym, and the two guys were carrying sports bags. Mmmm? His powers of deduction kicked in. Maybe he was getting the hang of this detective business.

The gym was called Benny's. It was up two flights of stairs, and the guy on reception sat drinking a tin of Bud, watching the Dodgers on a fifty-inch TV. He wore a Lonsdale vest to best show the world his collection of tattoos, which covered every inch of skin, and he had piercings in his nose and eyebrows.

Accardi badged him and showed a photograph on her phone of Angie Rogan. 'Seen this lady before?'

The guy did a double take on the badge, but didn't even glance at the photograph. 'Nope.'

Virgo leaned across the counter. 'Have another look, and try harder this time.'

'This is my place. Nobody tells me what to do.' The owner of the eponymous gym barreled his chest. He looked like he'd been a bodybuilder back in the day, but now a lot of the muscle had run to blubber.

Virgo grabbed a big handful of the Lonsdale vest. He pulled Benny over the counter, gripped hold of both ears, and pushed his face into the phone. 'Let me help you.'

'Get your fucking hands off me.'

'Seen her before?' Virgo yanked the ears.

'Aaargh.' Benny flailed his arms. 'I'm going to knock you out, asshole.'

Virgo shoved Benny back across the counter. 'Why don't me and you go into the gym and do this properly? See who gets knocked out?'

There was a moment's silence. Virgo saw the hesitation in Benny's face and then submission, camouflaged by an air of indifference.

Benny said, 'Don't want to waste my energy.'

A guy walked out of the gym, carrying a sports duffel and pumping out a strong smell of pine-scent deodorant. He seemed to sense the tension. 'Everything okay, Benny?'

'Everything's good.' Benny smiled. 'I was just explaining to these police officers that we don't get women in the gym.'

The guy smiled back and disappeared down the stairs. Virgo watched him go. He was dressed similar to the two men he'd seen get in the Cherokee. Smart khaki pants, and the same brand of polo shirt: the one where a man on a horse is about to strike your left nipple with a long mallet. Nothing unusual in itself except for the clean-cut blandness. In a city where everyone strives to exhibit their individuality, it was strange.

Back in the unmarked car, Accardi squealed the back wheels as she fishtailed it out of the parking lot and back onto the street. 'Don't do that again.'

'What?' Virgo tried to sound innocent.

'There's this quaint tradition in the LAPD — we don't assault or intimidate witnesses.'

'I'm trying to save a girl's life.'

'Okay, listen to me. I read your case file, and maybe that shitshow in Mexico happened because you got too emotionally involved.'

'Thanks, but I don't need any advice.'

Accardi grunted and lit a cigarette. 'Don't complain. It's not your car.'

The remainder of the journey was in silence. North of Culver City, Virgo felt the seductive pull of gravity on his eyelids and fought it off. But it had been a lifetime since he woke at 0400 hours in Federal Correctional Institution, Eagle

Valley, and if he wanted to be fresh and alert tomorrow, he needed sleep. At some point, Daniel Donovan was going to realize it wasn't a good idea to refuse help. When the call came, he had to be ready.

Accardi pulled up outside the hotel. 'Fancy going for a beer?'

'I can't.' Virgo made an apologetic smile.

'I'm not giving advice, but hey, take care of yourself.' Accardi screeched the tires again and left a cloud of smoke.

Virgo walked past the hotel reception, and had a hand out to press the elevator button, when a concierge dashed up to tell him he had guests waiting in the bar. It was gone midnight. Who knew he was staying there?

The bar was empty apart from two men in suits, whom Virgo didn't recognize, but identified as ex-Army. When he got closer, he saw they wore matching purple lapel pins, *IFS*. They must have known him, because they stood up and invited him over to their table. An unopened bottle of champagne sat in an ice bucket. The older one pulled out a business card and said, 'We're here to make you a job offer.'

Virgo studied the card. *David T. Mettam, Operations Director, Indigo Fox Solutions.* 'Send me an email, and I'll get back to you if I'm interested.'

Mettam was calm and unruffled. 'We're not a conventional company, with an oversized HR department.' His voice purred, like a Ferrari V8. 'We prefer to make a direct approach.'

'Why me?' Virgo folded his arms.

'Indigo Fox Solutions are all from a military background. Our operatives provide crisis intervention for private companies, the US government, and other friendly regimes. Right now, we need someone experienced in negotiation.'

'Sorry, I'm busy.' Virgo didn't have time for a bullshit sales pitch, or whatever was coming.

'That's okay. We are aware of your current deployment in relation to the young lady who had been abducted, and we are happy to sign you up now, but let you finalize that case.'

'What? How come you're aware?'

'We are trusted partners of all sectors within the US government.' Mettam signaled to a barman to come over and open the champagne. 'Salary 140 a year, plus expenses.'

'It's a generous offer. Let me sleep on it.'

'You drive a hard bargain.'

'I'm not trying to haggle. I'm tired.'

Mettam nodded to his colleague, who hadn't said a word. He was a bald guy with a purple scar that curled from the top of his left ear down to the corner of his mouth. First glance, you might think he was smirking, but he wasn't. The look in his eyes was controlled anger. He opened a briefcase and took out some papers. Slid them across the table.

Mettam said, 'In addition, I'm authorized to pay you a one-off sign-up bonus of $25,000.'

Virgo thought about it. Twenty-five grand might buy a small, half-decent RV, but what for? The reason for owning one was to get away from work and the aggravation of modern society. 'Thanks, but I'm not interested.'

'It's a one-off deal.' Mettam pointed to the contract on the table. The final pitch of a door-to-door salesman.

'You've got my answer.' Virgo watched the reaction of the two men opposite. Mettam seemed genuinely disappointed. Scarface looked like someone just took a dump in his Rice Krispies.

CHAPTER 15

STACY HEARD MUSIC. No melody or words, just the dull thump of a heavy, repetitive bassline from above the pit. It resonated in the base of her skull and sent shockwaves coursing through her scalp. She knew it was a tension headache, caused by stress and not being able to relax the muscles in her neck and back. She rotated her shoulders and stretched the knots out in her spine. How much longer would they keep her down here? How much more could she physically endure?

Time no longer existed. Her internal circadian rhythm, shot to pieces, didn't tell her if it was midday or midnight. She didn't care. The only thing she wanted was to go home and go to bed. Nothing else mattered anymore. The dreams of college success and building a new professional life were not in the least bit exciting and never would be. Relationships? No way. She didn't want anything that could cause more pain. Her resilience was too thin.

Even memories hurt: the loving touch of her mother, the first time she jumped a fence on a pony, the sun setting over the lake as she giggled her way down a joint. Somehow the scenes in her mind became foreign, as if they had happened to a different person or in a previous life. Was she going mad? Had the trauma triggered some kind of chemical imbalance in her thought process? She needed rest.

Then the sound changed. A scraping of metal on metal that heralded from above a light so bright it scalded the backs of her eyeballs. She clamped her hands in front of her face and knew that the gate to her prison was being opened. Why? Warmth flooded in with the fluorescent blaze and the oxygen-rich scent of fresh air.

Gradually, she pulled her hands away and squinted into the gap above. A figure loomed over. Was this it? Had her time come to be abused or put out of her misery like a wounded animal? She could hear the music properly now. Loud and booming. Couldn't remember the title, but it was by an old band called Blink-182, and the chorus was *la-la, la-la, la-la, la-la, la*, over and over. Then it stopped.

'If you scream or try and shout out, the playlist goes back on, and I close the hatch.'

Stacy forced herself to look. It was him. The weird bigfoot from the club, with the same baseball cap on. 'Why are you doing this to me?'

'Shut up and smile for your daddy.' A phone pointed down. It seemed small in the giant hand.

'If you're reasonable, I'm sure my father will pay you what you want.' Stacy tried to give the outward appearance of calm. Inside, she was a chaotic mix of terror and panic.

'That's the problem with rich folk. They think everything's about money.'

'Then what do you want?'

'Something more important.' Bigfoot bent down and grabbed something that looked like a sack of denim in both hands. 'Say hello to Dukes.'

Stacy knew it was a dead body as soon as the shape

appeared above her. She stepped back as it cartwheeled down and landed with a low thud on the other corpse like a sack of white cabbage. The body was that of a male, but the face was unrecognizable: a crimson explosion of blood and tissue; pieces of teeth and bone stuck out.

Now Stacy knew she was going to die in the pit. It was her tomb. She couldn't begin to imagine the sick motives behind why she had been taken, but it didn't matter. A ransom wasn't going to save her, and even if her father gave them what they wanted, they would kill her nevertheless. She had seen bigfoot's face. He wasn't going to leave witnesses to a killing spree. What had she got to lose? She took a deep breath and screamed, 'HELP ME. PLEASE SOMEONE HELP ME.'

Straight away the song filled the air: *la-la, la-la, la-la, la-la, la-la, la…*

The iron hatch screeched, and again it was dark.

CHAPTER 16

VIRGO WOKE AT 4:30, thanks to the prison routine, and checked his phone right away for any contact from Daniel Donovan. Negative. A hundred push-ups and a shower, and he was in a twenty-four-hour diner down the street, sat in a chintzy red booth, eating the Filler-Up breakfast of bacon, sausage, eggs, potatoes, gravy and pancakes à la the Leaning Tower of Pisa. As soon as the plate was clean, he took out his phone and rang a company in Berlin, called UMI Elektronik und Sicherheit. It was a front for the CIA and where Caleb Hawkins, a friend from Army days, now spent his time hacking into secure IT systems.

'It's Virgo.'

'Shit, you got a phone?' Hawkins laughed out in surprise. 'Only fuckers in jail got a phone are the ones dealing crack.'

'I'm out, and I need billing and cell-site on a number.'

'You still get tickets for the Kennedy Center?'

'I doubt it.' Virgo knew that was coming. Information is a currency to be bartered, and his buddy from the special forces was a three-hundred-pound African American with a penchant for opera. 'What about doing me a favor, just this once?'

'You said that last time.'

'Fine. Next visit to the States, I'll pay for the tickets myself.'

'Swear to God, on the creed of the Activity?'

The full name of the special force's unit was Mission Support Activity. A team so deep undercover, it was usually referred to by a project name that kept changing: Task Force Orange, Centra Spike, Grantor Shadow, Opaque Leaf, Cemetery Wind, Intrepid Spear.

Virgo said, 'I swear.'

An hour later, he was killing time, sat on a park bench watching joggers, and Lycra-people cross-legged on the grass meditating, when his phone lit up. *Hartman.*

'Any news?'

'What the fuck are you doing getting arrested? I told you to sit tight.' It sounded as though Hartman was eating.

'I got bored.' Virgo was surprised it had taken so long for Hartman to find out about the incident at La Souris.

'Why do you always find trouble and land up in a pile of shit?'

'What can I say? I guess it's a gift.'

'And I have to dig you out. Do you want to go back to prison, is that it?'

'We need investigators here on the ground.'

'They'll be with you early afternoon.' Hartman sighed and took a deep breath. 'And get used to being bored, or I'll find someone else who likes it.'

Virgo was about to hang up when he remembered something. 'Hey, Nick. Did you send the head hunters?'

'Wha…?' Hartman had taken another mouthful of something. Consonants couldn't form because of the bulk in his mouth.

'Two guys from a private outfit. Wanted me on the books as a negotiator.'

'Ha, ha, ha.' A piece of food caught in Hartman's throat, and he choked it up. 'Sorry.' More coughs. 'Best joke I've heard in a long time. They must be desperate.'

'Thanks.' Virgo ended the call. If it wasn't Hartman who recommended him to Indigo Fox Solutions, who was it? How did they know where he was, and on the very day that he had been released from prison?

When contact came from Caleb Hawkins, it was a What-sApp message, which included screen-shots of a spreadsheet and a map, and Virgo said, 'Interesting,' to nobody but two pigeons scratting around by his feet. It turned out Stacy Donovan had been using her burner phone on the night she disappeared. It had received a call forty minutes after she'd been abducted from a number belonging to Beth Hudson, the friend she'd gone to the club with. A call made to find out where she was. It was not answered, but tripped onto voice-mail, which was enough to mean it registered on the nearest cell-phone tower. Strike, game on.

Hawkins had shaded in a section of the map to look like a slice of pizza. It was the 120-degree triangle covered by one of the three antennas on the cell tower and indicated the area where Stacy Donovan's mobile had been when the call was received. There was nothing that could be done in terms of signal strength or cross-referencing with other towers, so there was no way of determining the distance away. It was an area pushing a hundred square miles, northeast of the city. The size was enormous, but applying logic could identify areas to prioritize.

Route 395 starts outside San Bernardino and runs all the way up to the state border in Oregon, but it was the section beyond the Mohave Desert and Edwards Air Force Base that was of interest, just before it skirted the Sequoia National Park, and headed off in the valley edge of the Sierra Nevada. The cell tower was located half a mile off the highway, and it was the antenna facing into the foothills that had picked up the signal from Stacy's phone. This was important. It meant the kidnappers had probably turned off the 395 and not carried on to Canada or somewhere else on the way.

The investigation team were due to arrive after lunch, which gave him time to recon the area and report back. They didn't know about Stacy's burner phone, and maybe that was a good thing, if there was a leak in the Operational Support Branch. He could make his own assessment of how much to share with them. Two minutes later, an Uber took him to the Hertz rental desk at LAX, and he hired a Mercedes C-Class convertible. Things were starting to move, and he had a feeling that whichever persons had taken Stacy Donovan weren't professionals. It's rare for a kid to have two phones, but even so, somebody had made a mistake and missed one of them for forty minutes or longer. Maybe they'd made other slip-ups.

It was going to be another hot day. ABC news said the wildfires in Fresno were getting whipped south by a Santa Ana, and warned against travel to the area. That wasn't a problem, since he was heading east of the danger zone. Just outside Claremont, he stopped off at a Barnes and Noble and bought a map, because paper was what he'd grown up with in the Army, not Google on a smartphone. Technology isn't always better than the old ways.

Just before the 395 cut between the Sequoia and Death Valley national parks, he found the cell tower and took the next turning on the left at a dusty crossroads. Twenty miles on from the junction, there was a sign:

Welcome to Marlberg, Population 13,035, Elevation 2,290 feet

He was driving through the town's main street when he noticed something that made sirens whoop and wail inside his head. He stopped the Merc for a closer look. Could it be a coincidence?

CHAPTER 17

A BLACK CHEROKEE SUV with Nebraska plates. It might not have been the same one he'd seen in the parking lot near Benny's gym, but once again there were other vehicles with out-of-town license plates: Alabama, Georgia, Montana, Wisconsin and Texas. It wasn't as though Marlberg looked like a honeypot tourist place. There was a single run-down motel and a bunch of stores that sold hardware and everyday supplies. Not the usual crap: artisanal handicrafts, local artwork, keychains or I-Love-Marlberg T shirts.

There were two diners facing each other on the main street. Virgo chose the Lucky Grill and stepped back into a vignette of 1950s nostalgia: checkerboard tiles, highway signage, two retro gas pumps and walls covered in advertising plaques. It had seen better days. The booths were threadbare, and the chrome tarnished. Most of the customers were a similar vintage: a dozen or so silver heads turned and checked him out before resuming their conversations.

Today's servers were Darlene and Fran. He sat at the counter, and it was Darlene came to take his order. She had the face of a septuagenarian, and the hair of someone forty years younger: it was thick and shiny, cut in a bob. If she rode a Harley in her spare time, she wouldn't need a helmet. Virgo ordered coffee and a slice of the classic apple pie.

While he waited, he checked out the clientele and noticed four men sat in a corner booth, who did not fit the demographic. They were mid-thirties, clean-cut and wearing polo shirts. Similar to the guys at Benny's gym, but this time with a laurel-leaf logo. A couple of them kept looking in his direction, and not making any effort to hide the fact.

Darlene came back with the coffee and pie, and said, 'What brings you to Marlberg?'

'I make and sell pottery.' Virgo smiled. Mr. Sincere. 'Thinking of opening a little boutique here.'

'Really?' Darlene's eyebrows went up, but the hair didn't move. 'We don't get a lot of sight-seers here; it's mainly just hunting and fishing.'

'Seems like a nice place.'

'It used to be.' Darlene shuffled off into the galley kitchen.

Under normal circumstances, Virgo knew that if he sat tight and kept ordering coffee, sooner or later someone would approach him to try and establish what his business really was, but he didn't have the luxury of time. Ergo, he took the initiative and walked over to the four polo shirts in the corner booth. Big smile. 'Excuse me, have you got a minute to give a stranger some advice?'

The four guys looked at each other, and one in wrap-around shades said, 'What about?'

'I'm considering moving my handmade pottery studio here. Wondered if there were enough visitors to make it worthwhile.'

A different member of the group, wearing a thick gold chain, jumped in. 'Can't help you there, pal.'

'Are you guys on vacation, or do you live here?' Virgo kept the smile going.

'What's it got to do with you?' This time it was number three, the toughest-looking one.

'Like I said, just trying to gauge tourist numbers.' Virgo hoped number four would get a chance to speak, but he didn't.

Number three said, 'Mind your own business, mister. We're busy.'

Virgo went back to the counter and ordered another coffee and one more slice of the delicious, classic apple pie. In a mirror at the far end of the counter, he saw one of the polo shirts on his phone. Two spoonfuls of pie gone, the door of the diner opened, and a man marched straight up to him and said, 'You ain't no fucking potter.'

The guy wasn't tall, but he was extra wide, wearing lime-green overalls badged Locke Transport. Black oil around his fingernails, and good-sized arms for hefting two-hundred-pound tires off commercial trucks. A monkey wrench rested in his right hand.

Virgo ate another mouthful of pie before speaking. 'I think what you meant to say was, *welcome to our friendly town – what can I do to make your stay here more pleasurabl*e. You are from the Marlberg Visitor Center?'

'What's the real reason you're in town?'

'I'm here for the hunting.'

'Wild pig or jackrabbits?'

'I only hunt two-legged animals.'

'You a cop?'

'If I was a cop, I'd arrest you for being an aggressive asshole.'

The four polo shirts left the booth and came over. The tough-guy one said, 'What did I tell you? He's another fucking journalist.'

Darlene leant over the counter, face pinched into a scowl.

'Come on, boys, leave the gentleman alone. He makes pottery.'

The mechanic started to pat the monkey wrench into his left palm. 'Another fucking journalist.'

Darlene said, 'Tommy Junior, stop right now, and get yourself back to work.'

Tommy Junior didn't move. 'Which magazine sent you?'

'Does it matter?' Virgo shrugged. 'One with writing in. Not the sort you'd buy.'

'Motherfucking scum.' Tommy Junior raised the wrench, but before it reached the zenith of its intended arc, Virgo's fist impacted the underside of his chin with such power, that, for a fraction of a second, TJ's feet left the floor. When they came back down, his eyeballs rolled into the back in his head, and he dropped deadweight onto the chequerboard tiles. Out cold.

There was silence. The gang of four looked at each other. Then all hell broke loose.

The first guy who came at him was the largest. Heavy shoulders. Big gut. Thick neck with a thick gold chain. A huge slab of ham in an XXL sports shirt that had never seen active duty on a playing field. Virgo waited. Barroom brawlers usually come in swinging, but this guy's arms were pinned to his sides. Eyes down. Body pivoting at where his waist should have been. Stubby legs propelling him head-first towards its target. The human battering ram.

Virgo was fast for a man of his physique, but not the quickest. It didn't matter. He had time. He judged the guy was aiming to strike him with the top of his skull on the side of the chest, to knock him off balance. Facilitate a pile-on. It's what the bad kids do in a school playground. Virgo took a step to his right and stopped the guy in his tracks with a solid fist angled up into his nose. Now the guy was upright. Blank eyes. Mouth open. Virgo swung an elbow. The bony point hit the jaw on one of its hinge joints, and made a muffled tearing sound.

The guy staggered sideways. His knees went. He bashed into a booth where an old couple were eating ranch chicken salad. He clutched at the table on his way down. Slap. His face hit the floor. A red gingham, wipe-clean table covering still in his hand. Romaine lettuce and sour cream dressing on his back.

Number two was the kid in the Ray-Ban wraparounds. Maybe he had sensitive eyes. Maybe he thought they made him look cool and mysterious. He was wiry. Tanned. Plenty of attitude, but no technique. Scrawny arms flailing. Spittle flying from his mouth. Virgo ducked a couple of wild swipes, then hit him once. Hard. Corkscrew right-hand flush on the bridge of the nose. No need for anything else. The kid crumpled like a punctured inflatable.

The next guy had already switched to defense. Hands in front of his face. Edging away. Virgo grabbed a handful of polo shirt in one hand, belt in the other, and threw him over the counter. The guy's head bounced off the coffee machine. The wall shook. Glasses rained down from a shelf. Bottles trembled. A vintage, metal Route 66 sign clattered to the floor. It went quiet.

Number four was already on his way to the door. It was the tough guy. Seen enough. Virgo let him go, and saw Darlene scowling from the kitchen doorway. He pulled an innocent face: *what did I do?*

CHAPTER 18

KERN COUNTY SHERIFF'S OFFICE, Marlberg substation. Virgo sat in the jail cell and wondered what Hartman would say this time if he found out. Probably not see the funny side. That's why he'd not called him and chosen someone else instead. A rattle of keys, and Sergeant Wozniak took him through to the front office where Detective Jenny Accardi was waiting with a look of reproach on her face.

She said, 'This is becoming a habit.'

'People keep picking on me.' Virgo snatched his belt from the property bag and threaded it through his jeans. Grabbed his wallet, scooped cash, USBs and the Merc keys into his pocket. 'Including the cops, who see that I've got a criminal record, and fall victim to their inner prejudice.' He smiled at Wozniak, who didn't bite. Finally, he fired up his phone and checked for contact from Donovan. Negative.

When they got out into the midday sunshine, Virgo said, 'Thanks, Accardi. See you around.'

She set off down the sidewalk into town. 'I'm hitching a ride back to LA with you.'

'You and Nash fallen out? I can't believe it. Such a charming guy.'

'No.' Accardi stopped, hands on hips. 'I've found out the connection between Benny's gym and Marlberg. It's the Snow Wolves.'

'Should that mean something to me?'

'I checked our intel system, and Benny's gym is one of their regular hangouts. Their leader, Tommy Locke, runs a road freight company out of a ranch here in Marlberg. Made his money carrying cocaine in secret compartments welded underneath the trucks.'

Virgo shook his head. 'I'm no wiser. The Snow Wolves?'

'White supremacist shitbirds. They flew under the radar for a long time, until the *Washington Post* did an in-depth feature. The kid you knocked out in the diner is the son of the chief shitbird, so they'll probably want to kill you.'

'They'll have to form a line behind the Aryan Brotherhood.'

Virgo plipped the locks on the Mercedes convertible, drove past the sign *You are now leaving Marlberg*, and back onto the 395. It was Saturday. Traffic flowed without blockage in the valley, most heading east into the hills for the weekend. On the radio, Starship said they'd built a city on rock and roll, even though the song was all synth with no guitars, and Accardi sat with an unlit Camel cigarette between her lips, with a should-she, shouldn't-she-light-it look in her eyes.

'Why would the Snow Wolves have anything to do with kidnapping?' It was Virgo, thinking aloud.

'Tommy Locke's a crook.' Accardi prodded the Camel back into its packet. 'Leopard, spots, and all that.'

'Money?'

'Nobody ever has enough, but he's got a lot more than most.'

'Maybe they need funds for rallies and propaganda?'

'They're not that sort of outfit. They want to blend in, so that's why they go for the short hair and sensible clothes.'

'Chameleons,' said Virgo. 'It's still a uniform.' He tapped the screen on his phone and changed the destination on Google Maps to the Ritz-Carlton Hotel. Maybe Daniel Donovan might know if there was a connection between his daughter and a group of racists dumb enough to call themselves the Snow Wolves.

When they got to the twenty-third floor, it was the same two private security guys outside the suite door. They recognized Virgo and let them in. Daniel Donovan was pacing up and down in front of the panoramic window, with red pouches beneath his big, blue eyes. He'd not slept or been rubbing his eyes. Maybe both. He was unshaven and had a glass of something that looked like it might be Jack Daniels in his hand.

Duncan Donovan sat at a bureau, working on a laptop, and was the first to speak. 'Please tell us you've come with good news.' He stood and walked over with the help of his silver-topped cane.

Daniel stopped pacing. A plea written large on his face that it wasn't bad news.

Virgo said, 'No. It's just a welfare visit. I don't suppose—'

'No.' Duncan cut him off. 'We've had no contact from the bastards.'

Daniel said, 'Excuse me, I need to go to the bathroom.' His face was ashen, and he looked like he might vomit.

When the senator had gone, Duncan lowered his voice. 'How long do these things generally take?'

Virgo frowned, *these things*. 'Some a few hours, and I worked one in Colombia that lasted ninety-eight days.'

'My brother needs to be back in Washington on Monday.'

'I'm sorry, is there something more important than the life of his daughter?'

The silver-topped cane shot up, pointed at Virgo's chest. 'Mind your attitude.'

'I served my country. I know there are matters that can take precedence over the life of an individual, but I also know that nobody in a command structure is irreplaceable. Maybe someone could stand in for the senator?'

'I know you served your country, Mr. Virgo. I know all about you.'

Virgo bit on his tongue. Was that a threat, or just a little warning shot to put him in his place? There was something about Duncan Donovan he didn't like, apart from the fact he was lying about there having been no contact from the kidnappers. He decided to change the subject. 'Have you ever heard of a white supremacist group called the Snow Wolves?'

'No.' Duncan slitted his eyes. 'What's this got to do with my niece?'

'Probably nothing, but we have to look at all angles.'

'I've told you already, the family are dealing with this.' Duncan did the cane-tap-along-with-each-word routine. 'Keep…away…and…let…us…resolve…it.'

Virgo resisted the urge to snatch the cane and turn it into matchsticks. 'Is that what the senator wants?'

At that moment, the senator wanted to empty the contents of his stomach down the toilet. There was a series of loud retching sounds.

Duncan looked a touch embarrassed. 'I'd better go and check on my brother.'

Virgo watched him go. Then went straight to Duncan's laptop and plugged in a USB flash drive.

Accardi came over to whisper, 'What do you think you're doing?'

'Uploading keylogger software. It'll let us monitor

Duncan's comms to see if he receives a ransom demand.' Virgo completed the installation and looked around the room. 'We could do with finding the senator's computer.'

'Don't you need approval from a judge?'

'I'm not a federal agent, remember? Look away if you're squeamish.'

'Me? I didn't see anything.'

There was a MacBook folded shut on a table in the bedroom. Virgo didn't have time to reach it before the bathroom door opened and the Donovan brothers were back in the room.

Daniel managed a weak apology smile. 'Must have been a bad shrimp in the omelette.' He looked a wreck.

Accardi said, 'I interviewed Stacy's friends up at UCLA. She's a very intelligent, strong and independent kid. You should be proud of her.'

'Thank you.' Water brimmed up in Daniel's eyes. 'I just want her back.'

'The agents were just leaving.' Duncan stepped in front to protect his younger sibling and indicate the meeting was closed.

Back on the sidewalk twenty-three floors down, Accardi lit a cigarette. 'The senator's brother is a hard-faced piece of work.'

'Duncan fancies himself as the power behind the throne. It doesn't make him a bad man.' Virgo pulled out his mobile. The two security guys outside the senator's suite had been wearing purple IFS lapel pins, which could mean only one thing: it was Duncan Donovan who had sent Mettam and scarface to try and recruit him on the Indigo Fox Solutions workforce. Why would he do that? There was someone he wanted to call who might have the answer.

CHAPTER 19

STACY LISTENED to the dull thud of music above as a distraction. Her stomach cramps came in waves, and she knew she had to empty her bowels to get relief. The blue LED shone bright. It meant he was probably watching or even videoing her. Did it matter? She was entombed with two slowly decomposing corpses and was going to end up dead herself. Of course it mattered. She didn't want to give the ugly freak the satisfaction.

The box of bottled water was by her feet. She tore off one of the rectangle flaps of cardboard and crawled on her hands and knees to where the two dead bodies were piled in an obscene embrace. There was a small pool of black viscous blood on the ground. It had dripped post-mortem from the mangled scalp of the new arrival. She took the cardboard and carefully bathed one side in the blood. It was thick as tar.

Then she crawled to the corner where the blue LED dot shimmered in the roof. Since she'd taken water bottles out of the box, it no longer supported her weight. So there were only two ways she could reach the ceiling. One was to drag the corpses over to the corner and stand on them. She didn't know if she had the strength, and it would take time. Bigfoot would intervene. The other option was to jump.

She started on her haunches and willed her legs to straighten and propel her upwards. She raised her arms and leapt. In her right hand was the cardboard. She held it out and slapped it against the thick Perspex casing that housed the camera. It stuck. A halo of blue light bled out from around it, but the lens and LED were covered.

Stacy collapsed onto the ground in triumph. She crawled around to the far corner of the pit and relieved herself. She felt better. Her body and mind could relax, and it was a victory, however small. She'd read at school that many slaves did not accept their bondage without some sign of resistance, such as damaging tools or pieces of farm equipment. Naturally, these acts were detected and soon rectified.

She sat and waited for the hatch to open. Nothing happened. The low grumble of a drum and bass rhythm carried on overhead. Time passed, and still nothing happened. Maybe he wasn't up there watching. A shiver went through her. What if she'd been abandoned altogether to die of starvation once the handful of protein bars ran out? What was her father doing? He must have people looking for her.

She lay down on her side. So much of the recent hours she'd spent moving, trying to keep warm. Now she needed to conserve energy. Fatigue tugged at her consciousness, and she closed her eyes. *BANG.* The sound of a bolt. Then the screech of the hatch being slid open. A torrent of burning white light flooded in. Brighter than that ball of nuclear fusion we call the sun. Now she could hear the music. '7 Nation Army' by the White Stripes. It filled the air with noise and then stopped.

He was there. Crouched down at the edge of the hatch. He leaned in, swatted away the cardboard that was over the camera, and wiped the Perspex shield. 'Naughty children get punished.'

'Fuck you.' Stacy stood up and backed against the wall. 'Kill me and get it over with.' She didn't want to die, but if he came down into the pit, it gave her a chance. Fight or flight.

'I don't want to kill you. I want to preserve you.' He stood up, then disappeared. Within a minute, he was back with a big, green wheelbarrow or agricultural cart. It was piled high with ice. Not cubes, solid blocks. He tipped it in and laughed.

Stacy watched, confused and stunned, as he tipped in three more loads. A cymbal crashed, and '7 Nation Army' blasted back out. Steel scraped against steel, and the hatch closed. Straight away the atmosphere changed. The chill bit into her skin and frosted the inside of her nostrils. There were clothes to be had, but dead people were wearing them. Would they save her life or merely prolong the pain? It didn't matter. Now Stacy knew how she was going to die. She lay down and closed her eyes. Soon Hypnos would carry her off to the underworld and oblivion.

CHAPTER 20

ELEVEN YEARS AGO, Brad Hooper had been driving a Special Operations Vehicle in eastern Syria, on a mission to identify positions held by a rabble-group of jihadis formed from the remnants of al-Qaeda in Iraq. He drove out of the compound at Hamdan military airport and onto the road toward Abu Kabal. It was an operation being conducted by the Activity, but he wore standard desert uniform. It was a clear, sunny morning. Half a mile down the road, someone detonated an IED that blew off both his feet and turned his legs into a jumble of bone fragments.

The After Action Review said the mission should have been aborted. A soldier in the rear of the SOV had noticed a lack of kids at the side of the road; on previous outings, there had always been a few, waving to the Americans or begging. The master sergeant in charge made the decision to proceed, on the grounds that the risk identified was acceptable, and died in the explosion. The soldier in the vehicle who had flagged the danger was Eddie Virgo.

Nobody knew who'd carried out the attack. The AAR said it could have been the Islamists, or it could have been a group loyal to the Assad government or even the Russians. In *The Art of War*, Sun Tzu said *know thy enemy*, and to this day he keeps being proved right.

The Army looked after Brad Hooper. He got new legs and retrained as an analyst. They would have looked after Virgo, but he met a nurse called Crystal while he was being treated in the Womack Medical Center, North Carolina, and decided he wanted to stay put.

'Duncan Donovan was a captain in the 4th Infantry Division.' Brad Hooper read from a computer screen. 'Only lasted four years.'

Virgo grimaced at his smartphone. He hated video calls. 'I take it he got pensioned out?'

'You mean the leg injury?' Hooper laughed. 'He got drunk on leave and jumped into an empty swimming pool.'

'Deep end or shallow?'

'Not deep enough. There's intel on the system that when he left the military, he ran a business that went bust and left a bunch of creditors.'

'It's not a crime to be a crap businessman.'

'Rich folk should pay their debts.'

'Any mention of Indigo Fox Solutions?'

'The ex-military mafiosi?'

'If that's what you call them.'

Hooper took a while to scroll and scan. 'No, nothing. But there's been no new information added to his file for years.'

'I've put a keylogger on his computer.' Virgo smiled. 'Will you do me a favor?'

'Are you trying to take advantage of a disabled colleague?'

'Don't I always.'

'Send me the spyware login and password.'

'Thanks, Brad. You're a gem.' Virgo hung up. It was a pleasant change to deal with Hooper, unlike Caleb Hawkins, who wouldn't tell his own grandmother the time of day without something in return. Some people, eh?

They were sat in front of a truck selling coffee and donuts outside Richardson's Caravan and Camping Super Store, off the San Bernardino Freeway. It was the sort of place old people bring their parents to smooch around, not buying anything, when they're fed up with taking them to garden centers. Half a dozen bistro tables and plastic chairs. Accardi was chaining the Camel, and Virgo stared at the display of RVs that ran one side of the parking lot, wondering which one to buy when this was all done and finished.

It was why he'd chosen Richardson's to meet the bureau investigators that Hartman had sent. They were late. Some things never change. In the Army, a lack of punctuality was a disciplinary offense, but many employees of the federal government appeared to be chronologically challenged, and things had been getting worse in recent years. Or was he getting old?

He drank more coffee and watched Accardi light another cigarette. What was she still doing there? He was grateful to get busted out of jail, and for the intelligence on Benny's, but this wasn't an LAPD job. She was taking a risk. Was she hoping the two of them would eventually go to a bar and maybe end up in bed together? She was an attractive woman, but he was going to have to spell it out to her: there would never be anyone else after Crystal. Wait a minute. Who was he kidding? He was flattering himself. She was just a tough cop who believed that people who did really bad things should be brought to justice, even if, on occasion, that meant not sticking to the rule book.

A thought danced into his head, and he said, 'Can you do the financials on Daniel and Duncan?'

'Bank accounts, credit cards, loans, investments?' Accardi blew a smoke ring.

'Just bank accounts. Anything to indicate they've paid a ransom or are preparing funds for that purpose.'

'With a subpoena?'

'What do you think?'

'It won't be easy. Depends who they bank with.'

'Do your best.'

'There's an innocent girl's life at stake. Of course I'll do my fucking best.' Accardi stubbed the Camel out with a wedge-heeled slingback and marched off.

Virgo sat quiet and chastised. Fifteen silent minutes later, a black Chevrolet Impala drove into the parking lot, and he knew immediately it was the bureau investigators. A man and a woman got out, waved, and walked towards him. He rubbed his eyes. Maybe he was hallucinating. He blinked and looked again. No, he wasn't mistaken. They really had sent Bailey and Whitlock.

CHAPTER 21

AT OAK HILLS, Virgo swung the Mercedes off Interstate 15 and took the 395 north. Checked the rear-view mirror to make sure the Impala had followed suit, then called Hartman, who answered, 'Speak,' like he was in *The Sopranos*, not the FBI Critical Incident Response Group.

'What the fuck you doing sending Bailey and Whitlock?' Virgo had recovered from the shock and was now angry.

'I'm sorry, what do you mean by that?' Hartman, the innocent.

'The two most incompetent agents we've got.'

'Things change. You're not up with the times.'

'Because last time I checked, neither of them could find their own ass with a mirror on a stick.'

'Bailey's on a career development program.'

'So you can get rid of her to another department.' Virgo banged the steering wheel in frustration. 'Whitlock isn't even an investigator, he's intel-support.'

'I trust them. They're good agents, and that's what matters.' Hartman's tone switched from defense to attack.

'You think you're something special. Maybe I made a mistake doing you a favor and putting you on this case.'

'Is that a threat?'

'Don't be stupid. I'm not going to see you go back to prison.'

Virgo sensed an undertone that didn't fill him with reassurance. 'If you want a *yes*-man, you should have got someone else.'

'I chose you for a reason.'

'Because I'm useless, like Bailey and Whitlock?'

'Shut up, and have some respect. I've got eyes on the ground out there now, and they won't hesitate to let me know if you go off-piste.' Hartman ended the call.

Virgo checked the rearview again, to make sure the stool pigeons were still there. Forty minutes later, he pulled off the 395, and they followed him into Marlberg. The motel was called the Edelweiss Inn and Suites. They booked three rooms at $55 a-piece, unpacked, and met in the lobby-cum-bar, beneath the head of a stag mounted on a plaque on the wall.

Bailey and Whitlock sat and made notes while Virgo filled them in on events at La Souris nightclub, the cell phone activity, and his encounter with the Snow Wolves at the Lucky Grill across the road. Bailey's face had a permanent frown, which could have been the concentration she needed to write, or could have been displeasure at her being sent to the backside of nowhere when she was on some kind of fast-track promotion scheme. Whitlock was like a kid in a candy store and couldn't believe he was out of the office on a live field operation. He had wide eyes and a big grin, but no suggestion of a plan regarding how to pursue the investigation.

It was as Virgo had feared. The only reason this pair were trustworthy was because they were too dumb to be corrupt and get away with it. It was down to him to take the initiative. He explained that hostage-takers use a variety of criteria to select their ideal stronghold, depending on how many of them there are. It needs to be secure. Not overlooked by neighbors. Accessible by vehicle. Views that give prior warning of visitors. Self-contained. A temporary residence that cannot be connected to anyone involved at a later date.

Virgo spread the map out on the table, drew a circle, and set out the priorities: Realtors, abandoned properties, empty houses, Airbnb, and any other agencies offering short-term lets. They needed to be methodical. Grid the map. Identify the potential strongholds, grade them high-medium-low, then cross them off once checked and verified that Stacy Donovan was not there. When he'd finished, he opened it up to questions, and Whitlock asked if they should start with the properties graded high. Even the stag on the wall looked embarrassed.

First job was to compile a list of properties. Whitlock volunteered to check letting agents and websites, Bailey chose to phone around utility companies and identify places that were vacant. That left Virgo with the Realtors. There was one agency just outside town and a few on the internet who covered the region. Where to start? Sitting on a phone trying to get through to another human being was not his idea of fun, so he decided to visit Chaz Moseley Real Estate Agents, the only physical business on his schedule.

Outside, it was cooking. The Merc was in the shade, but the hood was hot enough to fry onions. He plipped the locks, then remembered what he'd forgotten to do.

When he walked into the Lucky Grill, Darlene was behind the counter. She turned, and shouted into the galley kitchen, 'Hey, Fran. It's the pottery guy.'

Fran came out wiping her hands. 'I don't think he makes pottery, Darlene.'

Virgo took a stool at the counter. There were a couple of polo shirts he'd not seen before sat at the other end. When they saw him, they smacked a $20 note down, and walked out with their noses screwed up, as though keen to escape a bad smell. Word must have spread. They didn't fancy a rumble.

'Classic apple pie?' Darlene's hair looked a different shade of metal this afternoon.

'No, I've come to pay for the damage that was caused earlier.'

Darlene smiled. 'Oh, that's okay. It was nothing.'

Fran said, 'Two hundred bucks should cover it.' No smile.

'A pleasure.' Virgo counted it out. 'Least I can do.'

'You could try taking your business to the diner across the street.' Fran picked up the cash and disappeared into the kitchen.

'Ignore her.' Darlene set down a plate of classic apple pie. 'On the house.'

Virgo wasn't hungry, but the Army had taught him to eat when the opportunity presents itself, like a grizzly before hibernation. Besides, it would be rude not to. He tucked in and said, 'How do you get along with the nazis?'

'I'm sorry, dear?'

'The men who come here to hang out with Tommy Locke.'

'Business is business.'

'You mean their dollar is worth the same as anyone else's?'

'We're all born sinners, dear; the Bible tells us that. Everyone has evil as well as good in them, and God is the only judge of a person's character.' Darlene leaned across the counter. 'But if I'm honest, I don't care for them. They come and go. The only one who ever spoke more than two words to me got killed, so I just smile and take their money and know that one day they will face a reckoning before the Almighty.'

It was a giant slice of pie, but Virgo cleared the plate in four visits. 'Who got killed?'

'Jerome.' Darlene's eyes focused on a spot on the wall as she reminisced. 'He used to sit where you are now, and just chat.'

'How long ago was this?'

Darlene thought a moment. 'Maybe three weeks.' Then she dropped her voice and leant over the counter again. 'On the news, it said he died in a car accident, but the sheriff told me not to believe everything I hear on the radio.'

'Wise words.'

'He was a nice boy, Jerome.'

Virgo left the Lucky Grill, and keyed *Chaz Moseley Real Estate Agents* into Google Maps. He turned the AC in the Merc to max and drove down the main street, wondering what a nice boy like Jerome was doing associating with a herd of racist meatheads. If indeed he was a nice boy, because Virgo only had Darlene's word - the lady who still thought he was *the pottery guy.* He took the first left, then the second right at a 7-Eleven store, and cruised through a residential neighborhood until he reached a junction that marked the edge of the town. That's when he noticed the pimped-up Chevy Silverado in the mirror, with Tommy Junior behind the wheel, and a kid with a shotgun stood in the cargo bed. There was a loud explosion and the rear window of the Merc shattered into a million pieces.

CHAPTER 22

Virgo felt stabs of pain shoot down his right bicep from the shoulder. He floored the gas pedal before the second barrel came his way. When he checked the mirror, the Silverado was pumping out black smoke in pursuit, and the kid in the cargo bed was clinging on, the shotgun swinging on a rope around his shoulder. The road twisted down into the valley bottom. Steep. He slewed the hire car through the first bend and nearly lost it on a patch of pine straw. Overcorrected, and felt the back end waggle and spit.

A straight stretch, and he booted it again. The Silverado was no match for the acceleration of a Mercedes C-Class, but no car is faster than lead pellets from a 12-gauge shell. Distance was the safest option. Just before the next bend, he stood on the brakes and then hit the gas pedal to power all the way through the corner and out the other side. He was flying. The trees went by in blurs of brown and green. Up ahead came a chicane, and the road dropped again. He zig-zagged down, ready to floor it once more, but instead shouted *shit* and hit the anchors.

There was bridge over the river, and it was blocked. An

eighteen-wheel freight truck was parked in the middle. He couldn't read the signage, but no doubt it said *Locke Transport*. To one side, stood four men. One had a shotgun, another had a three-foot tire lever, and the other two just posed with their arms drifting away from their sides, trying to look tough. Welcome to a Snow Wolves ambush.

Virgo let the Merc slow down to a steady pace. Here we go — OODA time: observe, orient, decide, act. Not long. Behind him, he heard the tires of the Silverado screech through the bends. In front of him, the guy with the shotgun put the stock to his shoulder. Gullies either side of the road. No way out. He ran through the options. There was only one that didn't involve him getting shot or beat up. That would be the favorite then, if it worked. Decision made.

He hung back and waited for Tommy Junior's pickup to appear. Timing was key. The bridge was thirty yards ahead, and the road was true as an arrow. If he could position the Merc between the shotgun in front of him and the one behind, it would take out the threat. They wouldn't risk blasting each other with pellets. That left the problem of the men themselves.

They had two firearms, an iron bar, and who knew what else. The only weapon Virgo had was the one he was driving. Hertz special, weighing in at 1.5 tons. He had to make the most of it. The four men up ahead stood shoulder to shoulder in a show of strength. Great optics, but not a smart choice from a combat perspective. There was obviously no bowling alley in Marlberg, or they might have realized that targets that are spread out are harder to hit in one go.

He coasted another ten yards, until he could see Tommy Junior's hate-filled face in the mirror. *Now. Go, go, go...* The wheels of the Mercedes spun, then gripped. It tore up the strip towards the bridge. The four men froze. Not expecting a suicide maneuver. He kept going. They tried to starburst, but the split-second hesitation cost them. Virgo felt the hood crack, and two bodies bounce off the windshield up into the air. Only half the target group, but not bad.

Before the bodies landed, he had the driver's door open. The Mercedes smashed through the fence, cannoned off a stone arch, and into the river. Virgo was already on the bank. He lizard-crawled through the prickles and scrub to the underside of the bridge. Watched the hire car think about floating, then sink.

From up above came shouts.

'Is he still inside?'

'I think the door was open.'

'Watch for bubbles.'

'Why didn't one of you shoot the motherfucker?'

The last voice belonged to Tommy Junior. Virgo hunched his way to the other side of the bridge. He needed to get up. There was a supporting pillar. It was weathered, and on one corner a strip of concrete had flaked away to reveal the iron-rod reinforcement. Virgo used the welded wire to pull himself up by the fingertips, then scuffed the toes of his boots to gain leverage. Pain bolted down his right arm, and he lost his grip. For a second, he hung by one hand. He closed his eyes and overcame the agony. With one final effort he heaved and scrambled his way up.

On the bridge, he rolled under the 18-wheel truck. Waited. A few minutes went by. He waited some more. The voices became more distant. He saw two sets of feet cross the road. The Snow Wolves were splitting up to search the riverbank, both sides of the bridge. The one time they should have stuck together, they did the opposite. Real amateurs.

Virgo inched his way past a double wheel to get a view. He wanted a shotgun first. There were other ways to pick off the remaining four, but they would take longer and involve more risk. He was still aware of the burning in his right shoulder, where he'd caught some pellets. How bad was it? He didn't know, and there wasn't time to make an assessment. Best assume that his hand-to-hand combat capability was not one hundred percent. It shouldn't matter. Fifty was probably enough.

Tommy Junior and his friend from the cargo bed were a long way from the bridge. They'd followed the direction the current flowed. The two who'd gone upstream were much closer. One in a Ralph Lauren shirt and pants was less than half a football field away, and his buddy in the wraparound shades was even closer. He was scrabbling down the bank to take a look below the bridge. Four paces and he would be directly underneath. Shame he wasn't the one with a shotgun. Still, it wasn't an opportunity to let slip by.

Virgo counted to five. Rolled out. Vaulted the low side wall of the bridge and dropped down onto the bank. Let his knees cushion the impact. Ready to fight, but the guy was looking the other way. Peering into a patch of reeds. Virgo darted up behind him, grabbed the back of his neck, and slammed his head into a concrete support pillar. Hundred-dollar pair of Oakley sunglasses snapped in two.

The guy was too stunned to shout. Virgo had a hand over his mouth anyway and pulled him backwards onto the ground. He was still conscious. Virgo dropped to one knee and delivered a volley of three short punches to the jaw, one after another, rapid repeats, like a piston. Threat neutralized. Virgo picked up the iron bar and took the easy way back up onto the bridge via the blacktop. Swift. Keeping low.

It wasn't long before Mr. Ralph Lauren came looking for his pal. Virgo heard shouts of 'Scotty?' and, 'Come on, Scotty, what the fuck you doing?' It was getting closer. Virgo knew he had to strike before Scotty's limp body was discovered in the mud beneath the bridge. He shouted, 'Up here,' not knowing if it was a passable imitation of Scotty's voice, but it didn't matter. He had the high ground. He crouch-crawled between the truck and the low side wall, to the end of the bridge.

Ten seconds later, he heard the sound of feet scrabbling up the riverbank to the roadway. A head appeared. One swing of the tire lever, and the head disappeared. Split open. Next came the sound of a body crashing back down through the undergrowth on the bank. Virgo launched himself after it. He didn't want the shotgun ending up in the river. He smiled with relief when he saw body and shotgun had come up short. Better still, the gun was a Beretta under-over, best 12-gauge hunting weapon on the market, and he had a bit of hunting to do.

He checked the guy's pockets for spare shells. Negative. Cracked open the gun, and saw there were two in the spout. That would have to do. By the time he resumed his position behind the double wheels of the Locke Transport freight truck, he could see the last two remaining targets had abandoned their search and were heading back. He wanted them close. Shotgun pellets start to spread as soon as they leave the muzzle, more than an inch for every yard traveled. A faraway target might be easier to hit, but it might not put them out of action. The spread could be too wide.

He waited on his belly until he could see the stitching on their shoes, then got up and walked out real casual from behind the truck, with the stock of the Beretta 12-gauge on his hip. 'Looking for me?'

The kid with the shotgun on a rope round his neck went wide-eyed and made to lift the barrels. Virgo squeezed the trigger, and a barrage of lead-shot hit the kid in the groin. He doubled over and went down. Tommy Junior was straight onto one knee, trying to wrestle the shotgun away from his prostrate pal.

Virgo skipped forward and swung a desert boot. It

connected with Tommy Junior's left ear and clattered him sideways. He rolled onto his stomach, and groaned. Virgo brought the stock of the Beretta down on the back of his head. It was a lightweight model, but still did the trick. Tommy Junior was out cold for the second time in one day, and it wasn't yet four o'clock. Some guys never learn.

The keys to the Silverado were in the ignition. Virgo drove back up towards town and dialed 911. He said there'd been some kind of accident down by the Silver Oak crossing. No, he didn't want to leave his details. No, he hadn't seen anything. He was just a concerned citizen, trying to help. Then he hung up and threw the Beretta 12-gauge far as he could into a deep ravine.

CHAPTER 23

THE EDELWEISS INN and Suites was a two-story lump of stucco, built in an angular U-shape around its parking lot. Virgo sat on one of the two queen beds in room number 17 and studied the ancient, dark stain on the ceiling. Maybe a body had decomposed in the suite above and seeped through the floor, or somebody in his room had once blown out their brains upwards onto the ceiling. It was the sort of place travel guides call *authentic*.

He winced as Accardi used a pair of tweezers to pull a lead pellet from his shoulder. 'Where did you learn to do this?'

'Saw it in a movie.' She bathed the wound with hydrogen peroxide.

'That's reassuring.'

'This is the part where I say *stay with me*, or *don't die on me, you bastard.*'

Virgo laughed and started to look through the thick wad of papers that Accardi had brought with her: the last twelve months' bank transactions of the brothers Daniel and Duncan Donovan.

Accardi said, 'What do the fancy words mean?' She touched the tattoo of a double-handed sword on his forearm, circled by the inscription *Veritas Omnia Vincula Vincit.*

'Truth conquers everything.'

'The ghost unit, right?' Accardi hovered the tweezers over another pellet. 'I read your file when you got arrested at the club.'

'The Activity is not really a ghost unit. It exists, and *aaargh.*' He clenched his teeth. Felt like someone had pushed a red-hot poker into his shoulder and wiggled it around. 'Shouldn't I be drinking from a bottle of Scotch while you do this?'

'Relax, it was the last one.' She taped a big, square dressing over the little holes.

Virgo put his shirt back on, taking care with his right arm. It felt sore. He went back to work on the bank statements. The account he was looking at was Duncan Donovan's, and on every page there were one or two transactions that had been highlighted by a pink fluorescent marker. 'Whose is that account he's paying money into?'

'That's Daniel's. Don't you think that's a strange work arrangement? Usually if you work for someone, they pay you, not the other way round.'

'And the big sums coming into Duncan's bank. Where are they from?'

Accardi shrugged and brushed a strand of black hair off her face. 'An account in the Caymans. Don't know whose, but I've got a guy working on it.'

Virgo flicked through a few more sheets and did the calculations in his head. Every time Duncan received a sum of money from the Caymans account, he paid exactly half to Daniel, and they weren't small amounts. Maybe it was some family trust. It didn't explain why Duncan appeared to be employed by his brother, but received no financial recompense. Perhaps it wasn't about the money. It was about family pride and trying to get a Donovan into the White House.

He moved on to Daniel's accounts. No indication of funds having been withdrawn to pay a ransom. In fact, the over-riding impression was that Daniel Donovan suffered from the same monetary struggles as the average Joe in the street. Either he wasn't as rich as he made out, or he had his fortune stashed away somewhere out of sight. There were more trans-actions highlighted, and this time they were fluorescent green. Four thousand dollars a month he paid out to an account at Wells Fargo.

Accardi was watching, and anticipated the question. 'I don't know, but I'm going to find out.'

'Not just a pretty face, eh?'

'No, I'm good in bed as well, but I guess you're not interested.'

Virgo laughed. Impressed by the direct approach, but trying not to blush. 'You're out of my league, and—'

'It's okay, don't bother with the excuses. I know about your wife. Read your file, remember?' She opened her arms and gestured around the room. 'How about we meet up here in exactly one year's time?'

'Make it five.'

'Forget it. You're too old for me.' She tidied the gauze and tape into a green first-aid box.

'Maybe one day.'

'I don't think so.' Accardi swapped the first-aid box for a bag. 'Shame, because I brought you a present.' She pulled out the Glock and dropped it on the bed.

'What about the *you're a convicted felon bullshit* you and Nash gave me?'

'Next time they come for you, it won't be with just shotguns.'

Virgo walked to the window and pulled the curtain back.

The Chevy Silverado had gone. He'd left it outside the motel in plain sight, because there was no point trying to make a secret of where he was staying. You couldn't pass wind in a place like Marlberg without jungle drums letting everyone know. Tommy Junior or one of his crew had fetched the pickup, without calling in to say *hi*, and maybe they'd come back again later, maybe not. The more he saw of them, the more convinced he was that they weren't smart enough to have abducted Stacy Donovan. His phone buzzed a notification.

It wasn't Senator Donovan. It was Brad Hooper boarding a flight from Tucson to Los Angeles. He was based at the US Army Intelligence Center for Excellence at Fort Huachuca, Arizona. The message said, *ETA LAX 1820*. Virgo knew that Hooper must have got some information that he believed was too important to pass over the phone. The problem with intel types is they become overly secretive, thanks to the hours they spend bugging and eavesdropping on other people. Paranoia is an occupational hazard.

Traffic still flowed good in the valley. Accardi drove fast, with the window down an inch to let the cigarette smoke trail behind them on the 395. Just north of Riverside, she took a call, no Bluetooth, the handset cricked between her shoulder and ear. She listened and once or twice said, *Okay, thanks, Bernie*, then, *Bye, Bernie, I owe you*, and hung up. The next mile, she drove with her eyebrows knotted together, like two little black leeches kissing.

Virgo said, 'You look puzzled.' The astute former federal agent.

'That was Bernie in our Commercial Crimes Division. The Wells Fargo account Daniel Donovan has been paying four grand a month into belongs to a lady called Kat Mason in Virginia Beach.'

'Is she known?'

'No criminal record, but last week she reported her son, Ryan Mason, as a missing person.'

'You think he could be involved in Stacy's abduction?'

'Blackmail?' Accardi shook her head. 'Maybe not, but there must be some reason Senator Donovan is paying the Mason family, and one of them has gone missing.'

Virgo said, 'Let's see the senator and ask him the question.'

CHAPTER 24

THE SAME TWO security guys stood outside Donovan's suite on the twenty-third floor. Looked like Indigo Fox Solutions' operating policy was to get their pound of flesh out of the workforce, or perhaps this pair were particularly trusted by the client. Virgo greeted them with a nod and was about to walk past when they both took a step forward and blocked his path. He eyeballed them. 'Is there a problem?'

'Sorry, sir, we've got orders not to let you enter.' It was the shorter guy. Buzz cut, ear-piece and a tight, gray suit.

'Orders from the senator?'

'From his brother, Mr. Duncan.'

'We're not here to see him. We're here to see the senator.'

'I'm sorry, sir. You're not going in.'

'We need to speak to the senator. Now.' Virgo grabbed a lapel on the tight, gray suit. 'It's really kind of important.'

'Please remove your hand from me, sir.'

Virgo was about to throw him down the hallway when Accardi jumped between them.

She took hold of Virgo's arm. 'Time out. Let's have a team talk.'

They retreated down the corridor, to the elevator lobby. Accardi squared up to him, hands on hips. 'What do you think you're doing?'

'Trying to save a girl's life.' Virgo shrugged. Was he supposed to have done something wrong?

'You can't assault guys who are just doing their job.'

'What if the ends justify the means?'

'You crazy? My grandfather was Italian, but I'm no fan of Machiavelli.' Accardi pressed the button to summon the elevator. 'Besides, what's the point of fighting your way in there if the brothers don't want to talk to you? Come on, let's go.'

Virgo knew she had a point, but it didn't make walking away any easier. He swallowed his pride and felt it burning away in his chest all the way down the twenty-three stories to the ground floor.

There were still forty minutes to kill until Brad Hooper's flight from Tucson landed. Virgo called in at the Hertz rental office LAX and let them know that one of their cars was on a riverbed somewhere up in Kern County. If they waited a few months, it might emerge into the Pacific Ocean near Long Beach, and in the meantime the insurers could apply for recompense to Mr. Nicholas Hartman, care of the FBI, Quantico. Virginia.

Then he crossed the Westchester Parkway to the Avis office to hire another vehicle, because he figured Hertz might be reluctant to do business with a person who had a history of using cars as amphibian vehicles. He asked Avis for a Mercedes C-Class convertible, but they were all out, so he had to make do with a BMW 8 Series. Still German, but not as good.

They were waiting in the cell phone lot when Hooper WhatsApped to say there were too many cameras around the airport, and he'd meet them at Clutters Park. When they got there, he was already getting out of a taxi, and his face burst into a grin like a split sausage as soon as he saw Virgo. 'It's been a long time.'

Many double amputees can walk unaided, but a piece of shrapnel had damaged Brad Hooper's spine, so he needed elbow crutches and a big reservoir of determination. It didn't slow him down. He dashed over on titanium prosthetics, gave a salute, and then pulled Virgo into a homie-hug.

'This is Detective Accardi, LAPD,' said Virgo.

'Can she be trusted?' Hooper stared at her and didn't look convinced.

'Do you think I'd have brought her if I wasn't sure?'

'I heard about the breakdown. It must have been tough.'

'I didn't have a breakdown.' Virgo felt himself tensing up. Took a deep breath. 'Look, just trust me on this.'

'Okay, anything you want. You got it.'

They walked into the park. It wasn't much of a recreational area, just a piece of fenced-off hillside in El Segundo, with great views over the airport runways. There were a handful of plane-spotters doing what plane-spotters do, with binoculars and notepads, and nobody else, apart from scabby pigeons. Virgo watched a United Airlines 787 coming in to land, and felt a pang of guilt at having contacted Brad Hooper in the first place. He shouldn't have done it. The only reason his old Army colleague couldn't say no, was because it was Virgo pulled him from the burning SOV in Syria. Any soldier would have done the same.

Hooper leaned on the chain-link fence, next to a coin-operated telescope on a swivel stalk. 'Is Duncan Donovan anything to do with the Pentagon?'

Virgo blinked. 'No.'

'I thought not. So, he shouldn't be privy to top-secret information?'

'Why?'

'I've been monitoring the spyware, and he's in communication with a guy called David Mettam.'

'Indigo Fox Solutions.'

'The two of them are worried. Something to do with Babylon Inferno, which not many people know about.'

'Including me.'

'And me, until I ran the name through the USAICoE systems, and—'

'USA what?'

'You know — United States Army Intelligence Center of Excellence – where I work.' Hooper waved a crutch southeast towards Arizona. 'Babylon Inferno is the codename for a joint project with the UK and Israel to develop the next generation of military drones. It's a controversial issue.'

Virgo thought back to when he served. Unmanned aerial vehicles were mainly used for surveillance, and no one called them drones. These days, it was common for them to deliver bombs, like in Ukraine, and everyone accepted them as part of contemporary warfare. 'Why the controversy?'

'Imagine a swarm of a hundred combat drones, each carrying a warhead big enough to obliterate an aircraft carrier or a small town, and all of them communicating simultaneously with each other, deploying shields and jamming radar, because these robotic locusts are being controlled by artificial intelligence, not a grunt sat behind a laptop.'

'Impossible to defend against, unless you can match it.'

'That's the future of warfare on this planet. Whoever's AI can make the fastest decisions wins.'

Accardi lit a Camel and blew smoke down both nostrils. 'Excuse me, gentlemen. I've never been in the military, but aren't you missing the point?'

Hooper glared at her, like she'd just accused him of slapping a nun.

'The ethics stink,' said Accardi. 'Who decides which

people get killed? A fucking algorithm? It should only ever be another human being.'

Virgo said, 'I don't understand why Duncan Donovan is involved in this.'

'Can't help you there,' said Hooper. 'All I know is he sent a message to Mettam, *don't worry, Babylon Inferno will go ahead as planned.*'

'Wait a minute.' Accardi went to work on her phone's touchscreen. Three minutes and halfway down a cigarette later, she held up the handset and said, 'Ta-da, the detective strikes again. Daniel Donovan is chair of the US Senate Appropriations Subcommittee on Defense. Who wants to bet that Babylon Inferno is about to get a few billion dollars approved?'

'That's why Duncan wants his brother back in Washington,' Virgo said, thinking out loud and staring off across the runways and Pacific to the horizon.

Accardi had her game face on. 'Do you want to go back to the Ritz-Carlton? This time I'll help you move the goons from in front of the door.'

'I've got a better idea,' said Virgo. 'I should have done it before now, but I guess the negotiator muscle in my brain has gone flabby.'

CHAPTER 25

JACOB CHEWED on a chunk of beef steak and studied the screen. The Donovan girl hadn't moved for over an hour, and he was getting worried. Had he thrown in one load of ice too many? He couldn't make out if she was shivering or not. If she'd stopped shivering, then hypothermia had commenced, and her brain and nervous system had become affected. Her organs couldn't keep the body temperature above thirty-five, and they would shut down. Either that or she'd suffer a cardiac arrest. In fifteen minutes, he was due to meet Locke, and he couldn't leave her if that were the case.

Another thing he knew sometimes happened was she might take all her clothes off. Medical staff call it paradoxical undressing and estimate it happens in up to half of all medium-to-severe instances of hypothermia. Jacob smiled. That would be worth watching. The problem was, he'd promised the Helper that he wouldn't kill the girl until he was given permission. He could not break that promise. It just meant that his own personal gratification would have to be delayed.

Still no sign of movement in the pit, and he knew what he

would probably have to do. Give her a hot drink and make her eat more protein. Just enough to stop her dying, but not too much, because she still needed to be punished for obscuring the camera lens. He knew all about the psychology of sanctioning disruptive behavior. One day, he might write his autobiography and make a fortune from Amazon sales, because twenty-first-century America is fixated by the anti-hero. Morality and virtue are so passé. He'd call it *The Kid from a Euphemism.*

He spat a piece of gristle onto the porch and hacked at another section of beef. He wasn't used to cooking for himself. Maybe it had been a mistake to kill Dukes, but he was another soul who needed punishing. Dukes should have found that second phone on the Donovan girl a long time before he did. Sloppy. Fortunately, it appeared the operation hadn't been compromised, but nevertheless, if it had, there was a contingency in place. Everything was still on course.

Movement. He saw it. The Donovan girl rolled onto her side. She was shaking. Her shoulders and knees quivering, and the muscles in her back locked into a kind of spasm. He watched her get up, eat one of the nutrition bars, and then march around the outside wall of the pit. The girl was a fighter. Good. It made his job easier. He threw what was left of the beef over the side of the porch and fetched the car keys from inside the farm.

The roads were deserted. Jacob didn't pass another vehicle on the way to the lake, but it was still a good decision to meet away from the farm. Everyone in the area knew the Locke family, and any sighting of Tommy Junior outside of Marlberg might become the subject of gossip amongst the locals. It was a town where people liked to stick their nose in other people's business.

When he got there, Tommy Junior's pickup was already parked off the road in a crescent of pebble and dirt, used by hunters in the day, and at night by illicit lovers who couldn't afford a room at a cheap motel. The moon was just up above the hill and shone a ribbon across the water.

Jacob was surprised to see the pickup was empty, and no sign of anybody nearby. He got out of the car and peered inside the Silverado. Nothing. Just some work gloves and tools. He put a hand on the hood and felt it was still warm. What was the kid playing at? He'd always been the weak link in the team. The one most likely to do something stupid, because everything he'd got in life was down to his father. He'd never had to study or work. Just parade through life like a peacock, knowing that the Locke name gave him a free pass. Daddy looked after him.

Fucking brat. Jacob laughed and kicked a panel in on the door. Nobody could accuse him of being a daddy's boy. It had been the years of abuse by his father that brought the sickness on. But the sickness taught him a valuable lesson. All humans have weaknesses that they hide by modifying their behavior, and ultimately, always act in their own self-interest. It's a subconscious thing. That's why, when he was aged fifteen, Jacob went into his father's bedroom with a lump hammer and killed him. He could still see the brains, like strands of scrambled egg, spattered up the wall.

There were sounds of twigs snapping in the forest, and Tommy Junior came out, holding a handgun. His eyes were everywhere.

Jacob leant on the Silverado, arms folded. 'What's the big deal?'

'Guy called Virgo is fishing around.'

'Cop?'

'No. He's a loner.'

'Then why are we risking meeting up like this? Deal with him.'

Tommy Junior swallowed hard. 'It's not that easy.'

'You've got a gun and a bunch of disciples who think your father is the new messiah. What's the problem?'

Silence. Then Tommy Junior puffed his cheeks out. 'Okay, I'll tell you what the fucking problem is: I don't take orders from you. This is a Snow Wolves operation.' His face was beetroot. 'I called Dukes today, and he never answered. What have you done to him?'

'He was a liability. I made sure he could no longer undermine the integrity of the operation.'

'That's what you said about Jerome.'

'Yes, because Jerome was an undercover federal agent.'

'But he introduced you into the team.' Tommy Junior raised the gun. It was an old Colt revolver. 'How do I know you're not FBI as well, or some other fucking government spy?'

'Do you think I'd have killed Jerome if I was?' Jacob laughed. The mental ability of the average Snow Wolf was abject, and the son of their leader was in the bottom percentile. 'Put the gun away.'

'Remember who's in charge of this operation.' A light bulb seemed to switch on behind Tommy Junior's eyes as he recalled what this was all about. 'Has the senator agreed to our demands?'

'Here, let me show you this.' Jacob took out his phone and opened up the photo gallery. He selected a video of Stacy Donovan next to a corpse in the pit. 'Take a look, and listen carefully to what she says.'

Tommy Junior was transfixed by what was on the screen. He leaned forward and tilted his head to one side, trying to make out the girl's faltering words.

Jacob said, 'Sucker,' and grabbed the barrel of the Colt revolver. He twisted it free and in one movement threw it into the lake. It would have been easy to use the gun and put a hole in Tommy Junior's forehead, but he didn't want to take unnecessary chances. There could be campers in the area, and the sound of a sidearm is different to that of a hunter's shotgun. Besides, why spoil the fun? Killing someone with a bullet is no different to using an electric chair or a lethal injection.

Jacob was slightly off balance from slinging away the gun. He couldn't dodge the fist that caught him square on the side of the chin and made his head swim. A little flutter of panic tickled his nervous system. *Whoa, interesting.* This wasn't supposed to happen. Then he remembered the Locke family mended trucks for a living and had plenty of muscle. So what? If that was his best shot, there was nothing to be overly concerned about. Stay calm. Move fast.

Tommy Junior was already swinging another right. Jacob stepped inside, and it just cuffed him around the back of his shoulder. The massive height advantage made the difference. Jacob had studied the work of William Fairbairn, the man who created gutter fighting. A technique taught to allied soldiers in World War II, to help overcome the repugnance of killing a man in unarmed combat. Time to see if it worked.

Now Tommy Junior was off balance. Jacob bent down, twisted his torso, and uncoiled himself, with an arm ripping upwards, as if he were trying to start a rusty chainsaw. The edge of his hand struck Tommy Junior between the jawline and neck, sweet spot to hit the carotid artery. The target was instantly immobilized. Next came the palm strike. The momentum started in Jacob's toes, welled up through his body, and culminated in an arm that shot out ramrod straight, faster than shit through a goose with IBS. The bony stem of the palm crashed into the front of Tommy Junior's chin, and his head snapped backwards. Perfect method to make the brain shake inside the skull and go into power-saving mode. Lights out.

Jacob stood over the unconscious body. He saw that the

left side of Tommy Junior's head was red and swollen around the ear. Was that Virgo? He made a mental note to message the Helper and find out who this man was. Then he took a rope from the cargo bed of the pickup, tied one end to the tow bar, and the other to Tommy Junior's ankles. The lake shore was only thirty yards away, but he'd had enough exertion. He climbed in the driver's seat and set off across the stones and dried mud, dragging the body behind.

When he reached the shoreline, he drove into the water, as deep as he judged possible without flooding the air intake, then swung the steering wheel around to get the Silverado back on dry land and leave the body in the water. He got out and sat on the hood. It took a while for the ripples to fade away and the lake to become a flat mirror once more. He waited a few minutes to make sure the job was done, then went back to the farm. The team of four was history. Now there was one.

CHAPTER 26

VIRGO WAITED for the server to leave the table, then dialed the number on his phone. While it rang, he took a giant swig of Tiger Beer and gulped it down. These calls were always tough. No amount of Dutch courage made them easy, but communicating with distressed relatives was part of the job, and it wasn't something he was going to miss. Roll on, days when it was just him, the RV, and the sound of the ocean.

'Hello, who is this?' Fiona Donovan sounded wary.

'I'm sorry to trouble you, Mrs. Donovan. My name's Eddie Virgo. I'm with the FBI, trying to secure the safe return of your daughter, Stacy.'

'Oh my God, is she all right? Tell me she's all right. Have you got her back? Where's Daniel?'

'We don't know where Stacy is, but we're doing everything we can to find her. We just need a little help.'

'Help? What kind of help? Has something happened to her? What's happened to her? Oh my God, please, no…'

Virgo guessed Fiona Donovan didn't suffer regular panic attacks, and the acute anxiety was due to the situation, but he needed her calm. 'Mrs. Donovan, will you do me a favor?

Take a deep breath in through your nose, hold it in your chest while you count to five, then let it back out slowly through your mouth.'

Silence on the line.

'Do it three more times.'

A longer silence.

Virgo took the opportunity for another hit of Tiger Beer. Swirled it around in his mouth, and, when it had gone, said, 'Mrs. Donovan, your husband Daniel is declining to cooperate with the FBI on your daughter's disappearance.'

'What? Why would he do that?' There was genuine incredulity in her voice.

'I'm not sure, but I think he's being influenced by his brother, Duncan.'

'I see.' Fiona Donovan was calm now. The mention of Duncan had added a chill to the tone. 'Go on.'

'He thinks the two of them can get Stacy back on their own.'

'That's ridiculous.'

'He seems to want to make sure your husband is back in Washington Monday morning.'

'Well, yes, that's committee day. Daniel never likes to miss one, but there's a deputy chair, and...hey, wait a minute... what the fuck, this is our daughter we're talking about, our only child; who gives a shit about a meeting? It should be me in LA with Daniel, not that parasite.' The calmness had gone. 'They won't even let me out of the house without two gorillas escorting me to the grocery store. I'm sick of the macho crap and pretending everything is okay. I just want my daughter back.'

'I'm going to find her.' Virgo, the over-promiser. Sometimes, even he was appalled at his own bravado, but nobody likes negativity, or even indifference. 'Mrs. Donovan, will you help me?'

'What can I do?'

'I'm in a bar called Little Saigon, across the street from the Ritz-Carlton. Call your husband and tell him to give Duncan the slip. I'll be here for the next fifteen minutes.'

The bar did small plates. Virgo ordered summer rolls, crab tacos and loaded fries, along with another Tiger Beer. Then he waited. The window seat gave a view of the sidewalk, but not the hotel entrance, which was blocked by traffic. He watched the great and good of the city walk by on their way home or out for the night. The saucers of food arrived, but Senator Daniel Donovan didn't.

Accardi rang. Said she'd checked NCIC and the local databases for anyone called Jerome who'd died in an accident near Marlberg. There was one match. Three weeks ago, a guy called Jerome Thomas had failed to negotiate a bend on the road between Marlberg and Wilson Creek. No other vehicles involved. There was something strange about the entry in the database, in that a lot of the usual information was missing. She was on her way to the sheriff's office in Kern County to find out why that was.

The summer rolls were crammed full of prawn, mint, and cilantro, but the taco was disappointing: no sour cream or chili. Virgo pushed the empty plates to one side and toyed with the last of his beer. Pushing half an hour since he spoke to Fiona Donovan, and still no sign of the husband. Did the brother hold more sway than the wife? That would be unusual, but then the Donovans were no ordinary family.

Glass empty, Virgo thought it was time to call it a day, when he snatched a glimpse of blond curls on the sidewalk. Daniel Donovan came into the bar like a gust of wind and sat down across the table, breathing heavy. He looked crushed. The pouches under his eyes were darker and more creased, and his jacket was crumpled, as though he'd slept in it. There was also a small cut on his bottom lip, which glistened with a speck of blood. So much for slipping away from his brother unnoticed.

'In your own time.' Virgo leaned back.

'What?' The senator avoided eye contact.

'I know that whoever took Stacy has already been in communication with you.'

Donovan said nothing. Stared out the window, the cogs in his mind on overdrive.

Virgo knew the senator wanted to talk, but needed a push. 'They don't want money, do they?'

Donovan glanced across the table, then went back to pedestrian-watching. He shook his head, as though there was a struggle going on inside that he wanted to clear.

Virgo seized the chance to resolve the conflict. He leaned forward. 'This is about Babylon Inferno, isn't it?'

The senator's head shot round. 'How do you know about that?'

'We know everything.'

Donovan gave a weak, sardonic laugh. 'I doubt that very much, but it doesn't matter. I'm done, finished, fucked to high heaven. All I want now is to get our daughter home.'

'Tell me what happened.'

'I got a WhatsApp from a number I didn't know. When I opened it, there was a photograph of Stacy, and she was, I mean, she looked, she was…' Donovan's voice cracked up.

'Did the message auto-delete once you'd seen it?'

Donovan nodded.

'Did it say they'd kill your daughter if you involved the police or FBI?'

Donovan nodded again.

'They're probably smart enough to make sure the number can't be traced, but may I have it anyway?'

Daniel Donovan had the phone gripped in his hand, like it had been glued there for the last thirty-six hours. He unlocked it with a password and thumb print and with a little reluctance, he pushed it across the table. 'Then I received another photograph and a message telling me to put a stop to Babylon Inferno. When the budget application goes before the committee on Monday, I am to use my veto as chair to make sure it is not approved.'

'Is that why Duncan wants you back in Washington?'

The senator snorted a laugh laced through with bitterness. 'He wants me at the meeting, only so I can make sure that the program gets the green light.'

'Even if it means your daughter gets killed?'

'No, of course not. He's talking about producing a false record of the meeting that shows Babylon Inferno did not get approved, and sending it to the kidnappers. To me, that's a big risk. The meetings are not held in public, and all documents are stored in the Sensitive Compartmented Information Facility, but if they've got a contact inside Congress, they'd soon know we tried to pull a fast one.'

An image of Duncan Donovan flashed up in Virgo's picture bank. The self-appointed chief of staff, doing everything he could to support his younger sibling out of the goodness of his heart. The battle-scarred veteran, struggling to walk, but who would do anything for his family or his country. Was it all an act? 'Tell me if I'm wrong, Senator, but do Indigo Fox Solutions act on behalf of any companies involved in Babylon Inferno?'

Donovan ran a hand through his short ringlets which were starting to go lank and greasy. He sighed. 'I don't know.'

'Does Duncan give you money to make sure some defense contracts get approved?'

'What the fuck are you saying?' Donovan's eyes went as big as the empty saucers on the table. He looked outraged and angry.

'Some people call it *lobbying*, others *bribery*.'

'Just who the fuck are you? My daughter's in the hands of some goddamned lunatics, and you're making allegations that could get your ass sued off. Bullshit, do you hear me?'

'I've seen your bank accounts, yours and Duncan's.'

'Those are donations from well-wishers and loyal supporters.'

Virgo knew money like that should not be in a personal account, but he didn't want to force the issue. He just needed Daniel Donovan to realize there was no point concealing the truth, and agree to collaborate for the sake of Stacy. He leaned forward, elbows on the table, and both index fingers making a church spire. 'I know about the money you pay every month to Kat Mason. I know about Ryan Mason.'

All the color in Daniel Donovan's face disappeared. His hands began to shake, and the quiver in his bottom lip was enough to make the cut glisten up blood again. Then he buried his head in his hands and began to sob. The convulsions grew, and soon the sobs were enormous chest heaves punctuated by sounds like the bark of a seal.

Virgo saw a couple in a booth opposite staring, and then when they noticed him watching, they went back to their food and pretended nothing was happening.

When Senator Daniel Donovan's face emerged from behind his hands, there was a look of visceral sorrow in his eyes. 'They killed my son, Mr. Virgo. Please don't let them kill my daughter.'

CHAPTER 27

THERE HAD BEEN a bad accident on the Foothill Freeway, so Virgo cut south to Rialto and back up through San Bernardino. His mind was racing. Okay, Daniel Donovan wasn't the squeaky-clean family man he liked to portray to the voters of Oklahoma, because twenty years ago, he'd had an affair with his secretary and fathered a child. Such a cliché. Kept it a secret from everyone, including his wife, but someone must have found out.

What bothered Virgo wasn't Donovan's double standards, but what this meant to the investigation. Someone had kidnapped two siblings and immediately killed one of them to show they meant business. What special sort of monster would do that? He was aware of only one other case, and that had happened a long time ago in eastern Europe: Armenia or Belarus. Maybe it was a copycat or a coincidence. Either way, it cast a whole new complexion on the case of Stacy Donovan. Whoever had taken her had done a great deal of research and preparation, and the chances of them not killing her at the end of this were infinitesimally small.

Virgo rang Nick Harman to see if his old mentor remembered the double-kidnap case, but it tripped straight to voicemail. He left a two-word message, *call me*, and turned the radio on. Springsteen was singing about *tramps like us*, and it made him think about when he took Crystal to see the Boss up in New Jersey. It had been her birthday present, and he'd rented a cottage near the beach. That was where they first talked about starting a family, as they lay in bed together, listening to the rain hammer down on the shingles. It never happened. Nature has a way of reminding you that not everything in this life comes down to our own personal choices and decisions. Fate plays a part.

There were days when Virgo wished they'd had a child, but this wasn't one of them. He'd just seen the pain paternal love can cause, when he walked Daniel Donovan back to the Ritz-Carlton. He'd spent half an hour in the lobby briefing the senator on how to respond when the kidnappers next made contact, but how much had sunk in? The three most important things to ask: number one, proof of life; number two, proof of life; number three, proof of life. And don't forget to take photographs of any message or image before they disappear. What were the chances the senator would be in a fit state to remember? He needed a professional advisor by his side, not a brother who was only concerned about his shady business clients.

It was dark when Virgo pulled off the 395 and bumped cross-country into Marlberg. Agents Bailey and Whitlock were waiting for him in the bar of the Edelweiss, and their mouths lolled open for much of the next fifteen minutes as he told them about Babylon Inferno, then Ryan Mason, the illegitimate son of Daniel Donovan, who'd been murdered simply to encourage compliance, and his body photographed alongside Stacy to underline the point. Nice psychopathic touch.

Bailey said, 'Does Hartman know?'

'Not yet.' Virgo yawned, shook his head. 'I've left him a message.'

'What did you tell Senator Donovan to do about the defense committee meeting?'

'The only thing he can do. Go to Washington and make sure that Babylon Inferno does not get the go-ahead.'

'Really?' Bailey's head went down. She was making notes. After a while, she stopped writing and looked up. 'Don't you think that's a matter of national security?'

'I think it's a matter of saving a young woman's life.'

'And nothing else?' More writing, then Bailey put the pen to her mouth. 'What about the President or Joint Chiefs of Staff? Shouldn't someone let them know what's going on?'

'I'll tell Hartman. That's his call, but if it was down to me, I'd keep it tight. The more people who know, the greater the risk to Stacy Donovan's life.' Virgo watched Bailey record his reply. He knew she was only covering her own back, and it didn't bother him. He was way past all that crap. The thing that concerned him at the moment was the loose nature of the ransom demand. What was to stop Senator Donovan from refusing to approve Babylon Inferno at Monday morning's meeting, and then, once Stacy had been released, getting the program brought back before the committee and approved? Kidnappers who were smart enough to get this far must have identified this flaw in their plan. What was he missing?

Bailey turned to a fresh page in her notebook. 'Why would the Snow Wolves want to stop Babylon Inferno getting funded? They're white supremacists, not anti-war campaigners.'

Whitlock was eating nuts. He paused with a handful cupped under his chin. 'It's the Israeli connection. They hate Jews as much as any other non-white race, and then throw AI into the mix, and that would send them into full paranoid mode. The perfect conspiracy.'

Virgo said, 'I'm not convinced this is anything to do with the Snow Wolves.'

Accardi walked in, smelling of cigarette smoke. 'Sergeant Wozniak sends his regards.'

'I hope I never see him again,' said Virgo. 'As a connoisseur of jail cells, I can tell you his was the worst.'

Bailey and Whitlock looked at each other, eyebrows up. Not sure if this was a joke that they weren't privy to. Bailey looked like she might write something down, then changed her mind.

'Jerome Thomas crashed his car with twice the legal levels of alcohol in his blood.' Accardi sat down and scooped a handful of nuts from the bowl on the table. Whitlock scowled. She carried on. 'The autopsy found injuries consistent with the initial impact and the vehicle cartwheeling down the steep hillside, but it also found something else.' She chewed a moment. 'Tiny red pinpricks inside the gums and on the surface of the eyeballs, where the capillaries had burst.'

'Petechial hemorrhage?' Virgo knew that meant only one thing. 'He was strangled?'

Accardi nodded. 'Jerome Thomas was dead before his car left the road.'

Whitlock scowled again. Maybe it was all too real for him, and he didn't like being an agent out in the field after all.

Bailey said, 'The accident a deliberate attempt to cover it up.'

'Wozniak knows shit because the case was taken over by the FBI.' Accardi finished the nuts and stood up. 'I need a drink.'

'Wait.' Virgo was trying to reconcile the FBI taking over the case with the lack of information in the database. It shouldn't have made a difference. 'Who identified the body?'

Accardi said, 'Wozniak couldn't trace the next of kin. He said it was like Jerome Thomas didn't exist. No place of birth, employment history, IRS, social security…'

Virgo went with Accardi to the bar and insisted on buying the drinks. She'd dug lead pellets out of his flesh and looked the other way while he played fast and loose with the inconvenient niceties of the law. Best of all, she'd given him back the Glock, and he could feel its weight now, strapped under his shoulder. More than ever, he wanted to use it to blast holes in the bastards who'd killed Ryan Mason, and do it to them before they killed Stacy Donovan.

He carried a round of beers back to the table and asked what progress had been made in the identification and elimination of potential strongholds. Bailey put her glasses on and skipped backwards a few pages in the notebook.

Whitlock picked up a beer and stared into it. 'I might be mistaken, but I think there's something you should know. In fact, I'm sure there will be another explanation, or my memory's playing tricks on me.'

Accardi said, 'Come on, shit or get off the pot.'

'What?' Whitlock looked offended. He must have gone to a different type of college to Accardi. 'When I worked in the analysts' unit, we used to process intelligence logs from an undercover agent with the pseudonym Jerome. It's not a common name.'

'Unless you live in France.' Accardi's top lip curled. 'Come on, what's your point?'

Whitlock said, 'His specialty was long-term infiltration of white nationalist organizations, both separatist and supremacist, and much of the intel he submitted was from over here on the west coast.'

'Well then, that might explain why there was only a skeleton report on the database.' Accardi turned to Virgo. 'What do you think?'

Virgo knew what he thought, but didn't say it, because now he understood the real reason why Hartman had sprung him from prison to work this case, and it had nothing to do with friendship or guilt. Someone had fucked up and didn't want anyone else to know.

CHAPTER 28

THE PHONE RANG at 4 a.m. Virgo was already half awake and swung his legs out of bed before he answered. It was Hartman.

'It's supposed to be my day off, but here I am at your beck and call, like Aladdin's fucking genie.'

'Stop right there.' The anger had sent blood pumping round Virgo's body, and he was wide awake.

'What?'

'Stop the false bonhomie. I know what you did.'

'I don't know what you're talking about.'

'Jerome Thomas.'

'Who?'

'Jerome Thomas, the undercover FBI agent, who was killed because of a leak from your unit. They throttled him and sent his body down a ravine. Remember him now?'

Hartman said nothing.

'He was deep cover inside a white nationalist organization, which appears to be involved in the kidnap of a senator's daughter.'

Hartman still said nothing.

'Tell me, am I missing something, Nick?' Virgo's head pounded. He dry-swallowed a couple of Tylenol. 'I've still got contacts at the *Washington Post,* or I could give the director of National Intelligence a call.'

'Alright, quit fucking me about. I'll be straight with you if you promise this goes no further than us.'

'Stop trying to negotiate with a negotiator. Remember, you taught me everything I know. No counter-offers, no best alternatives…'

'You have to understand something — far-right extremism, specifically white nationalism, is the number one threat to the national security of the United States at this time.'

'Thanks for the corporate bullshit.'

'There were reports from an undercover operative in Southern California that a group of neo-Nazis were planning to kidnap a senator's daughter. The CIRG were briefed, and I decided to let it roll. The objective of our operation was to secure evidence against the leadership of the organization and then make arrests before they had chance to carry it out.'

'Risky.'

'No. We had a man on the inside until…'

'Someone at Quantico fed him to the wolves. Literally.'

'We lost control. I had no idea which senator was the intended target, or we could have implemented a prevention strategy.'

'I hope that's true, for your sake.' Virgo hung up.

It was still dark outside. He reeled off a hundred push-ups, showered, and fixed some eggs in the kitchenette. Today was the day. The kidnappers would keep Stacy alive long enough to prove that she was still breathing to Senator Donovan, before tomorrow morning's meeting. It didn't give them long. Things might have been easier if Hartman had been truthful from the start instead of trying to protect the reputation of the unit and keep himself out of the shit. Cover-ups always make matters worse.

On January 15, 2010, two soldiers from Bravo Company in Afghanistan saw a fifteen-year-old boy tending crops and decided to have some sport. They lobbed a grenade at him and finished him off at close range with M16 assault rifles. Colleagues raised concerns, because the boy was clearly unarmed, but senior officers brushed it under the carpet. That's how the kill team started, which went on to murder civilians at random and collect body parts as trophies. God bless America.

What Virgo didn't understand was why Nick Hartman was so keen to hide the fact that security within the department had been compromised. Was it misplaced loyalty, or did he have skin in the game? He was currently acting head of the unit, and any catastrophic failure would reflect badly on him, but if it was true he planned to retire, what did it really matter? Virgo had spent ten years studying what motivates people in crisis situations, but sometimes the human psyche simply remains a mystery.

He put the radio on and lay on the bed. A smiley voice said the mercury was going to hit 95 in the Valley, and a sincere one instructed him to visit Kenyon's Auto Parts for the ultimate in quality and service. An iconic bassline filled the room, and then The Jacksons started 'I Want You Back.' He picked up the list of real estate for sale that he'd got from the agents, Chaz Moseley, which had already been pared down. Sixty-two within an area of approximately ninety square miles; more than could be checked in one day. He had to go over them again and re-prioritize. Be ruthless. It was easy to be like Bailey: cross every *t*, dot every *i*, and in the end produce a document that proves a thorough and well-reasoned investigation has been carried out. In law enforcement, they call it defensive decision-making. But he didn't want that. The only thing that mattered was finding Stacy Donovan, and fast.

It's possible to keep a hostage in the bedroom of a townhouse, provided that it is secure and soundproof, or other means of restraint and noise control are employed. But most kidnappers want something more remote, where neighbors aren't peeking over hedges or calling round to introduce themselves and ask annoying questions. Sometimes, folk pretend to be friendly just to gain an opportunity to pry into other people's business, because knowledge makes them feel important.

When they were first married, Virgo and Crystal lived in a small suburban house at Lorton, Virginia. He'd just started work at Quantico, and she was fifteen miles up the road at the Medstar Hospital, Washington. It was a close-knit community. A lot of families and retirees who liked to socialize, and he'd always end up fielding the inevitable question – and what line of business are you in, Eddie? He always said he worked for the government, doing a very boring job, and the neighbors assumed he was a tax accountant. If they'd looked closely when he set off to work, they might have noticed the gun under his jacket. Some taxman.

Light had started to frame the curtain edges. Sun-up was 6:30 this time of year, and he had managed to get the list of priority properties down to thirty-seven. The Beatles were singing 'Hey Jude' when he thought he heard a sound outside in the corridor. Before he could move, the door to his room exploded off the hinges, and three men burst in. Big, in checked shirts and jeans. Number four walked in behind them, carrying a Sig Sauer 365. Virgo lay on the bed and looked over at the holster hung over the back of a chair, the handle of his gun leaning his way. Worth a lunge? No. No chance. A viper couldn't move that quick.

The guy with the Sig Sauer was heavy-built, with slate-gray hair, and a crag-stone face. He said, 'I'm Tommy Locke. Where's my son?'

'How should I know?'

'I've been calling him all night.'

'Maybe he found a woman who likes little men with an attitude problem.'

'I'm told he had a run-in with you, and you assaulted him.'

'All I did was defend myself.'

'You turn up, and he disappears.' Locke took a step back and trained the Sig Sauer on Virgo's chest. Then he nodded to one of the other guys. 'Cuff him, Jonno.'

Virgo watched like a hawk for the opportunity to strike. Once his hands were tied, the chances of overcoming the odds diminished, and regular people always make one mistake. The key was to seize on it. Problem was, Tommy Senior looked like he knew the game. Maybe he was ex-Army or had learnt the hard way in the battlefield of life. No opportunity came. Virgo felt a lead weight in his stomach as they cable-tied his wrists and pulled him outside into the back of a truck. Once more a prisoner. This time there were no rules.

CHAPTER 29

SOME OF THE ice had melted, but there were no pools. The water must have drained through fissures in the rock. More than half of the chunks remained, making the air bite and chafe with the cold. The two corpses lay covered in them, like dead salmon on display at a seafood market, and gave an indication of just how low the ambient temperature still was. Stacy scratched at the red welts on the back of her hands and closed her eyes to ask forgiveness from God.

She knew that prolonged exposure to cold affects the brain and can lead to confusion, but she'd made up her mind. The evil human being in the room above was not going to have the satisfaction of ending her life. She was going to take it herself. The ultimate protest. She was going to die on her own terms, not be controlled by some power-grazed sadist. Like the thousands of heretics in medieval France who martyred themselves rather than live in a state of persecution, she had chosen freedom. The final liberation.

Stacy could feel that her lips and throat were puffy and swollen, and other parts of her body were starting to itch. She knew it was urticaria, caused by the cold, rather than an allergic reaction to pollen, food or an insect bite. Without anti-histamines or steroids, the symptoms wouldn't abate and could last for weeks. That was, if she lived that long, because urticaria lowers blood pressure and triggers inflammation of the organs. How long before she got dizzy and couldn't stand up?

If she was going to do it, she had to be quick. The dead man who had been dumped through the hatch was wearing a belt. She scraped the ice away and unbuckled it. Her fingers burnt from the numbness and wouldn't grip the leather. She kept trying and pulled harder. The bulk of the torso had it trapped, so she tried pushing instead to roll the corpse over, but it was a rigid, deadweight. It didn't budge.

She sat back, gasping for breath. So much for being quick. What if bigfoot was up there now watching? What would he think she was doing? She looked at the hatch and the blue LED. For some reason, she sensed it must be nighttime. Maybe he was asleep. What if they took turns and worked in shifts to make sure she was monitored at all times? How long before the hatch opened again?

The effort had dented her energy. She needed to rest. She looked around the walls of the pit. What was she going to do with the belt if she succeeded in removing it anyway? How can you hang yourself if there's no hook or beam to tie a belt on to? She could wrap it round her neck, then try and tighten it until it cut off her windpipe, but she would just pass out. A couple of minutes later, she'd come round and have to do it again, and then again.

She crawled over to the corner where she'd discarded the plastic water bottles, and picked one up. She couldn't break it with her bare hands, so she sank her teeth into the plastic and grunted as she ripped it open. It was thicker near the neck and too tough to puncture, so she worked on the body. She hacked and pulled. What she was after was a jagged edge.

She got one the shape of an isosceles triangle and twisted it free from the mangled remains of the bottle.

The first time she presented the point to the inside of her wrist, she hesitated. It made a tiny scratch. It's a common trait among suicide victims who sever arteries in the arms or neck: a little nick to test the water. Stacy closed her eyes again. *Be strong.* This time it had to do the job. She lifted her right hand and brought the shard crashing down at an angle onto her exposed left wrist. She screamed, but it was more in fear than pain.

Where was the blood? Nothing. The point of the triangle had crumpled on impact. She began to cry, and sawed at her wrist with the edge of the plastic. Some of the burrs caught in the flesh, and blood started to color her skin. She sawed faster, but the damage was to the soft tissue. It hurt. She slung the useless piece of plastic away and pulled her knees up under her chin. *Think.* ABC: Maslow's hierarchy of physiological needs for life to survive – airway, breathing, circulation. She'd considered trying to choke herself, and bleed to death. What now?

Circulation. Urticaria had already suppressed her diastolic blood pressure. If she didn't eat or generate energy by moving, then the cold would take it down even further. All she had to do was lie down and keep still. Go to sleep, and never wake up. In the end, it was all so easy, and it was her choice, not his. Stacy stretched out and made herself as comfortable as she could. Then closed her eyes for the last time and waited for eternity to take her in its embrace.

CHAPTER 30

THE PLACE SMELLED of synthetic rubber, overlaid with a delicate bouquet of sulfur. Tires and diesel. Virgo scanned the workshop for any potential exit as they frogmarched him in, past welding gear and an air compressor, to the back of the building, where thick iron chains hung from girders in the roof to help winch out truck engines. Then something hard struck him in the right kidney, and a heavy blow to the midsection of his spine sent him face-first into a rack of bolts and washers.

When he turned round, one of the team had a baseball bat, and another had the biggest open-end wrench he'd ever seen.

Locke had the Sig Sauer resting in the crook of his elbow. He lifted the barrel. 'Tell me what you've done with my son, or God help me, we're going to beat it out of you.'

'You're asking the wrong guy.' Virgo flexed his wrists in the cable ties, but they were still tight.

'That there an Army tattoo?' Locke nodded at the two-handed sword on Virgo's arm.

Virgo said nothing.

'Thank you for your service. I mean that.' Locke smiled.

The lines in his face were deep and didn't bend easy. 'But when it comes to my family, it don't mean shit.'

Virgo smiled back. 'Torture is counterproductive because it gives you false information. Read the CIA's report on Guantanamo Bay.'

'Yeah, but what if it makes me feel better?'

'It won't make you a better father.'

'You a fucking parenting expert?' Locke narrowed his eyes. 'This is your last chance. Talk.'

Virgo made a quick assessment of his predicament. Outmanned, outgunned, in enemy territory, without any means of communication, and no friendlies about to mount a rescue mission. If he sustained significant injury, he'd be out of action until after Stacy Donovan's death. It was time to negotiate, even if it meant treading close to the line. He said, 'Let me help you. We can work together to find your son.'

Locke laughed, then clenched his jaw. 'You've got a fucking cheek.'

'What do you think I'm doing in Marlberg? Do you think I'm here on vacation?'

'You DEA?' Locke closed one eye.

'Not government. I'm here trying to find a missing girl, and my guess is that if your son has disappeared, then it's connected to her.'

'What do you mean connected?' Locke looked interested, but skeptical. 'Connected how?'

'I don't know, but this town's too small for it to be a coincidence.'

'Name?' One eye closed again.

'I can't tell you her name. I'm working in confidence for her father.'

'Of course you can't tell us her name. It's a secret.' Locke laughed. 'The thing is, my boys here can be very *persuasive*.'

The boys glanced at Locke for permission to laugh also. It

was given. They chuckled and brandished the weapons in case there was any doubt about the meaning of persuasion in this context.

Virgo held out his wrists. 'Come on, cut me free. I can find your son.'

Locke thought about it for a fraction of a second, then his face went puce, and he nodded to his men. 'Let him have it.'

The closest boy was the one with the baseball bat. He stepped in and used his girth to swing it with enough force to launch a ball into space. Virgo stepped towards it to reduce impact, and met it with his forearms and hands in the shape of an X. The Shotokan cross-block wasn't textbook, and pain shot up his left wrist. The blow wasn't clean enough to snap the cable tie, but it had stretched and weakened it.

Virgo managed to wriggle his hands free just before the four-foot steel spanner broke his ribs. He swayed back, parried, and was already corkscrewing an elbow into boy number one's face before the wrench had traveled 180 degrees. Virgo groin-kicked number two and laid him out with a knee to the bridge of his nose. Number three was Jonno. He was unarmed, but big as a barn door with a full beard and nicotine-colored teeth, and he walked straight into the baseball bat that Virgo now jabbed out end-first. Jonno's head snapped back, and a few of the yellow teeth flew out.

No time to rest. Virgo was about to throw a punch when his sixth sense alerted him to danger. The natural intuition that he'd honed into a fine art in the Army. He aborted the punch and dived to his right as the sound of a gunshot cracked the air. Jonno pirouetted and fell onto his back, a bullet wound in his upper chest. Locke stood staring at the Sig Sauer, as though it were the gun's fault he'd just shot his pal.

Virgo grabbed one of the heavy chains that hung from the ceiling and launched it at Locke before he had time to gather his thoughts and refocus. At the last moment, the chief Snow Wolf saw the iron links swinging towards his head, and threw up his arms. Virgo charged, head-down, and struck Locke in the midriff. It was enough to dislodge the gun, and the two of them went sprawling into the oil and sawdust.

A hand clamped over Virgo's face, and he felt a thumb gouge his eye. He recoiled and rolled, felt a fist hammer into the back of his head. For a middle-aged man, Locke was strong and fast. How come his son was a tortoise with a glass jaw? A knee pinned Virgo's chest to the floor, and a right hook caught him on the side of his jaw. Locke grunted, 'I'm fucking killing you. Fucking killing you.' Another right hook. This time to the ear.

Locke pulled his arm back. Virgo saw his chance: he brought up his left leg and hooked it around the front of Locke's neck. Brought the right leg up behind, in a crooked pincer, and used his hips to twist and apply pressure. Locke arched backward, pawing at the thigh that had his windpipe in a vise. Virgo snarled and maintained the pressure until he felt the resistance dissipate; then he sprang up and kicked Locke hard in the stomach. The Snow Wolf groaned and rolled onto his back.

Virgo picked up the Sig Sauer and waited.

Locke wheezed and coughed, then opened his eyes and saw the barrel pointing at his head. He said, 'Before you do it, tell me what you did with my son.'

Virgo pulled out the mag, emptied it, and dropped the rounds into his shirt pocket, then threw the gun at Locke. 'I'm not going to kill you, and I don't know what's happened to your son.'

'If I find out you've harmed Tommy, I'm coming to get you. Do you understand?'

'Then you know where I'll be. I'm not leaving Marlberg.' Virgo marched out of the workshop into the morning sun, conscious that he only had until it set to find Stacy Donovan. A day is a long time in the life of a mayfly, but disappears in the blink of an eye when you're under pressure to beat the clock. He acquisitioned a heavy-duty tow truck that was parked with the keys in, and stamped on the gas pedal. It spewed smoke. The back wheels span, and he ripped up the dirt track away from the ranch.

When he got back to his room at the Edelweiss, the Glock was still there in its holster on the back of the chair. He strapped it on and unplugged his phone from the charger. That's when he saw the message from Senator Daniel Donovan.

> I can't stay here any longer. Come get me and make it fast.

CHAPTER 31

VIRGO HITCHED a ride down into the valley with Accardi. She was the quickest woman on four wheels since Penelope Pitstop, but more black denim and chains than pink turtleneck and white boots. He didn't have long. Whatever had happened at the Ritz-Carlton might seem unbearable to Daniel Donovan, but the priority now was to locate where his daughter was being held. Virgo had divided the real estate checks between Bailey and Whitlock, but it wasn't the same as doing the legwork himself. Hartman had only sent these two second-raters as a token gesture because he didn't want any competent investigators who might discover that this whole shitshow had its origins in the bureau itself. Too late for that.

Ritz-Carlton, twenty-third story. The same two guys stood guard outside the suite door. Buzz cuts, earpieces and light gray suits, just one size too small, to make sure their trapezoid upper bodies could be admired, if only by themselves. Once again, it was the shorter one who took a stride forward to block the corridor, and bristled. 'Did you not get the message? No entry.'

Accardi produced her badge. 'This time it's official. Get out of the way.'

The guy laughed. 'We've got orders. Do you think we'd ignore them because some cop tells us to?'

'What if I shoot your balls off?' Virgo held the Glock groin-high. 'Put your hands on your heads. Now.'

The two security operatives looked at each other, then slowly did as they'd been told. The shorter one looked real pissed. He snarled, 'Big mistake, pal.'

'Yeah, I'm just the king of the fuck-ups.' Virgo nodded to Accardi. 'Take their weapons.'

Both guys carried on their ankle so as not to spoil the cut of their jackets. Accardi took possession of two Smith and Wesson .380s and dropped them in her tote.

Virgo smiled and walked into the hotel suite without knocking,

Duncan Donovan sat at a desk by the window. He stood up with a wild look of outrage on his face and came limping over as fast as his cane allowed. 'What the hell do you think you're doing in here?'

Virgo scanned the room. 'Where's Daniel?'

'None of your goddamned business. Get out.' Duncan prodded Virgo in the sternum with the silver-topped walking stick.

Virgo grabbed hold of the cane and stared at the senator's brother. Sweat beaded on the older man's top lip, and his pupils were big as an emu's. Virgo twisted the cane. 'Where is he?'

'Getting ready for church. We never miss a Sunday.'

'Fetch him.'

'I can't.'

'Now.'

'I can't. He's in the bathroom and won't come out.'

Virgo instinctively walked over and tried the door. It was

locked. The next JFK had apparently gotten scared of his mean older brother and hidden in the john. What hope was there left for the country that led the free world? 'Senator, open the door now. We need to go.'

There was a fumble of hesitation; then the latch slid. Daniel Donovan looked borderline hysterical, red vacant eyes, and slack mouth. 'I've changed my mind. I think I should stay here.'

'Too late.' Virgo locked his arm around the senator's and ran him through the suite.

Duncan shouted, 'Hey, what's going on?'

Accardi opened the door, and Virgo charged through, clamped to his Siamese twin, and bolted away down the corridor. The security guys started to give chase, but changed their minds when Accardi pointed one of the .380s at them. She waited until the lift doors were closing, then tossed both of them back out into the lobby.

Virgo sat with Daniel in the back of the LAPD Dodge while Accardi gunned it through Chinatown and onto Ramona Park. The Fresno wildfires had flared up again, and the sky was the color of a yellow bruise that gets darker on the turn.

Daniel sat staring out the window. 'I told Duncan I'm going to refuse funding for Babylon Inferno.'

'It's the right call. Don't worry.' Virgo clapped a hand on the senator's shoulder.

'He wasn't happy.'

'With respect, fuck him. It's not his daughter.'

'It's not that easy.'

'What's more important, Stacy or an unethical business arrangement?'

'He said he'd tell Fiona about Ryan.'

'I think you should tell your wife about your son yourself.

Come on, do it today. It's something you should have done a long time ago, don't you think?'

'Want to walk a mile in my moccasins?' Daniel lifted his foot and offered up a loafer. 'You know nothing about the pressures in my life.'

Accardi turned her head in the driver seat. 'Stop making fucking excuses and feeling sorry for yourself. Grow a fucking pair.'

Virgo frowned. Diplomacy wasn't her strong suit, but she had a point. He messaged Bailey to see what progress they'd made on the addresses. Then he fired another one off to Hartman, asking for full access to the bureau's case file on Jerome Thomas. Maybe there was something in there that the Kern County Sheriff Office weren't privy to, that might provide a pointer to where the stronghold was.

Half a mile shy of San Bernardino, Accardi's cell chimed the opening bars of 'Highway to Hell.' She unlocked the screen and shouted over her shoulder, 'The money paid into Duncan's account from the Cayman Islands is from a holding company, with one of the directors listed as Mr. David Terrance Mettam.'

Virgo said, 'Indigo Fox Solutions. Tell me something I don't know.'

'Okay, give me a minute. Here we go — you're not as smart and tough as you think.' Accardi lit a Camel and buzzed the window down. 'Plus, you need to stop romanticizing the past and learn to live in the moment.'

Virgo said nothing. The truth hurts.

Daniel Donovan started to cry. Tears trickled down his fake-tan face into forty-eight-hour stubble, and his nose dripped snot onto his pastel-blue tie, which was already stained by droplets of blood from his lip. 'They came to see me.'

'Who?' Accardi and Virgo in stereo.

'Those people. Indigo Fox. That guy…he basically threatened me.'

Virgo said, 'Mettam?'

'No, the other one.' Donovan blew his nose. 'Burgess.'

Virgo said, 'Does Burgess look like he ran his cheek through a bacon slicer?'

Donovan nodded and blew his nose again.

That was scarface, Virgo was sure. The sidekick who'd tried to recruit him in the hotel bar, with promises of a top salary and supplementary sign-on fee. It was clear the only reason they wanted him on the books was to control him in the Stacy Donovan case and make sure he didn't do anything to put Babylon Inferno at risk. Shame. He'd thought they wanted him for his magnetic personality and world-renowned expertise. Either way, he was glad he'd said no and escaped the taint of dirty money.

Virgo unlocked his cell to check the time. Senator Donovan was booked on a United Airlines red-eye to Dulles at 10 p.m. Someone needed to get him cleaned up, keep him safe, and hold his hand all the way to the departure gate at LAX. That someone was smoking a Camel filter and kept turning round to stare at Donovan, as though he was a selfish brat who needed the vanity beat out of him. Tough love or personal dislike? Probably the latter, but who cares if the result is the same, and right now the senator needed firm guidance to stop him breaking down completely. He needed to make that meeting for his daughter's sake.

Twelve miles past the exit for Edwards Airforce Base, they turned off the highway and headed cross-country up into the hills. The Dodge bumped and rattled. Just outside of town, Accardi took a call and listened without speaking. Eventually, she said, 'Okay, Sheriff, I'll let you know if I see him.' Hung up, and pointed to the sign at the side of the road:

Welcome to Marlberg. Population 13,035, Elevation 21,987 feet

She said, 'Someone needs to change that to *Population 13,034.* They just dragged Tommy Locke's body from the lake.'

Virgo had a bad feeling. 'Why's the sheriff calling you?'

'Because you're their number one suspect, dumbass. Don't worry, I didn't grass.'

Tommy Senior and the Snow Wolves, now the Kern County Sheriff's Office. Marlberg was the last place he should be going, but Virgo shrugged. It was too late to walk away now, and besides, what did he have to lose?

CHAPTER 32

THEY TOLD him the sickness started a week before the incident with the dog, but he never believed them. He knew he'd always had it. As long as he could remember, there'd been an emptiness in that part of his internal workings where other folk had sympathy and compassion. Sometimes the smallest spark could ignite the blind mania, which burnt white-hot behind his eyes and could only be cooled by releasing the violence pent up inside his limbs. Funny thing was, that dog was the closest thing to an object of love he'd ever known, but even after he'd killed it, he felt nothing. No loss or regret. But when he'd dashed the old man's brains out in the bedroom, there was something: a sense of strange excitement.

Come on, for fuck's sake. Jacob stared at the screen. Why was the Donovan girl still not moving?

Other things had happened when he was young, but people made excuses for him. The time he bust a girl's nose in the school playground because she'd called him stupid. They made out he was some kind of mental defective, even though he shit all over the other kids in written tests. Reading, writing and math. More fool them, because not long after that he put the teacher in the hospital with a punctured lung, and nobody did anything because he said he'd been abused. Abusers, victims: swings and roundabouts.

Don't die on me, bitch. Jacob checked his watch. How long had it been?

Of course, when the thing with his mother happened, everything changed. Most bad, but some good. He'd met the Helper. This single encounter was worth all the years of darkness, because finally somebody understood what it was like to be Jacob. The Helper knew because he had been the same. They were true kin.

Get up and move your stupid, rich butt. Jacob knew it was getting close.

The judge had sent him to the Euphemism. So what? It had made him stronger and meant he could spend more time with the Helper. Time is a human construct, but he'd used the years well, improving his mental and physical capabilities. This was the culmination. Jerome, Dukes and Tommy Junior were just pawns in the game, and had to be sacrificed so that the Helper's plan could be implemented. The queen's gambit.

That's it. Too late. Fucking dead. No. *Do something. It's too soon.*

Jacob ran into the farmhouse and heated a pan of water until it was not quite ready to boil. Poured it into a plastic bottle and grabbed a towel. Then jogged over to the icehouse and slid open the hatch. Immediately, he could feel the difference in temperature scratch the back of his throat. He lowered the ladder and climbed down. Rolled her onto her back, and she didn't move. The skin on her cheekbone looked gray and waxy. He felt it with the back of his hand, and it was cold.

He wrapped the towel around the bottle of hot water and pressed it against her neck. That's the place. Heating up the arms or legs forces cold blood back towards the heart and lungs and will prove fatal in cases of severe hypothermia. He held it against one side, then the other. Left, then right. Left, then right.

Come on, breathe. What are you doing? Breathe…

He lifted up a limp arm and felt for a pulse. That's when he saw the shallow cuts on her wrist and realized what she'd tried to do. What she might have succeeded in doing. Depriving him of the exercise of his power.

Really? You'd rather choose death? You don't choose. I do.

Jacob wrapped his hand around Stacy's hair and pulled up her head. He flat-handed her across the face once. Then again, and again.

This is your fault. Slap. *Not mine.* Slap. *You should have behaved.* Slap…

Stop. Listen. What was that?

A groan. Faint and low, but there it was once more. A subconscious reaction to pain. She was alive. Now he needed to keep her alive because she had one more important act to perform. Just one, before tomorrow's senate committee meeting.

CHAPTER 33

THE HOUSE WAS a five-bed mountain lodge, nestled in a four-acre parcel, perched above a canyon on the outskirts of Marlberg. Virgo reckoned it wouldn't be long before Sergeant Wozniak came knocking at the Edelweiss Inn and Suites, so had moved base. It was one of the rentals on the list he'd given to Bailey, and she'd suggested it as a suitable bolthole, having checked it out earlier in the search for Stacy. The agent had agreed they could use it for forty-eight hours, as long as someone picked up the cleaning tab.

Bailey had checked out over half the properties on the reprioritized list and catalogued the steps she'd taken at each site to search and eliminate it as the place where Stacy was being held. She'd gridded the map and worked methodically and efficiently to ensure the list was dealt with in the quickest possible way. Everything logged and evidenced. It was more bureaucratic than Virgo's approach would have been, but speed had not been sacrificed. She'd done a good job. Maybe he'd underestimated Bailey, or she really had developed in the twelve months he'd been sitting in a prison cell.

Whitlock was a different matter. There was still a question mark over the ex-analyst's capability to be a field agent. He liked to play the part, but being a federal agent is more than just posing in a nice suit and wearing aviator shades. Hard work and resilience are still the keystones to being halfway effective, with initiative and people skills added bonuses. TV series are to blame, but so what, Whitlock was young, and maybe one day he'd realize that nothing in real life is superficial or scripted: you have to quit acting and be yourself. Virgo often wished he were someone else, but he was stuck with being who he was: a person with a guilt complex, who overcompensated by trying to save other people. Nobody's perfect.

He watched Accardi boss Daniel Donovan around in the kitchen of the lodge. Making him take off his jacket and tie, wash and shave, drink and eat, and keep monitoring his phone. She was the opposite to Whitlock: strong, streetwise and confident enough not to give a shit about the fact that the man she was pushing around was a senator. She'd make someone a good wife or partner, even though she smoked like a chimney and swore like a sailor on shore leave. In another life, she could have been the one, but he had no interest in that direction. Fidelity to Crystal's memory was nonnegotiable.

Whitlock shouted, 'Incoming, two o'clock.' A warning more fitting to the Great War trenches than a mountain lodge in the hills of southern California. On this occasion there was no artillery barrage about to land, just a black sedan coming up the driveway.

Virgo checked the mag on his Glock 19, holstered it, and went outside to the front of the house, where there was enough limestone-chip parking for a dozen vehicles. In the middle of the turning circle was a fountain, with a smiling cherub statue casually recirculating the water via his penis. An attempt at Roman classical, oddly out of place in the SoCal hills.

The black sedan crunched over the gravel and came to a stop in front of Virgo. Three suits got out. Burgess with the scar and a couple of Indigo Fox goons, trying to look like they were businessmen and not ex-grunts who'd swapped one uniform for another. Both of them were carrying.

A thought shot into Virgo's brain: who had told them the location of his new basecamp, and how so soon? Then he realized the senator's cell must have been fitted with a tracker. So much for hiding out, but at least it wasn't the Kern County Sheriff's Office arriving on the doorstep.

'We've come to collect Mr. Donovan.' Burgess got straight to the point.

'That won't be necessary.' Virgo let his jacket hang open to show they weren't the only ones armed. 'We will make sure that the senator gets to the committee meeting.'

'I'm not here to argue with you, Virgo.'

'Then go back to good old Duncan and tell him his brother is old enough to make his own decisions.'

'I'm afraid that's not possible.' It looked like Burgess was smiling, but it was hard to be sure. The sickle scar from the left corner of his mouth curled up to his ear and gave him a permanent half-grin. 'Duncan had an accident and hasn't regained consciousness.'

Virgo was suspicious. 'What kind of accident?'

'He fell down some stairs at the hotel. Looks like his cane gave way or something.'

Virgo smiled: *or something*. That was more like it. Somebody wasn't pleased that they weren't getting good value for their dirty money. Served him right. Drink with the devil, and you'd best be good at holding your liquor.

Burgess took a step forward, and squared up to Virgo. 'The thing is we need to be sure that the senator does the right thing for his country.'

'You mean your clients?'

'The United States government does not negotiate with terrorists.'

'You work for the US government?'

'The Pentagon is one of our business partners.'

'But you're getting paid by one of the companies involved in the Babylon Inferno bid?'

'Our commercial contracts are confidential.'

'Then so is my relationship with Daniel Donovan. I will advise him what I believe is in his best interests.'

Burgess's face went tomato-red, apart from the scar, which stayed white. 'You might be an ex-federal agent, who fucked up because he went soft in the head, but – by some fucking miracle I still don't understand — you are now representing the FBI, and I must tell you again that the United States government does not, I repeat does not, negotiate with terrorists.'

'Relax. Nobody's going to negotiate.'

Burgess frowned, said nothing.

'There's no need to negotiate.' Virgo gave a casual shrug. 'We're just going to do what they want. It's no big deal.'

'If Babylon Inferno is not approved at tomorrow's committee meeting, it could be months before it gets back in the appropriations schedule. Do you know what that means?'

'Your client has to wait for their money.'

'The Chinese or the Russians win the race, and we can't stop them furthering their strategic goals.'

Virgo laughed. 'The evil guys take over the world. I've heard it all before.'

'This time it's different.'

'Money and power, it's always the same.' Virgo shook his

head. 'If this new technology is so important, the US government will find a way of making sure we get it first.'

Burgess balled his fists. 'Get out of my way.'

Virgo didn't move. 'It might just be different companies who get the lucrative contracts.'

'Last chance.' A feral glare appeared in Burgess's eyes.

Virgo stood his ground. 'I'm just trying to help a father save his daughter.'

Burgess lunged forward, leading with an elbow. Virgo stepped back, stuck out his left leg, spun scarface over it, and dumped him on his backside.

The two goons were reaching inside their jackets when a voice shouted, 'Freeze, assholes.' Accardi lolled on the steps, LAPD badge in one hand, gun in the other. Bailey stood next to her, wearing an FBI baseball cap she must have kept hidden up her sleeve, feet planted shoulder-width with by-the-book precision, and both hands on the grip of her pistol.

Burgess got up off the floor, the seat of his pants and back of his jacket covered in chalk dust. 'You'll regret this.'

Virgo said, 'I'd rather regret bruising your ego than regret leaving Stacy Donovan to die.'

When the Indigo Fox delegation drove away in their black sedan, Whitlock appeared at the front door of the lodge and said, 'Did I miss something?'

'The chance to show you've got a pair.' Accardi lit a cigarette.

Virgo watched the car drive down the winding road towards Marlberg, and wondered what was going on in that town. First Jerome Thomas is killed, then Tommy Locke Junior. The first one made sense if his identity as an undercover agent became known to the group he had infiltrated, but why Tommy Junior? The boy was heir apparent to the throne of the Snow Wolves, so whoever was responsible knew they were making themselves a formidable enemy in this neck of the woods. Were the deaths connected to Stacy's abduction? Absolutely, they had to be. The question was who would do this, because Virgo didn't subscribe to Burgess's assumption that they were dealing with terrorists. Something didn't smell right.

CHAPTER 34

THE NEXT JFK HAD SHAVED, showered, and was now asleep in vest and boxers on a sofa in the living room of the lodge. Virgo sat in a winged-back leather chair opposite and reviewed the list of properties that Bailey and Whitlock had visited. Time was running out and giving them a wave goodbye from the express train window as she went. There were still forty places left to check before daylight ended, which meant the only feasible way of doing it was to split the list between the three of them: Bailey, Whitlock and himself.

Accardi needed to get the senator dressed and put him on the red-eye from LAX to Washington. Problem was, there'd been no further contact from the kidnappers, and so no opportunity to request proof of life. It was unusual for shit-bags who make ransom demands not to be in touch on a frequent basis, trying to up the pressure and reassure themselves that they were still in control of the situation. The assumption was that they'd keep Stacy alive until the committee meeting, but in the world of psychopaths and narcissists, there's never a guarantee.

Virgo's phone rang. The screen showed it was Nick Hartman. He walked into the kitchen before he answered. 'Anything from the intel unit?'

'What the fuck do you think you're doing?' Hartman was mad. The usual playfulness in his voice gone entirely.

Virgo said, 'Who have I upset? Tell them I'm not bothered.' Accardi was waving a coffee cup in his direction, and he gave her a thumbs-up.

'I just read the report Bailey filed,' Hartman said, through clenched teeth.

'I know, she's so efficient. Not like when I used to—'

'Shut up, Eddie. What the hell are you doing in Marlberg? Get back to LA this fucking minute.'

'I'm tracking down the premises where Stacy Donovan is being held, so we can rescue her if she's still alive.'

'I know what you're actually doing because I read Bailey's report. It was a rhetorical question, moron.'

'Just a minute…' Virgo didn't much care for the tone of the conversation.

'Don't you remember anything from your training?' Hartman had lost it. He was shouting down the phone. 'If the kidnappers discover you're out there snooping around, we've got a dead-fucking-hostage situation. Are you out of your goddamned, shit-filled mind? I can't believe I was stupid enough to trust you with a simple job.'

Virgo took a deep breath and tried to remain calm. 'Look, whoever's got Stacy has already killed her half-brother, probably an FBI undercover agent, and one other local guy. Do you think they're going to leave her alive when this is over? More chance of the Cardinals winning a Super Bowl. Come on, Nick, get real.'

'Oh yeah, and what chance is there of finding a needle in a haystack? Get back to LA and make sure the senator catches his flight. That's an order.'

'What's the matter, Nick?' Virgo knew something wasn't right. His old mentor was rattled. First time ever.

'You're the matter, Eddie. Just do as you're fucking told.'

'Department of Defense? White House? Our friends at Langley? Who is it that's leaning on you?'

'Hey, watch your mouth. Nobody influences my decision-making when it comes to managing a critical incident. *Nobody.*'

'What about Indigo Fox? Anyone from that outfit paid you a visit?'

'I don't pimp myself out to mercenaries.' Hartman dropped his voice and threw in a bit of menace. 'Now for the last time, listen very carefully to what I'm going to instruct you to do.'

But Virgo didn't listen carefully. He ended the call. When the screen flashed *Hartman* five seconds later, he didn't answer, and let it trip to voicemail.

Accardi held out a coffee. 'I heard every word. Do you trust him?'

Virgo had to think. 'I believe he means well, but on this occasion, he's mistaken. The best chance of saving Stacy Donovan's life is to find her before tomorrow's committee meeting.'

'He's mistaken?' Accardi made a pout of disbelief. 'Is this some rookie we're talking about?'

'He's about to retire. Maybe he's let his judgment get clouded by plans of holidays on the Florida Keys or a European cruise.'

'Did he sound like a man winding down?' Accardi pulled another skeptical pout.

'I guess not.'

'Remember, this is the man who started it all by letting an undercover agent conspire with white supremacists to kidnap a member of the US senate. Is that the action of someone who's dreaming of visiting the Eiffel Tower or the Coliseum?'

'I'm not sure it was Hartman made that decision.'

'The same guy now wants you to stop searching for the hostage. Ask yourself, why?'

'Like Hartman said, if the shitbags find out the FBI are involved and closing in, it might make them kill the hostage.'

'Stop making excuses for him.' Accardi stamped her boot and punched Virgo on the shoulder. 'Your loyalty has frazzled your logic. Think about it.'

Virgo knew she was right, but he had a stubborn streak that he'd inherited from his mother, an NYC redhead, with a penchant for Jameson whiskey. So, he chewed on some coffee and looked out the window, where Bailey and Whitlock stood on the terrace, engaged in an animated conversation.

Accardi hadn't finished. 'I don't know if he's working for someone else or just covering his own ass, but I'm sure of one thing — he's not got the girl's best interests at heart.' She punched his shoulder again. 'Are you listening?'

'Okay, Hartman might have an agenda. It doesn't change our operational plan: we find the girl and leave the recriminations until later.' Virgo looked out of the window and saw Bailey and Whitlock were now nose to nose on the terrace. Definitely arguing, not having an animated discussion.

The kitchen door opened, and Daniel Donovan zombie-walked in, still in just vest and boxers. There was a look of panic frozen on his face, and he clutched his phone like it was a de-pinned grenade. 'I think they've sent me a message.'

CHAPTER 35

THERE WAS no brilliant light at the end of a tunnel, or a sensation of hovering above her own body. Nor was there an overwhelming sense of peace, an encounter with a spiritual being, or a brief review of life revealed in flashbacks. In fact, Stacy had none of the supposed near-death experiences. She felt nothing and then dull pain as she realized the ghoul had climbed down into the pit and was slapping her face. If she'd had a modicum of strength, she would have gouged his eyes out, but she had none. Her limbs were useless.

Now she was on her own again. On her own if you didn't count the two corpses in their own little pile beneath the hatch. She'd given them names: the young one on the bottom was Sebastian because he looked kind of preppy and the type who makes out he's more refined and cultured than he actually is. The older guy on top was Hank. No reason, he just looked like a Hank.

Sebastian and Hank. Was she going crazy? Yes, probably, but she didn't care. What did anything matter? The bastard Bigfoot had taken away most of the ice and left some bottles of warm water and soft towels just lying there. She couldn't resist. Not so long ago, she'd yearned for death to sweep her away to a better place, and now she saw the ridiculous but irresistible appeal of life. Nature is cruel, but can be beautiful.

There was one reason more than any other that she wanted to live. Revenge. She was going to kill Bigfoot, and not until she had made him suffer so badly that he pleaded to be put down. Even then, she would prolong his pain: mutilate him with knives, drill holes in his joints, use acid to burn away areas of flesh, club him around the head with a bat. Nothing was out of bounds. The only limitation on what she could do was her own imagination.

The first thing she'd do when she escaped from the pit and got home was learn how to use a gun. Firing one had never interested her. It doesn't take huge muscles to squeeze a trigger, but it gives you the upper hand if you need to control someone physically bigger than you. Nobody likes to look down the barrel of a firearm, because the kinetic energy of a bullet can destroy internal organs with the shock waves. She would have to practice, enough to be confident. That wasn't a problem. When she set her mind on something, her self-discipline was so strong, it bordered on obsession.

Then she would have to track the target down, assuming he wasn't in police custody. That would be the hardest part. The best approach might be to cooperate with the police investigation and let them discover his identity and arrest him. Maybe even wait until he was charged and in the court system, where his name would become known, but then before the trial, she would refuse to give evidence against him, or claim she had been mistaken. She'd seen Jodie Foster do it in a movie once: go on a police line-up, and deliberately not pick out her attacker because she wanted to kill him herself later.

Next, she'd set a trap, the more elaborate, the better, and lure him to a specially chosen building. Make him believe he'd won a competition and had to go there to collect the prize; or a distant relative had died and left him something in the will; perhaps an ex-girlfriend wanted to meet up, or an old schoolfriend needed help selling a ton of stolen jewelry. Stacy needed to work on the fine detail, but planning revenge is part of the fun.

When he walked in, she'd jump out brandishing something symbolic, like an AK-47, and shout *surprise*, and then just for starters, shoot out one of his kneecaps.

Wait. What's that? There was a noise above, and Stacy stopped her fantasy. The hatch slid open, and light and warmth flooded in. She shielded her eyes, but knew it was him. In the same red cap and smelly shirt. What was it on this occasion? More ice, or another round of hot water and towels? Punishment or reward? This time she wasn't going to give him any excuse to mistreat her. She was going to play the part of the obedient captive, meek and respectful. She had to stay alive to kill the bastard.

She manufactured a smile. 'Thank you for the warm compress.'

Bigfoot grunted, taken aback.

Stacy followed up. 'I really appreciate it. You went to a lot of trouble.'

'Shut up.' He found his voice.

'I'm sorry. I just wanted you to know—'

'I said shut your fucking mouth. Now.'

Stacy buttoned her lip and tried to look suitably subservient.

Bigfoot threw something into the pit. 'Pick it up.'

It was a pad of notepaper. When she retrieved it, she saw someone had written something on the top sheet. The words were in capitals and squiggly, like they'd been drawn by a child.

Bigfoot pulled out a phone. 'When I say *read*, you start reading.'

'Whatever you say. Anything to bring this situation to a successful conclusion.'

'Shut the fuck up.'

'Of course.'

Bigfoot pointed the phone down into the tomb and touched the screen. 'Okay, *read*.'

Stacy squinted in the brightness. 'Colorado Rapids 3, San Jose Earthquakes 1; Sporting Kansas City 2, Houston Dynamo 0; LA Galaxy 4, Real Salt Lake 0.' She looked up. 'That's it.'

There was a pause as Bigfoot tapped the screen and said, 'Turn over the page.'

'Okay.'

'Read.' Another tap of the screen.

'I've got a message for you, Daddy.' Stacy felt the lump appear in her throat. 'A reminder, if you want to see me alive again. Go to your meeting tomorrow, and make sure Babylon Inferno is stopped.'

It had been a while since she'd thought about her family, and what they must be going through. Now it hit her again, but she fought it. She watched Bigfoot pocket his cell and close the hatch, and all she could think was, *One day, I'm going to kill you.* She'd set her mind on it, and there was no going back.

CHAPTER 36

DANIEL DONOVAN LOOKED HALF-HUMAN AGAIN. He'd got on fresh-polished shoes, a pressed shirt, clean tie, and a brush had tamed his bangs back into their curly Caesar cut. It was just his face and suit that were still crumpled. Virgo hadn't told him that brother Duncan was in a coma in the ICU of Cedars-Sinai Medical Center. The priority was Stacy, and anything that distracted from that overarching objective was to be avoided. Good news was she was still alive at the time Saturday night's soccer games finished.

Bad news was that Daniel was in no fit state to look after himself. Duncan was out of the picture, but Indigo Fox would be waiting somewhere to apply the pressure and blackmail him into complying with their wishes. It might be LAX, more likely Washington. Accardi had volunteered to stick with him overnight and all the way to Capitol Hill. Virgo felt bad because that was his job, but it was better if he stayed in Marlberg to locate Stacy, on account of the fact that he was prepared to break the law to get results, and she couldn't.

Accardi showed the senator into the back seat of the unmarked LAPD Dodge and opened the driver's door. Then she closed it again and marched back to the stone fountain, where Virgo was watching them leave.

She gave him a hug. 'Don't get arrested. I won't be here to get you out.'

Virgo hugged her back. 'Thanks for what you've done.'

'They fire me, I can always go back to fixing Kawasaki engines at my brother's repair shop.'

Virgo watched the Dodge disappear down the valley before he climbed into the BMW rental. He'd tucked his list of real estate into the sun visor and tapped the first address into Google Maps. It was an isolated holiday let a mile out of town. The type of place city dwellers like to go to be at one with nature, and get disappointed when there's no drive-thru Starbucks. It was also in the middle of the 120-degree slice of pizza that Hawkins had shaded on the map to indicate where Stacy's burner phone had pinged off the antenna, and which was why he'd prioritized it.

The Merc's wheels churned up some gravel. He gunned it out of the gates and onto the road that snaked down into Marlberg. The sky was blue, with less of the pumpkin-soup tinge and a lot more sun. Growing up in the Lower East Side of Manhattan, Virgo had never developed an interest in wildlife and didn't know a pelican from a plover, but he was good at spotting some things that were airborne. That's why he knew that the black object in his mirror, levitating four hundred feet off the ground, was a surveillance drone, not a bird of prey. It could be some harmless geeks trying out their new toy, but he didn't think so.

Immediately, his level of tactical awareness ratcheted up to maximum. Every vehicle was a potential threat; every person out hiking a potential enemy asset in disguise. A major red flag would be anything out of the ordinary, such as a broken-down car or a woman in distress at the side of the road. Something innocuous that might appeal to a person's better nature, or an incident that would require him to slow down or stop. The best way to pick a person's pocket is to appear friendly: same applies sometimes if you want to kill or cause them physical injury.

The road straightened out, and he saw something in the trees. When he got closer, he could tell it was an old-school VW campervan. He accelerated past, ready to react to any danger, but it was just a family with young kids having a picnic on a blanket. A little farther on, there was an unoccupied, red Tesla parked off the road, alongside a path that ran off into the woods. He approached it with caution, then sped up and passed it without incident. The occupants must have been out in the trees, reconnecting with nature on a Sunday afternoon before having to go back to another soul-sapping week in the office.

Up ahead, the road hair-pinned left and nose-dived downhill before leveling out. Fifty yards farther on, Virgo saw something catch the sun, up on the hillside. Sniper sights? It was too late to stop and turn back. He yanked the steering wheel left and right and slalomed like Bode Miller going for Olympic gold. *Crack.* The first bullet shattered the windshield and filled the car with a thousand safety-glass pebbles, the next put a neat hole in the headrest of the passenger seat, and a third took out the nearside headlight.

No point trying to go further. The guy with the rifle knew how to use it. Virgo swerved off the road and into a rough clearing beneath the branches of some pitted oak trees, which obscured the view from up on the hill. He killed the engine and ducked out of the BMW with the Glock already in his hand. He crouched down behind the back wheel and waited. It wasn't long before he heard the high-pitched buzz, like a swarm of bees on helium, and saw the drone descend below the treeline, searching for its quarry, less than twenty yards away.

Virgo rested the barrel of the Glock on the trunk of the hire car and waited for the drone to maintain a steady hovering position. As soon as it did, he pulled the trigger and watched as it exploded into pieces of metal and plastic. Whoever was after him had lost their eyes, and that evened things up. The sniper still had the higher ground, but they wouldn't know which route of approach Virgo would take, and might not be equipped for a handgun shoot-out if they'd been expecting an easy kill shot.

The red Tesla he'd passed was obviously their vehicle. From where it was parked, it was an easy ruck through the woods to the rock outcrop that overlooked the road below and made it like shooting fish in a barrel. Virgo considered getting back in the BMW and tearing back up there, but that could be a fatal mistake if the sniper hadn't moved. So instead, he distanced himself from his last known position, and when sufficiently far enough where they wouldn't expect an attack from that angle, he scrambled up the hillside toward the road above.

Halfway up, he stopped and listened for movement. Nothing. Just the hot breeze rattling the leaves. He set off again, but more cautious now, so as not to give away his location. He was likely dealing with a team of two: one to operate the drone, and one to kill. They could have split up, to cover each other, or they could be heading back in convoy to the Tesla. Shame they drove electric, because he wouldn't hear the engine fire up. At least they were saving the planet, even though they had a nice sideline in the assassination of fellow humans.

Another few paces, and Virgo heard a metallic snap some way off to his right. He cut sideways at speed, across the hillside beneath a ten-foot face of granite, then climbed up a fissure in the rock. When he popped his head above the edge, he was just in time to see a man jogging away into the trees with an aluminum rifle case in his hand. He didn't want to lose him, so shouted, 'Hey, you missed, asshole. Try a closer shot.'

The sniper dropped the flight case and spun round with his hand reaching inside his jacket. Virgo hauled himself up onto the plateau and was already rolling away when the first bullet kicked up the dirt where his head had been a fraction of a second earlier. Lying on his belly, both hands on the Glock, and arms stretched out in front of him, he fired back. The guy caught it somewhere near his right hip, and it spun him onto the ground.

Virgo waited.

After a while, he heard a howl of pain, and the sniper shouted, 'Jesus Christ, get me a fucking medic.'

Injured fighters are dangerous. Virgo kept quiet and maintained his position. If the wound was serious enough to have immobilized him, it wouldn't be long before blood loss and shock impacted his reflexes.

Another howl, then, 'Come on. I was just doing a job.'

Virgo pushed up onto his knees, gun still trained on its target. Once on his feet, he approached with patient circumspection, keeping one eye on the woods beyond for any sign that an accomplice was lying in wait. Nothing moved in the trees. He took a few more cautious steps and saw that the injured man on the ground was wiry, with short black hair, and a pencil mustache. There was a large red stain on his gray trackpants, and his eyes were clamped shut in pain. No sign of the gun.

'Put your hands on your head.' Virgo took another step. He was less than ten feet away.

The sniper opened his eyes, and in that moment, Virgo recognized the intent behind them. The guy was no poker player. He didn't make to put his hands on his head, but pulled out a handgun from underneath his body. That was as far as he got because Virgo was waiting and pumped three bullets into his chest. Threat eliminated.

No sooner had the gunshot reverberations died down, he heard a car door slam on the far side of the woods. The Tesla. He ran through the trees, getting gouged and scratched by brambles and saplings. When he reached the road, the car had gone. Nothing he could do; the drone pilot had got away.

He retraced his steps and searched the dead sniper's pockets. Nothing to indicate who he was working for, but a wallet with bank cards and a driving license that said his name was Michael Nunez. Virgo used his phone to take a photograph of the dead man, then took the wallet and slid back down the hillside to the hire car. Now was not the time to be hanging about for an ambulance, or calling the cops to argue justifiable homicide. Not with his record. Someone had just tried to kill him, and the question was, why did they want him dead? Was it to stop him giving advice to the senator, or was it because he was getting close to finding Stacy? He needed an ID on Nunez.

CHAPTER 37

THE PROPERTY WAS A SPRAWLING, one-story ranch house that squatted on the hillside behind a razor-wire fence. It was advertised on different vacation letting sites and currently showed up as available to rent. Virgo left the BMW out of sight and covered the last mile on foot, hugging the treeline to minimize his exposure. The ideal approach would be to keep the place under surveillance for a few hours to monitor any activity, but they didn't have the luxury of time. Risk could be reduced, but not avoided.

Closer he got, he could see there were no vehicles at the property or nearby. The blinds were up at the windows. No recent tire tracks in the dirt. This was not the place, he was sure. To be a hundred percent, he vaulted the gate and ran around the back into the yard. There was nothing apart from a rusted barbecue and some outdoor furniture with the paint flaking off. No wonder the place wasn't rented out. He peered inside through the grime-filmed windows and saw no signs of recent occupation. Another one to strike off the list.

As he headed back to the car, his phone vibrated, and the screen showed a German number: Caleb Hawkins at the

CIA's cover-company UMI Elektronik und Sicherheit, returning his call.

Virgo swiped up. 'What you got for me?'

'That depends on what you've got for me.' Same old Caleb. Nothing for free.

'Tickets to the Kennedy Center, I told you. They're putting on The *Marriage of Figaro* at Christmas.'

'It's one of my favorites.'

'I know.'

'Saw it once at La Scala in Milan, Italy. Not the town in Michigan. Romantic comedy at its finest, and in my humble opinion, Mozart's greatest work.'

'How absolutely fascinating.' Virgo, Mr. Sarcastic. 'Come on, have we got a deal or not?'

Hawkins laughed. 'We're brothers; of course we got a deal. The photo of the stiff you sent me checks out. He was Michael Jaydon Nunez, ex-private in the 4th Battalion, 23rd Infantry Regiment. How'd he die?'

'Tripped and fell on four of my bullets.'

'Don't mess with the Activity, or accidents will happen.'

'What about any recent intel on Nunez?' Virgo was back at the BMW. He took the opportunity to clear some more glass pellets off the driver's seat.

'After leaving the Army, he freelanced. Worked for us in Afghanistan, on supply from a private contractor we did business with.'

'Indigo Fox?'

'Affirmative. Not used him for three years.'

Virgo nodded to nobody but himself and a squirrel, which was eyeing him with suspicion from the bough of a jacaranda. Things were starting to make sense. Indigo Fox had taken out Duncan because he'd lost control of his brother and was no further use to them, and now they were after him because he'd got Daniel Donovan's ear and was advising him to block Babylon Inferno. They could see their big payday disappearing. 'What about that other issue?'

'Next-generation drone shit?'

'Babylon Inferno. The one that's going to make soldiers redundant.'

'I'm glad we served when we did.'

'Who stands to lose most financially if the program doesn't go ahead?'

Hawkins laughed. 'Seasons change, but some things never do, eh? Money is always the prime motivator, just like in Verdi's *Falstaff*. The only difference on this occasion is it's not the big boys who are getting their own way.'

'Meaning what?' Virgo didn't follow.

'There's five defense companies that dominate the market: Lockheed Martin, Raytheon, Boeing…'

'General Dynamics, Northrop Grumman, I know. Which one is Indigo Fox working for?'

'None of them.'

'Are you kidding me?'

'Negative. The big five will no doubt be involved in Babylon Inferno in terms of hardware, but artificial intelligence is a different kind of software to what they're used to, and some new companies are leading the world.'

'And one of these AI companies has employed Indigo Fox to lobby on behalf of their interests?'

'You mean apply some palm grease?'

'Call it what you want.'

'The firm is called Bagshaw-AI, based in England. One of the highest-ranking new listings thanks to some major investment capital.'

'Anything unusual about the board or major shareholders?'

'Just the usual faceless, rich bastards.'

'What's the contract worth to them if they get it.'

'A few billion? But that'll be split with some other companies.'

'Still no luck with that screenshot I sent you?' Virgo had photographed the latest app message from the kidnappers on the senator's phone.

'No chance tracing the number. It's a prepaid SIM purchased three months ago, and was used online only, routed through a server in Switzerland.'

'I thought you were the best?'

'I'm not a magician.'

'See you at Christmas.' Virgo hung up. Disappointed that there was nothing in Bagshaw-AI's company profile to indicate why they might employ extreme measures to win a contract. But then again, they probably didn't know. They employ Indigo Fox to make sure that their bid is approved by the Senate's Appropriation Committee for Defense, and they're not concerned how that is achieved. Business is business. For their part, Indigo Fox are paid a huge sum of money, but it's results-based, and if Babylon Inferno doesn't get the green light, they don't get the x number of million dollars that will otherwise come their way. Yachts in Bermuda, ski chalets in Aspen, duplex overlooking Central Park, beach house in Malibu – all gone.

The next property on the list was a house for sale in Marlberg itself. He tap-touched the address into his phone and drove there as fast as he could without a windshield to keep the breeze and bugs out of his eyes. As soon as he turned onto the street, he knew it wasn't the one. It was a dead end, with just a dozen small bungalows either side of neatly trimmed verges. The kind of place grandparents move to when they've sold the family home and given the cash to their kids or blown it in Vegas.

Number 2, Acacia Avenue had a real estate agent's sign on a post in the front lawn, and Virgo wondered whether it was even worth getting out of the car. The house was over-looked by neighbors, and he'd already seen one old couple in the bungalow opposite, sneaking a look at him out of their kitchen window, as though he might be a cat burglar or serial killer. Maybe it was the bullet hole in the hood that concerned them. They were probably on the phone right now to the Kern County Sheriff's office. He hoped they weren't, because they were the last people he needed to show up and drag him in for questioning about Tommy Junior.

In the end, conscience got the better of him, and he decided he ought to check out the property, for the sake of being thorough and meticulous. He parked up outside the picket gate, then smiled and waved to the couple across the street, as he climbed out of the car. Before he made it halfway down the path, his phone buzzed. Whitlock, the wannabe agent.

'What do you want?' Virgo was a little abrupt. He made a mental note to try and be more patient with junior colleagues in future.

There was silence on the phone.

Virgo tried again. 'Come on, I've not got all day.' The new resolution hadn't lasted long.

'Hi, Virgo, it's me, Whitlock.'

There was something strained about the kid's voice. 'I know who it is. What's the matter?'

On the line, Whitlock coughed to clear his throat. 'There's a man pointing a shotgun at me; says you killed his son.'

Virgo shook his head. 'What's he look like?'

'It's Mr. Locke.'

'Tell him it wasn't me.'

'He's going to kill me unless you agree to take my place.'

'Put him on the phone.'

There were muffled noises. 'He says no talking.'

'Great. Tell him I'll be down at his workshop in ten minutes.' Virgo ended the call.

He checked out the bungalow, which, as he'd anticipated, was not where Stacy was being held, and spun the BMW around at the end of the cul-de-sac. Then he smacked both palms on the steering wheel in frustration. This was exactly what he didn't need at such a vital time; an agent from the government unit that investigates kidnaps getting actually kidnapped himself by an unreconstructed Fuhrer figure.

Of course, the option was there to press control-alt-delete and stop the operation to find Stacy, while this hiccough was resolved through the official channels. He could press the red button and call in the department's SWAT team, but the rescue mission would take thirty minutes to plan and six hours to get the paperwork signed off by the back-covering top brass. Time he didn't have. Also, he was more convinced than ever that the Snow Wolves were not holding the senator's daughter because of some racist objection to Babylon Inferno. There was something else at play. Tommy Locke was just a distraction, but it was a distraction he was going to have to deal with on his own.

CHAPTER 38

THE POSSE WAS THERE WAITING for him, just as he thought they might be. Four pickups and two saloons lined up in the dirt outside the workshop of Locke Transport. He knew he was driving into the lion's den, but not that long ago he'd been a professional negotiator, doing it day in, day out, usually with shitbags meaner and more dangerous than this bunch of misguided rednecks. He backed himself to talk his way out of most tight spots. It was the word *most* that bothered him.

Virgo pulled on the parking brake to lock up the back wheels, and slewed round slightly to a stop. A little theatrical, but if the boys wanted a showdown, it was the least he could do to play the part. Then he tucked his gun under the driver's seat, took off his shirt, and walked bare-chested over to the motley crew, to show he wasn't carrying, hands held up over his head.

'What did I say I'd do to you if I found out you killed my son?' Tommy Locke came to meet him holding a shotgun and flanked by two of his generals.

'I told you the truth. It wasn't me.' Virgo saw Whitlock

with two younger guys in polo shirts on either side, holding his arms, and another stood behind him with a handgun.

'These good friends here of Tommy Junior saw you beat him up.' Locke tossed his head back over his shoulder to the polo shirts.

'I was defending myself.'

'Now he's dead.'

'Killed by someone else, not me.' Virgo slowly lowered his hands, but kept his palms out on show. 'Come on, what do you want? Do you want to find out who killed your son, or do you want to take your anger and grief out on the nearest scapegoat?'

'What if it's the same thing, smartass?'

'It's understandable someone in your position needs to be seen to take action — doing nothing can be seen as a sign of weakness, but think about it, why would I kill your son?'

'Because you got lucky first time, and he was going to teach you a lesson, good and proper.'

Virgo did his best to stop himself from smiling. 'This might be hard for you to accept, although I suspect subconsciously you had a good idea yourself, but your son couldn't beat an egg.'

'Put your fucking hands back up.' Locke kept the barrels of the shotgun pointed firmly at the center of Virgo's chest and took a step closer. He called up his generals. 'Show him how we make an omelette.'

Virgo knew what was coming, but was all out of options. If he put up a fight, Locke had a good chance of getting him with the shotgun, and Whitlock wasn't the kind of teammate you could rely on in a brawl. He glanced over at the young agent, who all of a sudden couldn't look him in the eye. That's how it was. Either he felt bad for getting him into this position, or he didn't want to watch what was about to happen. Same difference. Virgo clenched every muscle in his body, majoring on those in the neck and abdomen, and let the first punch catch him on the side of his jaw.

Next came a barrage of blows to his stomach from one guy while the other was round the back, working on his kidneys. It was fair to say the negotiations weren't going to plan. After what seemed an age, but was likely two minutes, it stopped, and he could feel the metal taste of blood in his mouth. The two generals stood bent at the hip, gulping for breath. Their hands must have hurt, but not as much as his body. It was on fire.

Locke watched through narrow chinks in his basalt face. 'Ready to tell me what happened yet?'

'No.' Virgo managed a crooked smile. 'Think I'll pass.'

'How about I blow your fucking balls off?' Old man Locke dipped the barrels of the 12-bore down a few degrees.

Virgo spat a slug of saliva-blood onto the ground and wiped his mouth with the back of his hand. 'You know your son's acquaintance Jerome didn't die in a car accident, don't you? Someone killed him.'

'I have friends in the sheriff's department.' Locke looked pleased with himself on that account. 'Sure, I knew that there was more to it than they let on.'

'So who murdered Jerome, because two weeks ago, I hadn't even heard of Marlberg?'

'You saying it was the same guy killed Tommy Junior?'

Virgo said nothing. Let the possibility sink in. 'I don't know; it's possible.' Then he took a punt. 'Any other of your son's acquaintances dropped off the radar lately?'

Locke scowled, starting to lose patience. 'Kids come and go all the time. The Snow Wolves is a network of folk who want to maintain their race and culture. They stay with us to build connections and learn the values; then they go back to their home towns and spread the word.'

'So, nobody unusual?'

'What do you mean, fucking unusual?'

'I don't know.' Virgo could feel himself grasping at straws. 'Somebody who didn't fit the profile or disappeared without saying goodbye.'

Locke shrugged and looked at the two generals. They stopped panting and shrugged back. Locke said, 'Looks like your attempt to blame someone else just turned to shit.'

Virgo tensed up his muscles for round 2.

'Excuse me, sir.' It was one of the polo shirts guarding Whitlock. A guy in his twenties already going bald, and compensating with an ass-fluff goatee.

Locke turned round. 'Someone say something?'

The goatee put his hand up, like he was a kid in class who needed a pee. 'What about Jacob?'

'Who the fuck is Jacob?' Locke's face turned more granite than Stone Mountain.

'The big dude from DC, who Jerome introduced to us.'

'Pizza face?'

'Yeah, he had kind of old acne scars.'

Locke was interested now. He walked back towards the line of vehicles where Whitlock was being held, and squared up to the goatee guy. 'Okay, tell me about Jacob?'

'Him and Tommy Junior were tight. Real tight. Then Jerome had the accident, and Jacob disappeared, and you know...' The goatee hesitated, searching for the right word. 'He was different.'

'What do you mean fucking different? Dolly Parton's different. Tom Cruise is different. Jerry Seinfeld is different. It means shit.'

'No sense of humor, aggressive, obsessed, I don't know, not right, not normal.'

The kid holding Whitlock's other arm was short and stocky, in a phlegm-colored Fred Perry and matching bucket hat. He nodded along and then said, 'And don't forget about Dukes.'

'Dukes?' Locke turned to him. 'That cowboy who always smells of weed. What about him?'

Bucket hat said, 'He went AWOL same time as Jacob.'

Goatee said, 'I'm sure Tommy Junior spoke to him recently.'

Bucket hat said, 'Or was it Jacob on the phone yesterday?'

The two polo shirts screwed their faces up to show they were scouring inside their brains for any better detail. It went quiet.

BOOM. The air molecules within a hundred yards shook. Tommy Locke had fired the shotgun into the ground inches in front of their toes. The dust swirled up and got taken away on a gentle Santa Ana. He swung the barrels of the 12-bore a full 360, to make sure everyone got the message. 'Go and find Jacob and Dukes. Do it fucking now.' Then he pulled the trigger again and blasted a hole in the door of his own flat-bed Ford, his face contorted in rage and grief.

Virgo spat out some more blood, glad that Locke's attention had shifted away from him. A relief that he didn't have to set a new world record as the human punchbag. Good thing was, he now had two names: Jacob and Dukes. It was Jacob he was interested in because of the description. But who was he? Was he getting paid by a rival company to Bagshaw-AI to sabotage their contract? Find Jacob, and he'd find the answer.

He'd also be able to solve another puzzle. It was something one of the polo shirts had said when describing Jacob: *the big dude from DC, who Jerome introduced to us.* What was an FBI undercover agent doing getting someone like this involved in an operation? The only people undercover agents bring into a long-term infiltration are other undercover agents, to give distance, so that when the arrests are made, the cover story of the original agent remains intact, and he or she can move on to the next long-term op. The new arrivals are the evidence-gatherers who will give testimony in court, with their short-terms covers burnt. But it didn't sound as though Jacob was an undercover agent. Either Jerome Thomas had gone rogue, or someone had set him up with a ringer.

CHAPTER 39

JACOB'S EARS picked up a new sound. He stopped reading and held his breath. It was a car engine, a long way distant, but still the first vehicle that had been this close since he moved into the farm. He put down his book and picked up the binoculars. The car was a black sedan, kicking up dust clouds out on the fire road that ran past the entrance to the estate before climbing up into the forest and going nowhere. The track was rough and better suited to outfits with off-road tires and suspension.

He walked over to the edge of the porch and watched the car turn into the gateway of the farm. It triggered one of the sets of motion-detection sensors he'd rigged up inside the boundary, and an alarm blared from a speaker until he hit mute. The car weaved towards him on the driveway between the old cornfields. Single occupant. He relaxed a little. Probably a hopelessly lost urbanite whose satnav had gone batshit crazy. Any minute, they'd realize Google or Waze had sent them into the back of beyond, and make a K-turn. The car kept coming. It was a Honda Accord, with California plates, and the single occupant was a woman.

It wasn't the cavalry coming to rescue the Donovan girl, but it was an interference Jacob didn't want. It was approaching the crucial hours, and there were two tasks left to perform. The second one he was particularly looking forward to. It was better than getting paid. Now, here was this stupid woman who couldn't read a map, probably wanting directions to the Hollywood Walk of Fame or Disneyland. He needed to get shut of her quickly in case the final instructions came through.

The Honda drove all the way up to the steps of the porch, and the woman got out. She was dressed smart in a navy suit and cream scarf. Short chestnut hair, and carrying a leather, business satchel. Maybe she was a religious freak, about to try and convert him.

Jacob closed the MacBook, which served as a video monitor for the icehouse and walked down the steps. 'Can I help you?'

'Hi, how's it going?' The woman smiled, like an over-friendly store assistant. 'I thought this place was empty and up for sale?'

Jacob had a bad feeling. 'Why do you want to know?'

'I'm thinking of buying it.'

'It was my grandmother's place, but she died, and I'm just looking after it.'

'Oh, I'm sorry for your loss.'

'There was a glitch with the will, and some cousin is claiming they own half of the place.'

'The Realtor never mentioned that.'

Jacob was uncertain. Real estate agents don't as a rule make appointments to view on a Sunday, do they? And the farm had been on the market for pushing two years, which was why the Helper had chosen it. There was some kind of argument going on within the family about inheritance, and the asking price was way over the top for such a run-down jumble of buildings and land. He needed to know who else might be coming. 'Did you make an appointment to view this afternoon, because nobody called me?'

The woman smiled and went bashful. 'No, I'm sorry. I thought I'd just call by and get a feel for if it was the right place for me.'

'You local?'

'No, me and my partner are relocating from Philadelphia.'

'That's a long way to come to just get a feel for a place without an appointment.' Jacob was getting edgy.

The woman laughed. 'No, I've already started my new job down in Riverside. That's why we're relocating.'

She sounded plausible. Jacob just wanted her to go. 'Make an appointment with the agent for next week. It'll give me chance to fix the place up a little.'

The woman dipped her eyebrows and pursed her lips, the way some women do when they're play-acting hurt and want a special favor, like a six-year-old girl. 'Pleeeease, could I have a quick look around now? I'm flying back to Philly tomorrow to start clearing the old house out.'

Jacob stood with his feet planted. 'No, I don't think so. The place is a real mess.'

'I don't mind, honest. I can look beyond the superficiality. I just want to see the structure: the blank canvas for me and my partner to turn into our own little masterpiece.'

Jacob was getting angry. She was too pushy. 'Sorry, lady. My grandmother would never forgive me if I let a stranger see her place in this state.'

The woman looked disappointed. 'Oh, well. Thanks anyway. I guess I'll give the agency a call tomorrow and arrange to come back in a couple of weeks.' She started to walk back to the Honda, but stopped and came back. 'Hey, why don't I take your number, and we can arrange it between ourselves.' She took out her phone and smiled.

Jacob knew if he gave her a fake number, and she tested it out, then that would lead to an unpleasant situation, but there was no way he was giving her his correct number. That was the problem these days: no privacy. Everyone knows that if you're a certain age, you've got a cell. There were probably other excuses, but he didn't know them, because he hadn't been allowed a cell for twenty years. Hospital rule. Jacob made a big play of checking his pockets. 'My phone must be inside somewhere. I'll tell you what, let me give you a quick tour of the old place, but it'll have to be real quick, mind.'

'Thank you so much. That's so kind of you.' The woman hugged her satchel, and marched around Jacob and up the steps.

'Not that quick, lady.' Jacob went after her.

He showed her through to the kitchen, which was decidedly the worst room in the house. It was a temporary doss, so he hadn't washed any plates or put garbage in the bin. The room stank and buzzed with flies attracted by leftover food and the giant dead rat that was decomposing on the floor tiles next to the sink. The woman screwed up her nose and walked straight through to the living area and the bedrooms. She didn't spend much time looking around any room, just in and out, but then Jacob had probably become acclimatized to the rank odor, and she was in a rush to get outside into fresh air.

When they got back out on the porch, she said, 'Can I take a look around the back?' And set off without waiting for a reply.

'There's nothing there. Just disused barns and scrubland.' Jacob hurried after her.

'What's that place?' The woman pointed to the icehouse.

'Nothing. Just an agricultural storage place.'

'It would make a great cabin or summer house.' The woman was already taking big strides down the path. 'Let's have a quick look inside.'

'No, I don't think it's safe.' Jacob set off after her.

She found the door unlocked and went inside. 'Wow, so cute.'

Jacob followed her in and saw her eyes dart around, noticing the items that shouldn't have been there, in an unsafe, agricultural ruin. The laptop he'd set up on a camping table to monitor the pit camera, the Wi-Fi router, the spare box of protein bars and water bottles, the phone he'd been using to video the Donovan girl, and the big pool of dried blood and hair, where he'd stomped Dukes's head along to 'American Idiot' by Green Day.

He saw the woman reach into her satchel, but he already had his gun out. He didn't wait. The first bullet hit her in the ribs side-on and put her down. He finished her off with a headshot. Then he yanked the satchel off from around her shoulder and pulled out the Glock 19 she'd been about to pull on him. Somehow, he didn't think this lady had been telling the truth about relocating from Philadelphia.

When he tipped the satchel out, there were pens, papers and a wallet. As soon as he opened the wallet, he recognized the FBI badge: blind justice holding the weighing scales and sword. This was not good. He had to tell the Helper.

CHAPTER 40

THERE WAS a full-size steel-drum band inside Virgo's skull, playing 'Colonel Bogey' at full volume and marching along to it in hobnail boots. He'd not slept, eaten or drunk, and the AC wasn't too effective now that the front windshield was gone. He chewed a trio of Tylenol and coaxed the BMW through a tight, uphill bend and onto the track leading to the next property on the list. It was a remote plot right on the edge of the pizza slice shaded on the map.

What was making the headache worse was the creeping realization that Accardi had been right all along about Hartman. Not that Virgo would admit it if she happened to call him up and say *I told you so*, in a whiny voice. Everything Hartman had done was aimed at making sure they didn't identify the location Stacy was being held. It was as though he wanted the kidnappers' demands to be agreed to without any attempt at negotiation.

Mrs. Google Maps told him he'd arrived at his destination. The house was a rustic, A-frame mountain cabin hidden in ten forested acres. The listing agent said it was *a rare opportunity to acquire a stunning, private retreat surrounded by the beauty of nature and abundant wildlife.* Virgo thought it was an overgrown, rodent-infested shack. It took less than a minute to establish that there were no signs of recent human habitation. He tapped in the next address and spun the car around.

Okay, at first, he'd thought Hartman was engaged in a damage-limitation exercise. The unit had got their fingers burnt by letting an undercover operation run too long, or run without the required supervision. Maybe there'd even been an element of entrapment along the way, with Jerome being told to talk up the ethnic dangers of Babylon Inferno to the Snow Wolves. Whatever way it went down, Virgo had originally thought Hartman was trying to resolve it in the shadows so as to preserve the reputation of the FBI and the careers of one or two senior managers.

But hallelujah, Virgo had seen the light. Until now, it had been blocked out by the sense of loyalty he felt to his former mentor and erstwhile friend. Why did Hartman want him out of Marlberg? Simple, he wanted the Babylon Inferno program to be stopped because presumably somebody was paying him big bucks. Retirement approaching, and overlooked for the final promotion, money can help salve the feelings of bitterness.

Virgo gunned the BMW down the mountain road and felt like laughing, but the bugs would have splatted into his teeth. A sick joke: Hartman was doing his best to make sure the senator blocked the AI drone program, and Indigo Fox were desperate for him to get the bid approved. Virgo was caught in the middle. The filling in a sandwich he would never be able to negotiate his way out of because there could only ever be one winner. His priority remained: find Stacy.

The road straightened out, and he called Accardi.

'How's he doing?'

'Better and worse.' Accardi sounded a little off. 'He's constantly worrying about how he's going to tell his wife about Ryan Mason, and what the voters in Oklahoma will think. I'm ready to smack him round the face.'

'He should be more worried about his daughter, and the DA prosecuting him for taking bribes.'

'The senator says he's never accepted dirty money.'

'With a straight face?'

'He's convinced himself that any payments Duncan received were for legitimate lobbying. It never affected his integrity.'

'He's lying.'

'It's all relative in politics.'

Virgo heard the sound of a match being struck. 'Where are you? Is he there?'

'Relax.' A pause while she no doubt dragged on a Camel filter. 'I've got eyes on him.'

'I've got two names for you to run through the LAPD intel systems: Jacob and Dukes. I'm guessing the first is a forename.'

'There'll be too many hits. I need filters.' Accardi was shouting now. In the background, there was the roar of an airplane taking off.

'Both from out of state. Connections to white nationalist organizations.'

'Leave it with me.' She exhaled, then coughed. 'Want to know something else in the meantime? I didn't like to mention it because I know what a big pal of yours he is.'

'Not Hartman again?'

'The reason your two agents were arguing amongst themselves was because Hartman had told them to decamp back to LA, but Bailey decided to stick with you and your plan, unlike little prick, who wanted to bail out.'

Virgo was about to share with Accardi his Saul-like conversion on the road to Marlberg — the one about his big pal, Hartman — when something above the tree line caught his eye. 'Got to go. Don't lose Donovan.'

He slowed down for a better look. *Come on, not again.* A black insect with four rotor legs, and a sleek video-camera body, built for short-range reconnaissance. These guys were persistent, if nothing else. The question was, where was the ambush up ahead this time? Another sniper on the hillside, or would it be something more subtle like road works or a fallen tree blocking the route. *Whiskey Tango Foxtrot.* The answer was neither. Right then, a Sikorsky S-70 helicopter swooped down over the ridge, and the tarmac alongside the car danced with high velocity slugs.

Virgo swerved and slammed on the anchors. The first pass missed him. He looked behind to see the Sikorsky turn for another run. Three on board: pilot, and a couple of wingmen with assault rifles. Problem was, he was exposed. It was a wide and straight section of highway, which was why they'd chosen it. He needed to get down the valley and into the town center where buildings offered protection, and members of the public were more populous. Even Indigo Fox didn't want collateral casualties or getting captured on Smartphones and going viral on X and Insta.

He slammed the gas pedal to the floor and left ten pounds of rubber smoking on the asphalt. The engine screamed up through the gears. A needle on the tacho dial flew up into the red zone, and the steering wheel started to judder. Accardi would have been proud. Problem was the Sikorsky S-70 has a cruising speed of 160mph, whereas a BMW 8 Series tops out at 150, and that's assuming it's driven on a straight and flat surface. That's why Virgo was setting himself a sequence of milestones to help achieve the goal of sanctuary. Baby steps.

The first milestone was reaching a plantation of big-cone spruce, which would give temporary relief. It was best part of a mile away, a big patch of green on the hillside. He tensed his forearms, fighting the bumps in the road, and kept the accelerator floored. Fields flashed by, and a hurricane tore at his face. In the mirror, he saw the chopper closing him down. Touch and go whether he'd make it to the plantation before he was in range. Fifty yards short of the spruce, he heard the assault rifles open up. *Shit, too late.*

There was nothing he could do except hope the shooters were regular ex-Army guys and not experienced in attack helicopter operations. Speed, angle and altitude have specific effects on the trajectory of bullets because rifles have a spiraled barrel and spin their projectiles clockwise. If firing down from a chopper to the right, aim straight but high, to compensate for the bullet's rotation, and if the target is on the left, aim left and low. There was one other thing he could do, and that was pray, but he wasn't sure God existed. Maybe, he was about to find out.

The first rounds to hit tore two lines in the roof of the car. Add a ring-pull, it could have been opened like a tin of sardines. Virgo felt the air fizz. Pieces of upholstery exploded like party poppers, but he didn't feel pain or any blood running down his limbs. He could still think, so there wasn't a hole in his brain. All good. He made the plantation and threw the car up a narrow track used by loggers. Mounds of woodchip and mulch slowed him down. The tire ruts were deep, and the sump of the BMW bottomed out on the center section. For a second, the rear wheels spun in fresh air, and it looked like he was marooned, but momentum carried the car onto dry land.

Come on. No, wait. Abort, abort. Too late. Virgo had been hoping to make the far side of the plantation before the pilot knew which direction he was heading, but progress had been slow. He could see the chopper up ahead through the branches, waiting for him to emerge. There was no way to K-turn in the ruts. He pushed the stick into reverse and shot backwards. As soon as he was in the thickest part of the trees, he stopped and killed the engine. Listened and waited. After a few seconds, the Sikorsky peeled off and made its way back to the start of the loggers' track, looking for him. Virgo fired up and gunned forward once more.

When he broke cover, the sky was clear. He rejoined the road and focused on the next milestone: a plugged and abandoned oil well, with its buildings and nodding donkey still standing. It was a couple of miles down the winding road, but he wasn't going by road. He was going route one. There was a silted-up riverbed that ran straight down the hill, and all the way down one side was a line of towers carrying high voltage wires, tall enough to keep the chopper at arm's length. He bumped the BMW across the road and set off.

The ground disappeared, as though he'd driven off the edge of the world. Then gravity kicked in, and the car plummeted nose-down into the abyss. He hit rocks and branches and stumps and more rocks. It didn't make a difference which way he yanked the wheel. The BMW plowed its own furrow, using the wall of the bends to maintain its course, like a bobsleigh on the Cresta Run. There was a massive crash as the front end of the car hit tarmac, about to rejoin the road at 90 degrees. *Oooof. Shit.* The airbag deployed. Virgo peeled his face off it and tried to push it away, but it bounced back, making driving impossible. Some irony: a safety device was going to cost him his life. It would take a couple of minutes to deflate. He bailed out of the BMW and ran for the edge of the nearest building.

It was a big, stuccoed warehouse covered in peeling white paint, high windows with smashed glass. He reached it just as a succession of bullets ripped chunks out of the cement. He dived round the corner and sprinted to the main entrance. The double doors had been clamped by iron bars and padlocks. He pulled out his gun, and when the Sikorsky appeared, he used the doorway as part cover and fired. He kept firing until the mag was empty. Early on in his Army career, he'd won a pistol-shot badge for the accuracy of his target shooting, but time must have taken its toll. Because he'd just been aiming at the pilot, but had hit one of the riflemen hanging out the side. No prizes this time.

It was enough to make the chopper back off while they assessed the injury and administered initial first aid, but he was still stranded. He didn't have a spare magazine, and none of the other buildings on the orphaned oil-well site provided any cover. If the Sikorsky came back, the situation was fucked up beyond all repair. Time stood still. The chopper maintained its position three hundred feet off the ground, one hundred yards away, across a stretch of cereal crops. He racked his brain, but there was nothing rattling around in there. The engines of the Sikorsky growled, and it banked around, heading straight back at him.

Come on, observe, orient, decide, act.

Done. The only opportunity of escape was the BMW. He put his head down and ran. It was still a suicide mission because the next stretch of road, which dropped gently into Marlberg, was unprotected by trees or high cable-carrying posts. He flung himself into the driver's seat and batted away what was left of the airbag. Pointed the hood towards the center of town, and looked in the mirror, expecting to see the skids of the helicopter homing in. Wait. Nothing. They'd gone. Then he saw why: two RVs in convoy cruising down the road — families heading home after a weekend in the hills. He slowed down so they could catch up and shield him all the way back down into Marlberg.

The town was dozing after a long, hot afternoon. Virgo parked up, and went in the Lucky Grill. He needed a drink and food. Must have been Darlene's day off, because his server was a young, surly woman called Abi, who was chewing gum. He ordered beer and a steak sandwich. If was only when he turned around that he saw a full pack of Snow Wolves taking up three booths down one wall. Looked like some of them had been sat there drinking most of the day. One of them said something and pointed to Virgo, and the others laughed.

Tommy Locke stood up and raised a hand to stop the noise. He ambled over to the counter and took the stool next to Virgo. 'Have you found them? Jacob and Dukes?'

'Not yet, but I will.'

'Or you'll die trying.' Locke closed one eye. 'I heard they found a body up on the hills, with a sniper rifle close by.'

'Heard it from your friends in the sheriff's office?'

'Remember, when you find Jacob and Dukes, you call me first.'

'I've got you on speed-dial, under A for Adolf.'

Locke's top lip curled. 'Don't make fun of folk with different values.'

'I'm tired, I'm hungry, my body is bruised and aching, thanks to your henchmen, and now a bunch of mercenaries are trying to blow me away. Excuse me if I'm not attuned to your cultural sensitivities.'

'Stop talking shit and find the fuckers who killed my son.' Locke trundled back to the boys in the booths.

A plate slid along the counter and struck his elbow. The steak sandwich. At the other end of the counter, Abi pulled a sarcastic smile. 'Enjoy.'

Virgo took a bite and watched two black sedans pull up outside the Lucky Grill. Eight doors opened, and eight men in black combat fatigues got out. Indigo Fox. The first one into the diner was Burgess, shaking his head, as though this was all somebody else's fault.

He walked up to the counter, seven acolytes crowding in behind him, and said, 'It's over, Virgo. The United States does not negotiate with terrorists. I'm afraid you're going to have to step outside and come with us.'

There was no way out this time. Virgo was unarmed and outnumbered beyond realistic hope. He stood up, shoulders drooped in submission, and took a farewell bite of steak sandwich. Then he headbutted Burgess on the bridge of his nose and launched himself into the wall of wannabe ninjas. No point going quietly.

CHAPTER 41

IT HAD BEEN a long time since the gunshots, maybe an hour. Stacy was sure that's what they were, even though the hatch deadened the sound. At first, she'd thought it might be the police come to rescue her, and they'd fired three bullets into Bigfoot to kill him, but if that had been the case, they would have found her by now. There had been voices before the gunshots, but faint and muffled. With every minute that had passed since the shooting, an ounce of hope drained from her body.

Not that she was scared. At med school they'd done some work around dealing with the close relatives of deceased patients. Specifically, the Kubler-Ross model, also known as the five stages of grief: denial, anger, bargaining, depression and acceptance. Since she'd been in the pit, she'd passed through the whole series and was now comfortably in the acceptance zone. It was just strange that she was mourning her own death, not that of a loved one. Still, it didn't stop her experiencing hope, no matter how slight, and it didn't stop her wanting to live so that she could exact revenge on the lanky bastard who'd done this to her.

Twenty was no age to die, but some kids don't make it to their teens. Others have debilitating diseases, or tragic accidents. Stacy was worried about what her death would do to her parents' marriage. She was an only child. There was an unspoken thought in the back of her mind that said they'd only ever stayed married because of her and possibly her father's career. They weren't like her friends' parents. Her mom was distant, but strong-willed, and her dad was warmer, but more high maintenance. They never argued, which she also found a little strange, but perhaps she didn't know what went on when she wasn't there. Would losing their only daughter bring them closer together or tear them apart?

Stacy cracked the top off a water bottle and took a long drink. She'd lost the feelings of shame and anger about peeing in the corner, underneath the gaze of a video camera. Funny, how it doesn't take long for humans to lose their cultural inhibitions and revert to the ways of nature. She was pulling her trousers back up when the sound of metal clanking signaled the hatch was about to open. There was more scraping of steel on steel, and once again a deluge of light poured in, followed by the sweet scents of air that smelled like countryside.

He was there. Even before she could fully remove her hands from her eyes, she knew. Just from his size and shape. The last scintilla of hope that he had been the one on the receiving end of the shots disappeared. Who had been? She was about to find out. Bigfoot bent down and lifted something heavy and unwieldy.

Stacy backed herself up to the wall of the pit. The body landed plumb on the two prostrate corpses, but slid to one side and rolled off. It was a woman. Dressed smart. She had the look of a schoolteacher or maybe even a doctor. What slice of misfortune had befallen her to end up here? Wrong place, wrong time, or was she part of the kidnap gang? No. Even with the blood-soaked blouse and scarf, and a rear section of cranium missing, she had the appearance of a professional lady. Not the sort to have anything to do with the sadistic bastard who'd just thrown her into the makeshift tomb.

'Get over here where I can see you properly,' Bigfoot barked. He vanished for a second, then came back with a phone.

'Whatever you say.' Stacy edged around the bodies, to the side of the hatch where he stood. Still playing the good girl.

'Why are you doing that?' His voice dripped with suspicion.

'Doing what?'

'Cooperating. Behaving yourself.'

'I thought that's what you wanted.'

'People aren't nice to me without a reason. What's yours?'

Stacy wanted to say that she hoped to lure him into a reverse Stockholm syndrome, and then, when he wasn't on his guard, grab a weapon and chop his head off. It was the fantasies that kept her going. But instead, she said, 'I'm just trying to stay alive.'

'Then it's your lucky day. It's nearly over, but there's been a change of plan.' Bigfoot knelt down with the camera on the phone primed. 'We need to record a new video message for daddy.'

CHAPTER 42

VIRGO KICKED out with his heels, hoping to fracture a shin bone, and thrashed his head around, trying to make contact with any unguarded face. But it was no use. Four men had him, two on each arm. Then he caught sight of the stun gun and knew what was coming. *Fuck, fuck, fuck…* fifty thousand volts, delivered in pulses over five seconds. His muscles contracted and went into spasm, and he dropped to the floor. All voluntary control of his limbs gone, and searing pain to the core of his body.

Now he was being half-dragged, half-carried across the diner floor. His face bashed into one of the vintage gas pumps, and the toes of his boots scraped across the chequerboard tiles. The ignominy of defeat. What were they going to do with him? Keep him locked away until after tomorrow's meeting, or drive up into the hills and put a bullet in the back of his head? It didn't matter. He was out of the game and only hoped that Accardi could stop Indigo Fox getting to Daniel Donovan. Or Bailey and Whitlock could find Stacy first.

The door to the street opened, and he was about to get drag-carried over the threshold, when there were shouts and swearing. He was dropped onto the floor. A chair cart-wheeled past his head and shattered the front window. A Formica tabletop frisbee'd into one of the Indigo Fox ninjas and caught him square in the mouth. Bottles and pint glasses rained down, most of them still full of beer. More chairs clattered into the shell-shocked ninjas, followed by the metal bases of stools ripped up from the floor.

Finally, when there was nothing left to throw, came the Snow Wolves themselves, led by Tommy Locke. He plowed straight into Burgess and floored him with one punch, even though the Indigo Fox man was thirty years younger. Without pausing, Locke windmilled into another one of the private contractors, and soon there was a melee of twenty men exchanging blows, grappling and using anything to hand as improvised weapons. One of the ninjas got crowned by a table lamp, and one of the older Snow Wolves got doubled over and puked his guts up on the tiles.

Behind the counter, server Abi stood and watched, a look of insouciant ennui on her face, as though mass brawls between quasi-military units and white supremacists happened every Sunday afternoon. At one point, it looked like she was going to call the cops, but then changed her mind and shuffled behind the coffee machine to dodge the flying projectiles.

Virgo felt the long muscles in his body relax, and hauled himself up onto his feet, using the door handle. The Snow Wolves had put up a decent show for a disparate group of civilian thugs, but it was clear that after the initial exertion, they were going to be no match for a group of physically fit ex-servicemen.

He was about to help even things up when Tommy Locke yelled at him, 'Go.'

Virgo hesitated.

Locke yelled again. 'Go and find them.' As soon as the

words were out of his mouth, an arm wrapped around his neck, he fell backwards onto the floor, and a boot struck the side of his head.

Virgo opened the door and ran. Jumped in the battered hire car, drove around the block, and parked up in a quiet side street. Nerves still jangling from the electricity. He took a few deep breaths to collect himself, and heard the sirens of the sheriff's cars on their way to the Lucky Grill. Someone had called them about the riot, or maybe someone who knew he was wanted for questioning about Tommy Junior's death had contacted them. Either way, he was well clear.

There was no sign of the Sikorsky, and with the rest of Indigo Fox snarled up in town, it was a good opportunity to head out and check the next property on his list. He was tapping the address in his cell when the screen lit up with an incoming call from Accardi.

'Don't get mad. I lost him.'

'What?' Virgo thought there was an undertone of humor in her voice, but it could have been anxiety. 'You are kidding, right?'

'I saw him looking at his phone, and his face changed. When I asked him what it was, he told me it was nothing. Just his wife getting upset.'

'You weren't supposed to let him out of your sight.'

'Hey, I said don't get mad.' Accardi sighed. She sounded out of breath. 'He went to restrooms in the airport. I waited outside. After ten minutes, he'd not come out, so I went in and checked all the cubicles, getting stared at by a load of men stood pissing, and then saw there was another exit.'

'How long until the flight?'

'Forty minutes. We'd checked in, but not done security.'

'He might still make it.'

'I'm on my way to the gate now, but he won't be there. I think he's deliberately shaken me off and left the airport.'

'Check the flight, and call me back.'

Virgo tried to clear his mind, which was still reverberating with the aftereffects from the stun gun. If it was Indigo Fox who had got to Daniel Donovan at LAX, why would they still be trying to get him in Marlberg? And if it wasn't Indigo Fox, the only other reason for such an abrupt change in behavior was if the message he'd received was from the kidnappers. But if Senator Donovan didn't make the plane, then he wouldn't be chairing tomorrow morning's appropriations committee meeting, and Babylon Inferno would in all likelihood receive approval. It didn't make sense.

CHAPTER 43

THE RADIO STATION had more ads than music. A baritone voice said, *sponsored by Belvedere Pet Cemetery: your number one animal funeral directors,* then a jingle, which segued into Jagger complaining he couldn't get any satisfaction. Virgo had only switched it on to see if there was anything on the LA news. He didn't know exactly what. He just had a feeling something bad was going to happen.

He called Daniel Donovan's mobile, and it tripped straight to the message box. For a moment, he didn't know what to say, then he shouted over the Rolling Stones' classic, 'Stay strong, Senator. Do what's best for your daughter, and give me a call to let me know you're all right.'

High pressure over the desert had turned up the dial on the wind machine, which now blew dirt and sand westward through the hills. Virgo was heading north, cutting across the dust balls on the way to his penultimate address, when his cell buzzed a notification. Text from Accardi:

> Plane departed for Washington. Donovan not on board.

So that was it. The senator wasn't going to make the meeting. What now?

Up ahead on the highway he saw blue lights coming towards him, and then three black-and-whites flashed past, sirens wailing, on their way to Marlberg. The altercation at the Lucky Grill must have sucked in the entire law enforcement resources of Kern County. Virgo called Accardi, then canceled it when in the mirror he saw one of the cop cars peel off and U-turn. No time to panic. He checked his speed was in the limits and carried on. Maybe the cop car had been diverted onto another call.

Or maybe not. The police car drove right up behind, with the blues and twos still blaring. The headlights flashed. Virgo could try to outrun an officer trained in pursuit-driving, who had a police radio to summon other resources, but he didn't fancy his chances. The alternative was to pull over and rely on his silver tongue to work its magic, just as it had done at Tommy Locke's transport depot, but preferably without being prefaced by a severe beating. He decided to pull over. It would be quicker to explain how he had nothing to do with Tommy Junior's death than engage in a lengthy car chase through the mountain passages of Southern California.

Virgo turned off the highway, with the police cruiser still right up his tail. He climbed out and cursed when he saw the officer coming towards him was Sergeant Wozniak. Some people you meet for the very first time and strike up an unspoken bond of kinship, whereas others you encounter on life's rocky journey and immediately despise for no reason. The sergeant was in the *others* category.

Wozniak already had his gun clasped in both hands. 'I don't think your detective friend with the cute ass will get you out of jail this time.'

'Say that to her face, and she'll knock you out.'

'Way-hay.' Wozniak grinned. 'You two got something going on?'

Virgo gritted his teeth. 'Stop messing me around. The guys you want to interview about Tommy Junior's death are called Jacob and Dukes. You might also want to speak to them about the murder of Jerome Thomas.'

'Is that so?'

'Ask Tommy Senior. He seems to have very close connections within your office.'

'What's that supposed to mean? Are you alleging impropriety?'

'Come on, I'm not accusing anybody.' Virgo could feel the frustration making his teeth itch. 'Just ask me what you want about my run-in with Tommy Junior, and let me get on my way.'

Wozniak grinned again. 'What makes you think this is about the death of that retard TJ?'

Virgo said nothing. There was a hollow feeling in his stomach.

'Edward McKinley Virgo, I am arresting you on behalf of the federal government for breaching the conditions of your release from prison.'

'What?' Virgo was stunned. 'There must be a mistake.'

'Notice came direct from the FBI this afternoon, together with the DOJ paperwork.'

'Wait a minute. *Hartman*. The contact at the FBI, was it someone called *Hartman*?'

'Could have been Homer Simpson; doesn't matter who it was. Turn round and get your hands on the hood.'

Virgo didn't move. 'This man Hartman is doing all he can to stop me locating a girl who has been kidnapped and whose life is in imminent danger.'

'Sure, I believe you. He's a senior FBI agent?' Wozniak curled an incredulous sneer.

'Acting head of the Crisis Negotiation Unit.'

'Wow, even better. And why would a bureau manager not want to rescue an innocent girl?'

'I don't know.' Virgo shrugged. 'Somebody must be paying him.'

'There you go again, throwing around accusations of corruption.' Wozniak jabbed the barrel of his gun. 'Hands on the hood.'

Virgo was in the last chance saloon, drinking a final Scotch while the barman cleared tables. 'Look, the girl who's been abducted is the daughter of a well-known senator, who I'm acting for. I'm sure you don't want to be known for the rest of your career as the guy who got the senator's daughter killed.'

A speck of uncertainty flickered in Wozniak's eyes. 'This senator. Can he vouch for you?'

'He's gone missing.' The words were out of Virgo's mouth before his brain had time to realize how crass and contrived it sounded.

Wozniak laughed, then went full attack dog. 'Turn round, asshole. Hands on the hood. NOW.'

Virgo's shoulders slumped. This time the game was well and truly up. He reluctantly shuffled around, and placed his palms on the paintwork of the BMW, which was hot enough to fry an egg.

Wozniak growled, 'Feet wider apart.'

Virgo complied.

'Wider.' Wozniak getting off on the authority.

'Don't worry. I'm not going to cause any trouble.'

Virgo's gun was under the driver's seat, but he got patted down anyway. Standard procedure. No cop wants to share a patrol car with a prisoner who has a concealed Derringer. He peeked under his armpit and saw Wozniak holding his Glock 17 in his right hand. He waited until he felt the officer frisk his leg down to the ankle, then snapped his forearm backwards and sent the pistol rocketing into the underbrush that lined the highway.

Wozniak was quick. He pulled Virgo's legs away from under him and racked open his expandable baton. Police training is clear: an ASP should only be used to strike the primary nerve clusters in the thigh, or major muscle groups like the biceps, with a view to causing transitory neuropraxia. The sergeant had either forgotten or decided the only way to subdue Virgo was to kill him. Either way, he went straight for the skull strike.

Virgo rolled, and the baton smashed into the dirt-covered bedrock, hard enough to cause an avalanche in the Sierra. An inch from his head. He knew a follow-up wouldn't be long. He saw Wozniak raise his hand, then used his arms and back muscles to drive the sole of his foot upwards and into the underside of the officer's chin. Contact was clean. It gave him time to regain his feet.

The sergeant staggered backwards, and when he blinked, there was blood leaking from the side of his mouth, like he'd bitten his tongue or lip. 'I'm going to make you regret that.'

Virgo smiled. Wozniak was talking. Fighting is an activity that requires total focus and application, to the exclusion of all other peripheral thought. Only the Greatest could talk and fight at the same time, and Wozniak was no Muhammad Ali. He waited for the sergeant to come onto him again with the ASP. Three, two, one, here it comes.

Wozniak had the baton raised high above his head, in anticipation of a strike so widely telegraphed that most of SoCal saw it coming. Virgo fired out a straight left and felt his knuckles nestle into nose gristle, then followed up with a precocked right, twisting his body and sending it out on a wider trajectory so it delivered maximum power. The haymaker hit Wozniak on the side of the jawbone. He rocked and dropped to his knees.

Virgo grabbed the baton and was about to finish it, but there was no need. The sergeant's eyelids went half-mast, and he fell unconscious face-first into the dust freshly arrived from the Mohave Desert. Virgo walked over to the black-and-white and used the ASP to smash the police radio. He threw Wozniak's personal radio and cell into a drainage ditch, then dragged his deadweight over to the driver's door and attached him one-handed to the steering wheel with his own cuffs.

Under any other circumstances, Virgo would have apologized to a law-enforcement officer for being forced to assault them, even if they were out cold, but on this occasion, he didn't feel like it. He respected the uniform, but not this man's attitude. No wonder cops get a bad name if the only ones the public encounter are the Wozniaks of this world. Maybe the FBI were no better, or he was just getting old.

He'd missed a call from Accardi during his tussle with Kern County's finest. He pulled back onto the highway and called her back. 'Any news on Donovan?'

'He's still in LA.' Accardi was driving. She had to shout over the noise. 'I got a friend in Major Crimes. He requested a trace on the senator's cell phone.'

'Location?'

'After he left the airport, he headed north through Playa Vista, then east to Culver City.'

'Last known position?'

'Hey, watch where you're fucking going, dickhead.'

'Sorry?'

'Not you.' Accardi switched from angry-driver voice to the professional. 'After Culver City, he about-faced and turned back west into Rancho Park, and for the last twenty minutes, he's been pinging off a cell tower on Mississippi Avenue.'

Virgo had no idea what the senator's movements meant,

but knew it must be linked to the phone message he'd received. He didn't know LA too well. 'What is there in the neighborhood?'

Accardi laughed. 'It's Los Angeles. We have the entire world in every neighborhood. If you live here, you don't need to go traveling to see life.'

'Something significant? Government offices, arms suppliers, financial institutions? I don't know.'

'It's just a regular mix of business and residential. I'm on my way there now.'

Virgo smiled. 'Don't tell me. You've got another friend with an IMSI-catcher?'

'He's called Donny, from Gangs and Narcotics. Going to meet me there with the Stingray. We should be able to isolate Donovan's cell signal and get a precise location.'

'Thanks for going the extra mile.'

'Yeah, well, I feel bad.' Accardi coughed. 'How was I supposed to know some men's restrooms have two fucking exits. I've never seen so many dicks.' She ended the call.

Virgo hadn't traveled half a mile before the screen of his cell lit up. Whitlock. He swiped up. 'Everything okay?'

'I can't get hold of Bailey.' His voice was high pitched. Panicky. 'I've been trying her for half an hour. Left messages. Nothing…'

'Maybe she's somewhere with poor cell reception.'

'I called the office to get a trace.' Whitlock's voice shifted up another octave. 'Her phone's switched off.'

'What was the last property she visited?'

'I need to check the master list.'

'Then fucking do it.' Virgo couldn't stop the rage detonating in his chest. They might just have found where Stacy was being held, but they'd lost an agent. Someone once said in the heat of war, *success is not final, failure is not fatal: it's the courage to continue that counts.* This wasn't over.

CHAPTER 44

THE KNIFE WAS twenty-six inches long and called a hirschfanger. German for deer catcher. A symmetrical blade, with buck-horn handle and silver pommel. Jacob had spent a lot of time choosing it, because most hunting knives aren't designed to kill. They're to skin, slice and gut, not deliver the coup de grâce. He wanted one that from the get-go had only ever been intended for one purpose: to kill an animal. It wasn't cheap. With international shipping, it was over a thousand dollars. So what? He had the money.

He spat on the blade and polished it with a rag. Not long before he could use it. It also wouldn't be long before the FIB woman was missed by her colleagues, and they would come looking for her, but the Helper said not to worry, the operation had been brought forward and a contingency plan put in place. The end was imminent. A man called Virgo was the only danger, and he was about to be taken out of the game. Once and for all.

Jacob sat on the porch and scanned the horizon. Nothing moved apart from the hot air blowing orange dust towards the Pacific, over where the sun shone the last of its rays. His instructions were clear from this juncture onward: if anyone approaches the farm, kill the Donovan girl because her father was doing exactly as he'd been told. That suited him. There was still a smear on the stainless steel of the hirschfanger, so Jacob spat on it again and rubbed. It needed to be pristine for the money he'd spent, and the job he was going to perform as its initiation in blood sacrifice.

Everything was under control again. The FBI woman's car was in the back barn, next to his own. A tight squeeze. He'd had to shuffle his pickup sideways, and it had taken time, during which he'd felt anxious and vulnerable. Not in control. The agent's phone was locked with a PIN, so there was no means of knowing whom she'd been in contact with recently, or any way of reading messages that might be relevant. The only thing he could do was turn it off. The episode had made him feel hot and short of breath, and the sound of the birds singing in the fields was too loud to bear. But now, all good.

He tapped the spacebar to get rid of the screen saver, and his MacBook lit up with the view of the pit. Getting pretty crowded down there. The Donovan girl had taken to walking round in circles again, a sign that she'd stopped trying to kill herself. Not that it mattered anymore. The pleasure would soon be his. He checked his cell, but the message from the Helper had not come through, even though he expected to have received it by now. No need to get jumpy. It was still all under control.

When he searched the agent's bag, he found a book where she'd been making notes and writing up draft reports on the case. This had also made him tense and feel like he was overheating. She'd made critical comments about the Helper and how he wanted her to leave Marlberg, and go to Los Angeles. Shame she didn't listen to her superior instead of thinking she knew better and choosing to carry on her foolish searches across the county. She thought this man Virgo was a greater leader than the Helper, and it was those poor decision-making skills got her killed.

There was the sound of an engine, and Jacob grabbed his gun, ducked level with the balustrade of the porch, and scanned the horizon. *Okay, and relax.* A light aircraft, over the next valley, probably headed for Bakersfield or one of the private strips in the area. Too far away to be doing surveillance on the farm before sending in a SWAT team, and in any case, the Helper promised there would be no SWAT team, and his word was good.

The day Jacob killed the pig who claimed to be his biological father had been the day he met the Helper. Kismet, naturally. The first person to understand the sickness and to show him respect and kindness without wanting anything in return. Throughout the years in hospital, he'd kept in touch, first as a visitor, then working pro bono as a counselor. It was only through the Helper's work, and recommendations to the board, that Jacob had been released. Everything he had now — his freedom, his inheritance, and the opportunity to slake the awful thirst that his sickness inflicted — he owed it all to the Helper.

Jacob sat back down on the porch and laughed as the thought of that day twenty years ago came crashing back in a memory tsunami. He didn't laugh at all the events of the day, because the bits where he killed his pet dog and his father, or took his mother hostage, weren't funny in a humorous way. What made him laugh was the memory of when a man in an FBI baseball cap hopped over the fence into the back garden and shouted to him through a megaphone, *Hi, Jacob. My name's Nick, and I'm here to help ya.* Jacob had been distressed and confused, and all he'd heard was, *Hi, my name's Helper.* It had stuck ever since, a little joke between the two of them.

That fateful day, the Helper had stayed there in the garden

for eight hours, just talking to him and, more important, listening. Not putting any pressure on him, with threats or deadlines, and not making false promises, swearing that everything was going to be okay. It was the first time an adult had communicated with him as an equal. Everything he said was full of wisdom, perception, and insights regarding the issues in Jacob's life. It was inspirational. This man was the teacher and father he'd never had, and Jacob wanted to be in his presence and please him, to repay his faith.

A rogue ray of sunlight glinted on the blade of the deer-catcher. Jacob picked it up and began to rub it again with the cloth while he waited for the phone to buzz. Anytime now.

CHAPTER 45

THE HIGHWAY WAS LITTLE MORE than a track of compacted red cinder and rocks, zigzagging steadily up through the pine and oak: a service road that ascended to an aerial mast on the brow of a peak that didn't seem to get any closer the more you drove. Virgo gunned it, one hand on the wheel, the other on the phone clamped to his right ear. He wasn't sure Hartman would answer, but then of course he did. Cocky bastard.

'What the fuck?' It was the best Virgo could come up with. Outstanding wordplay from a man who once upon a time relied on language skills for a living.

'Hand yourself in, Eddie. It's over.' Hartman was calm. The avuncular voice of reason.

'You set me up, shitbird,' said Virgo. Anger made eloquence difficult. 'You never wanted me to save that girl's life.'

'I told you to stay in LA. You deliberately flaunted my directive, and therefore I had no option but report you as being in breach of your conditional release from jail.'

'I hope they're paying you well.'

'There is no *they*, Eddie. You're suffering from paranoia and psychosis caused by the grief at losing Crystal. I understand your—'

'Stop.' Virgo slammed the wheel with his one free hand and almost careened down a concrete storm drain. 'Keep my wife out of this. Do you know you got Bailey killed?'

'If she's dead, I'm afraid the responsibility lies with you.'

'Don't fucking gaslight me, Nick.'

'Why would I try to make out you're crazy when you already proved it down in Mexico.'

Ooof. Another blow below the belt. Virgo felt tired to the core. Disillusionment and betrayal the thieves of energy and spirit. 'What happened? I thought we were supposed to be the good guys?'

'Hope you like tortillas and beans, Eddie.'

'I used to look up to you.'

'That's because I'm good at my job. I can separate dealing with other people's shit without getting personally involved, unlike you, who's got the super-fucking-hero complex.'

A grain of truth? Maybe, but Virgo knew Hartman was obfuscating. Attack is the best means of defense. 'Okay, let's agree a deal. I'll go back and spend the rest of my sentence south of the border if the girl gets released. Or just tell me where she is.'

Hartman laughed. 'You're in no position to negotiate. You are going back to greaser jail, period.'

'Okay, try this one? Let the girl go, and I won't kill you.'

'What makes you think I've got her fate in my hands? You need help, Eddie.'

'Start running. I'm coming for you.' Virgo ended the call.

The track ran out on the summit, where a stubby aerial mast and satellite dish were hunkered down behind a high steel fence. Whitlock was waiting for him on the patch of concrete, which served as a parking lot and turning circle for the work trucks that serviced the telecommunications equipment. He was leaning on the driver's door of a standard-issue FBI Dodge.

Virgo pulled up alongside, grabbed the map from under the sun visor, and jumped out. He noticed Whitlock's face was drained of blood, and his hands were shaking as he messaged on his phone. 'No news?'

'She's still not replying.' Whitlock's voice quivered, and he looked like he might burst into tears. He scrambled the phone into his pocket. 'It's more than fifty minutes now.'

'Stay calm. It's okay to be scared.' Virgo unfolded the map on the hood of the hire car and placed the master list of addresses on it. 'Give me the names of the properties allocated to you, and I can work out which ones were Bailey's. We should be able to estimate which place she was checking about an hour ago.'

Silence.

'Come on, snap out of it.' Virgo spread his arms out across the hood to stop the wind taking the map down into the valley, and squinted as he tried to find their current location. 'Make it quick. The sooner we get there, the greater our chances.'

'Put your hands on your head, slowly.' Whitlock's voice cracked and squeaked. 'I'm sorry, Eddie.'

'What the?' Virgo turned round. There was a Glock 19 pointing at his chest.

'Hey, no sudden movements.' Whitlock coughed. It was like he had a golf ball caught in his throat. 'I said put your hands on your head, slowly.'

Virgo kept his hands by his sides. 'What the fuck do you think you're doing?'

'I've been ordered to detain you here until the sheriff's department arrives.'

'This is Hartman, isn't it?'

'You breached the conditions of your jail release. He had no choice.'

Virgo still hadn't raised his hands. The young agent should have made him do it by now or shot him, but it was easier to talk: displacement activity. 'Of course he had a choice. It was his decision, and the only reason he made it was to stop me finding Stacy Donovan.'

Whitlock coughed again. The golf ball was back. 'Why would he do that?'

'Don't you think something smells? The undercover op gets compromised, and then when a senator's daughter gets kidnapped, he doesn't put his best go-to negotiator on it, he gets me out of solitary confinement.'

Whitlock looked confused. 'Are you saying you weren't one of the bureau's top negotiators?'

'I shot a kid in the head. What do you think? That they gave me the annual award for best crisis resolution?'

'Then, why you?'

'Because I was out of the loop. I didn't know about the undercover operation, and Hartman thought he could control me.'

There was a speck of doubt in Whitlock's eye, but he shook his head, and it vanished. 'No. I can't believe Mr. Hartman would deliberately do something like that.'

'He must have called the Department of Justice by mistake.' Virgo realized he'd been wrong about Whitlock's readiness to talk. It wasn't displacement activity — he was playing for time until the cavalry arrived. 'Put the gun back in its pouch, or I'm going to take it off you and whack you over the head with it.'

Whitlock tensed. 'Stay back, or I'll shoot.'

'No, you won't.'

'I'm not afraid to shoot.'

'Everyone's a virgin until the first time, but you're not

popping your cherry today.' Virgo held his hand out for the gun.

Whitlock's knuckles went white, and his finger tightened on the trigger. 'Why are you so sure?'

'Because deep down, you think I might be right about Hartman.'

'We should let the Office of Professional Responsibility investigate his conduct.'

'Come on, give me the damned gun.' Virgo stepped closer. 'There's no time.'

'Back off.' Whitlock stood his ground. 'I'll shoot.' The barrel of the Glock was flitting all over.

Virgo took another step.

Whitlock scrunched his eyes tight shut and squeezed on the trigger.

A loud bang rang out across the tops of the pine trees and down into the dale beyond, like the sound of a sledge-hammer hitting sheet metal. Virgo already had hold of the gun, and the 9mm slug went a mile up into the hazy, blue SoCal sky. He twisted it out of Whitlock's grip and brought the butt's heel down onto the top of the agent's head.

'Aw, shit. Why did you do that?' Whitlock clasped the top of his crown. Blood seeped through his fingers.

'Give me your phone.'

'No.'

Virgo spun Whitlock around, spreadeagled him across the trunk of the Dodge, and fished the phone out of his pants' pocket. 'What's the security code?'

'Get lost.' Whitlock's face was pressed into the paintwork of the car. He could only speak out of one corner of his mouth. 'I'm not saying.'

This was not the time to deploy reasoned argument. Virgo spun him round again and hit him in the stomach with a punch that didn't leave much in the locker. The persuader.

Then he waited until Whitlock could speak. It took a while, but the numbers to the passcode came out one at a time, punctuated by loud rasps and sucks.

Virgo keyed them in, and when the cell screen lit up, he checked the messages and saw the last one was to Hartman:

> He's just driving up the track now. I'll keep him here until the cops arrive.

There was more chat. Virgo scrolled and saw one that made him stop:

> When he's in custody, meet me at the house.

Whitlock was doubled over, looked like he might puke. Blood ran down his forehead and dripped off his eyebrows onto his smart, leather loafers.

Virgo yanked on an ear to straighten him up, and thrust the phone in his face. 'What house?'

Whitlock's mouth opened and closed, but no sound came out.

Virgo reloaded his fist and cranked it back.

'Wait.' Behold, a miracle — Whitlock could speak again. 'It's a place outside San Bernardino. Jerome Thomas used it as a safe house to write up his intel reports and take time out from the Snow Wolves. The bureau have it on a twelve-month rental through one of their ghost companies.'

'Hartman's in Virginia.'

'No, he never left Los Angeles.'

'Son of a bitch.' Virgo let go of Whitlock's ear and massaged his own temples. The extent of the duplicity was greater than he'd thought, and it made his brain pound inside his head. 'What's the address in San Bernardino?'

'I don't know. I mean I can't remember.' Whitlock flinched

in anticipation of another blow. 'It's in the messages somewhere.'

'You've been there already?'

'Just once to update Mr. Hartman on the investigation.'

'Why you? Why not Bailey? She's more senior.'

'I don't know.' Whitlock used the sleeve of his jacket to wipe away a trail of blood that ran down his cheek. 'Mr. Hartman said he'd make sure I graduated my probationary period and get signed off to become a special agent. It's all I've ever wanted.'

'Do you still want to work out in the field, or do you think you're better suited to being an intelligence analyst?'

'I'm not sure.'

Virgo scrolled the messages until he found an Inland Empire address. He was about to close it down when a red light started blinking on his something's-not-right-radar. 'Hey, this phone number isn't Hartman's.'

'It's a personal number.' Whitlock shrugged: no big deal. 'He didn't want to use his work phone in case it had been compromised by whoever in the office had blown Jerome Thomas's cover. He said he needed to make sure all communication was secure and sanitized.'

'More like secret and off the books.'

A crease appeared between Whitlock's eyebrows. Doubt and confusion. He still wasn't convinced. 'Mr Hartman is temporary head of Unit, why would he take part in anything dishonest or illegal?'

'Why did Judas Iscariot betray the son of God, or Michael Jordan endorse burgers? What made Robert De Niro go from *Raging Bull* and *Taxi Driver* to all those shit movies?'

The crease between Whitlock's brows turned into a ravine.

Virgo folded the map back up and grabbed the two lists of addresses. He needed to work out the last property Bailey had visited, but he'd have to do it somewhere else because any minute Kern County's finest would be blue-and-two-ing it up the hill. Of course, the alternative was to drive down to San Bernardino and pummel Hartman nonstop in the face until he revealed the address where Stacy Donovan was being held. Tempting, but he didn't have time. He saw the keys were in the bureau Dodge and decided it was a better ride than the beat-up BMW.

He was in the driver's seat, stick knocked into reverse, when Whitlock's bloodied face loomed at the window. 'I want to come with you.'

'So you can rat me out to the cops?'

'I want to find Bailey and the girl.'

Virgo vacillated. 'Why should I trust you?'

'Come on.' Whitlock's eyes pleaded. 'I want to prove I can be an agent.'

Virgo sighed. There was something about idealistic naivety he couldn't resist, plus his instinct told him the kid was being truthful. He just hoped the old sixth sense was right. 'Okay, jump in.'

CHAPTER 46

VIRGO TOOK a route that skirted the western edge of Marlberg, hugging a barren valley side, strewn with boulders. They were on their way to Rosstal farm, an eighty-acre property that lay on a plateau near the county border. Accessible by a badly maintained dirt track. One way in, one way out. If his calculations were correct, this was the last place Bailey checked before all contact was lost. Up ahead, an ill-boding buzzard hung in the sky on a Mohave breeze, and Virgo looked around the Dodge interior for some wood to rap his knuckles on, but it was all PVC. Good job he was only partially superstitious.

In the passenger seat, Whitlock sat talking to himself under his breath, trying to screw his courage to the sticking place. The bleeding had stopped, leaving his hair in thick, congealed strands, and the tremors in his hands had all but disappeared. An aura of determination had settled on him, but he still looked more like a pumped, trainee accountant at a bank than someone in their probationary period to be a special agent. The curse of a fresh face.

Two more buzzards appeared from nowhere and floated

effortlessly above the granite outcrop. Another tingle crawled up Virgo's spine. It was the same one he'd had when the Special Ops Vehicle left Hamdan military airport on the way to Abu Kabul, although this time there was no tangible or logical reason for it. Pure instinct. Back in Syria, the after-action review concluded that the operation should have been aborted, but today that was not an option. Whatever waited for him at the end of the track was his fate. Good or bad. Not that he overly cared, because the times when a real and imminent prospect of death caused him concern were long gone.

They'd disappeared the day Crystal took her last breath on a Washington sidewalk. It seemed long ago, but still felt raw. Half of himself also died that day, and the remaining fifty percent he'd kept functioning out of respect and love for his wife; she would have wanted him to carry on and enjoy life, but it was the hardest challenge he'd ever faced. The world had lost its meaning and attraction.

The numbness in his soul meant he cared nothing about what destiny had in store, as long as it wasn't another seven years in a Mexican jail. One way or another, he wasn't going back. Like Thelma and Louise, he'd rather crash and burn in the Grand Canyon than subjugate himself to the authorities. What he'd done in Guerrero state was against the law, but not morally wrong. In war, there are always casualties, and nobody argues that some wars are not justified.

The track leveled out, and Virgo saw the farm in the distance. He slowed down so the tires didn't kick up so much sand and dust, and a mile out, he turned off the engine and coasted to a stop. The old crop fields were overgrown, but if he could get glimpses of the buildings through the vegetation, then anyone on the lookout could also see them.

Before he got out of the car, his phone burred, and the screen said *Detective Accardi*. It seemed a little formal now, but he'd added her to his contacts not long after his arrest at La

Souris nightclub. That was a two-day eternity ago. He swiped up. 'You found the senator?'

'I think so. Me and Donny have got the Stingray machine outside a building in the middle of west LA.' There was a lot of traffic noise. Accardi was shouting. 'It's indicating Donovan's cell is inside.'

'What are you waiting for? It's not too late for a private charter to get him into Washington in time for the committee meeting.'

'Yeah? Why don't you come down and drag him out?'

'Because I'm trying to find his daughter, and Agent Bailey.'

'Bailey's missing?'

'No contact for an hour.'

'Shit.' Accardi went quiet. Then, 'Hey, you don't suppose it's anything to do with that little prick Whitlock?'

'No, the little prick's sat next to me. We're going to find her together.'

Accardi hollow-laughed. 'Yeah, well, at the moment I've still got a chance of keeping my job, but if I set foot in these premises and haul Donovan's ass outside, then I can kiss goodbye to my LAPD service pension.'

'What is it, a church?'

'Not exactly.'

'Chapel, mosque, synagogue…?'

'Fox News.'

'What?'

'Fox News – it's a cable TV channel.'

'I know what it is. I mean, what the hell is he doing in there?'

'These Stingrays are great at grabbing cell-phone signals, but they're like crap when it comes to seeing through solid walls.'

'Try walking in through the front doors.'

'And asking at reception?'

'Why not?'

'Because the plastic blonde on the desk won't know, and the ex-cops working security are too smart to let us get past the first control point.'

'Go straight to the top.'

'Rupert fucking Murdoch?'

'Ask to speak to the duty manager or one of the producers.'

Accardi thought about it. 'Okay, but I'm not forcing my way in at gunpoint. If they refuse to cooperate, I'm walking away.'

'It's worth a try. He can still make the committee in Washington.'

'Yeah, if you've got a spare Lear Jet.'

'Cross one bridge at a time.'

'Platitudes don't help. Neither does the patronizing attitude, so thank you, but don't say anything else.' Accardi hung up.

Ouch. Virgo felt the burn of her tongue-lashing. He set off walking at speed, bent forward at the hip to keep his head and shoulders beneath the line of the vegetation, and with Whitlock's gun tucked in the back of his waistband. The wannabe agent ducked along in his wake. Virgo tried to remain focused on maintaining a concealed approach, but the revelation about Daniel Donovan's whereabouts kept intruding. Why would he go to a TV studio? Did he feel safe there, or have a friend he trusted who worked in the building? Maybe it was political maneuver: some kind of deal to save his career when the revelations came out about his unhealthy relationship with Indigo Fox and the illicit affair with his ex-secretary.

No, Virgo didn't think so. He was sure Donovan could be as cynical as the next politico up for re-election, but he'd seen the pain in this man's soul wrought by his daughter's abduction. Whatever he was doing in the Fox News building, he was doing it out of desperation to try and save Stacy's life. The problem was, desperation stops people thinking straight, and makes them do stupid things.

After a while, they reached a tumbledown brick structure in one of the fields that fronted the track, probably an old animal shelter or machinery store. Virgo hopped inside and used a gap in the broken glass to take a view of the target premises: it was a big, wooden ranch-style farmhouse, a hundred yards off the track down a private driveway. A cluster of outbuildings beyond it, and an antiquated windmill that had once been used to grind grain or pump water.

There was no sign of life, but he knew — this was the place. It was the perfect spot. No neighbors or passing traffic, and no way of approaching it in a vehicle without being seen. Is that what Bailey had done? Driven up to the main house and given some story about being a lost tourist or searching for a distant relative. She would have had something prepared because she was professional, and Virgo had underestimated her at first. Hartman had done the same when he chose to send her out to LA.

Virgo made a quick assessment of the best line of approach. It was something he needed to do on his own, without putting anyone else's life at risk. He gave Whitlock his gun back and told him to make his way to the end of the driveway and wait there. If anyone left in a hurry, shoot them, and if he didn't come back in ten minutes, call the SWAT team. Whitlock looked disappointed, but he took the gun and nodded.

Time to roll. Virgo's plan was to circle the property and approach from the rear. But he didn't have long, so instead of making a wide arc around the edges of the fields, he was going to have to bolt almost straight across, keeping low and using what natural cover he could find. Two strides after leaving the tumbledown shelter, his phone buzzed. Ignore or answer? He saw it was Accardi again and beat a quick retreat back inside the building.

It took a sweaty finger three attempts to answer. 'Have you got Donovan?'

'I'm watching him right now.' Accardi sounded unnaturally calm. Resigned.

'Get him.'

'On a big TV screen in the reception area of Fox News. He's gone public.'

'Shit.'

'Big time. He's doing an interview right now with the anchor on *Sunday Night Live*.'

'About his daughter?'

'Babylon Inferno. Hang up and take a look yourself; they're streaming it online.'

Virgo ended the call and opened up the TV app. The Fox News live stream was slow to respond, but then it filled the screen. In a blue, neon studio on a round, slightly raised podium, two men sat across from each other in comfortable, cream, leather chairs. Daniel Donovan and a clean-cut, teak-tanned news anchor called Jeff, who kept smiling at the camera. Maybe Jeff was proud of his dazzling teeth, but more likely he couldn't believe his luck at what had just landed in his lap.

At the bottom of the screen, the ticker read:

Senator blows whistle on government plans to hand over defense of our country to artificial intelligence and foreign powers.

Virgo unmuted the sound on his phone, and Donovan said, 'It's morally and ethically wrong to abrogate our responsibility in times of conflict and let unaccountable, self-taught computer programs decide whether to kill human beings and which ones to choose.'

Anchor Jeff said, 'And you say these machines will be piloting drones?'

'Not what you'd think of as a drone. Fifth- or sixth-generation UAVs: unmanned aerial vehicles. Thousands of flying bombs, with their own software brains.'

Jeff stopped smiling a second and pulled a stern face. 'It's a frightening thought. We all know computers can have bugs.'

'Or get hacked.' Donovan nodded. His face was stiff from all the makeup. 'Which is another reason why we shouldn't be getting into bed with other countries.'

'You don't trust Israel or Great Britain?' The ultra-white smile was back.

'No, I don't.'

'Care to expand on that, Senator?'

'I've seen confidential briefings from government agencies that leads me to that conclusion, but for reasons of national security, I can't go into detail.'

Virgo shook his head. *Wow.* The chair of the appropriations committee was doing his best to twist the dagger and kill Babylon Inferno before it got off the ground. Any second now, he'd swear the Jews organized the 9/11 attacks, and the Brits were after recolonizing the eastern states. The senator couldn't possibly disclose what he'd seen in a confidential briefing paper, but had no qualms about divulging a secret military arms program on live television. Brilliant. Only a politician could pull it off.

Corrugated lines appeared in Jeff's tanned forehead. 'You told our researchers that evil forces have been attempting to prevent you from telling your story – that your life has been threatened, and you had to escape your hotel in downtown

Los Angeles by hiding in a laundry basket and donning a chef's apron to exit a rear door in the kitchens.'

Virgo smiled. *Laundry basket? Chef's apron?* He could have sworn he and Accardi had bundled the senator into the elevator, but hey, if you're going to do a hatchet job, do it properly. Donovan was giving the media what they wanted: the quirky details that turned a potentially dry tale of politics, budgets and technical information into an intriguing drama of human risk and adventure. They'd taken the bait, and he was playing them.

Daniel Donovan cleared his throat and looked down the camera lens. There was a sorrowful, but earnest gravity in his face, like he was preparing for the day when he was the President of the United States and had to tell the nation he'd just pressed the nuclear button. 'US annual defense spending is $900 billion, and I'm afraid where you get that kind of money, there will always be bad actors. The people behind this project stand to lose fortunes if it if doesn't go ahead, and I guess I was seen as the biggest obstacle in their way.'

Even Jeff looked surprised. 'Excuse me, Senator, are you alleging that one or more of the companies involved in developing this technology threatened to kill you?'

'I can't hand on heart swear who it was.' Donovan oozed sincerity. 'I was kept imprisoned in my hotel room by these ex-military types and told I must approve the AI program at tomorrow's senate committee.'

'Or else?'

'Me and my brother, Duncan, would pay the price. I took that to mean the ultimate price.'

'And just to recap for viewers who may have just joined us, Senator Donovan, you are the chair of the Senate Appropriations Subcommittee on Defense?'

'I am.'

'And tomorrow, the subcommittee will be asked to

approve the development of a new weapon, which you believe is not only immoral and un-American, but actually poses a danger to our great country?'

Daniel Donovan's tight curls nodded. He shrugged, as though he had no choice in the matter. 'I thought people should know. All it takes for evil to blossom is for good men to say nothing.'

Jeff stacked his papers and tamped them on his knee. 'We'll be right back after this message from our sponsors.'

Virgo switched off the app. Daniel Donovan had given a good performance. He'd stopped or at least disrupted Babylon Inferno as good as if he'd chaired tomorrow's meeting and used his veto to deny funding. In fact, no, not *as good as*, but better. He'd thrown the issue out into the open and, with a mixture of half-truth and innuendo, colored the debate for the foreseeable future. A lot of people would now assume it was an inherently wicked program, and that there were active conspiracies to implement it against the wishes of the American people.

The senator had done precisely what the kidnappers wanted, without having to go through the process of chairing a subcommittee meeting. The problem was, he'd just taken away the only reason for his daughter to be kept alive.

CHAPTER 47

MINUTES DRAGGED, like the interminable embrace of a dentist's chair. Sun half-sank beneath western hills, and the shadows stretched over the icehouse and barns, creeping up to the timber wall of the farmhouse. Jacob sat on the porch with his index finger in a polishing cloth and made hundreds of tiny circles on the blade of the deer-catcher. His eyes darted across the fields and along the perimeter, looking for the slightest movement, and he ground the molars in the left side of his mouth. How much longer?

Twenty years in the Euphemism – a prison pretending to be a hospital – had taught him patience, and he closed his eyes for a moment. Relaxed and forced himself to stop grinding his teeth. He'd read about the Stanford marshmallow experiment on delayed gratification, where if kids could resist a sweet treat for fifteen minutes, they were given double portions. Of course, some couldn't resist and just stuffed the first marshmallow in their greedy mouths straight away, but they were the dumb, dim-witted ones. Not like Jacob. He could wait, and it would make the reward greater. He'd studied a lot during his time in the Euphemism, and it had helped him conceal the thing that made him different from other people: the sickness.

It was a strange beast. The counseling sessions, which forced him to reflect on what he'd done, had made him realize he could kill his pet dog, which he loved, and his father, whom he hated, and experience the same absence of lasting emotion. A brief but ecstatic rush of euphoria, followed by an even shorter twinge of regret and then absolutely nothing. It was like when he paid for sex. The thrill, the shame, the emptiness.

Something moved on the track. Jacob grabbed the binoculars and stood up. A reflection of light on a moving surface, where the sun still reached beyond the edge of the fields. He closed his left eye and turned the focus wheel until the image on the boundary was sharp, then closed his right and adjusted the other diopter. There was a dilapidated shack, overgrown with knapweed and broom. He kept watching, but nothing budged. He checked both sides up and down the track. All quiet. Maybe it had been a bird skimming the tops of the rye grass.

The phone purred and shimmied on the table. Jacob froze for a second, then snatched it up. Message from the Helper. He grinned and nodded his head. It was the delayed gratification he'd been waiting for.

> It's done. Clean up and get out.

Jacob grabbed the deer-catcher and set off for the icehouse. A ripple of excitement wrapped itself around his bowels and danced up into his stomach. It was a familiar feeling. The sickness coming on. He couldn't help himself. The only cure was to surrender to its obscenity and let it run its cathartic course. He would be purged and restored, as before. If the place where they'd locked him away was really a hospital, they would have made him properly better, wouldn't they? Instead, they'd just given him injections to make their jobs easier.

The door to the icehouse was locked. He opened it with a key chained to a loop on his jeans and stepped inside. *Clean up and get out.* Jacob laughed at the coded language. Oh, yes, he was going to clean up, but it was going to be a messy business, and that was why he had made preparations. He put the deer-catcher down and unhooked the grocery bag that hung from a rusted nail in the back of the door. It contained his XXL disposable, white coveralls. He pulled them on and felt his hand tremor a little as he coaxed up the zipper.

A sharp perfume of disinfectant mixed with dried blood and old coffee grounds grubbed away at the back of his throat, and he realized he was on sensory overdrive. Smell, touch, taste all cranked up to maximum because of the torrent of chemicals his brain was blasting out. He steadied himself and took a deep breath. No point rushing the best part. The massive high of anticipation is something to be savored, not cast aside in a chase for the finish line. Once the deed is done, there's no going back, only in the vicarious medium of memory, which is never the same. He breathed in and out, slow, twice more, and closed his eyes. It was time.

Jacob hauled the cast-iron hatch to one side. It felt as light as a sheet of aluminum foil because of the pent-up energy fit to burst free of his body. The light shone down into the pit below, and he immediately did a double take. *What the fuck?* The Donovan girl wasn't moving. She was facedown in the corner she'd been using to piss and shit. Dead or dying? It didn't matter. The bitch had tricked him into thinking she no longer wanted to take her own life, and then done something to herself.

He sat down on the edge of the opening and lowered himself down into the hole. This was not how he had imagined the ending. Not at all. It wasn't meant to happen here, with three stiffs giving him the open-dead-eye stare. It was supposed to be in the farmhouse's main bedroom, on the mattress where he'd been making himself sweat thinking about what he was going to do to her. Maybe she'd enjoy it, maybe not.

The disruption to his plan was disappointing, but not catastrophic. No need to panic and lose control. The only question was whether there was time to hoist her out of the tomb and carry her across to the main building. Or do it here? Was the risk of acting out his fantasies worth it? Did he have a choice? Nothing could put out the fire once the dry twigs of brutal desire had caught a spark.

Jacob bent down to drag her up, and that's when he heard the alarm: the motion-detection system he'd rigged up at the far end of the driveway. He planted a boot on the chest of Dukes's corpse, using it to reach the hatch and heave himself back up into the icehouse. He rushed over to the MacBook, muted the alarm, and selected the camera covering the sensor that had just activated. There was a figure. The quality of the image was poor in the failing daylight.

He shot out of the icehouse and around the rear of the barns. Entered the farmhouse through a back door and made his way through the kitchen and hallways to the front. He edged along the wall and took a sideways glance through the window. The figure was still there. Moving slowly, using the overgrown cornfield as cover. No apparent company, but acting too suspicious to be a lone hiker who'd taken a wrong turn.

Jacob eased the door open and commando-crawled out onto the porch. With the binoculars, he saw the figure was a man in his late twenties, taking tentative steps and swiveling his head side to side, as though he expected to be ambushed at any moment. Definitely not a hiker. Apart from the behavior, the smart suit and gun in his right hand were giveaways. Then the man's demeanor changed, and he began marching faster. He was closing in.

The Helper had said someone would come, and here they were. He'd said it wouldn't be a SWAT team, and he'd kept his word. He'd said *you can handle it*, and he was right. Jacob wasn't the biggest fan of guns, but sometimes they were a necessary evil. He drew the Colt Python from its scabbard and began the final countdown: ten, nine, eight, seven, six, five…

CHAPTER 48

VIRGO VAULTED a cedar rail fence and rolled straight onto his belly, deep in the long grass, just as a gunshot rang out on the other side of the ranch buildings. *Bang, bang, bang.* Three more in rapid succession. This was the place. As if there'd ever been any doubt. The explosions were too far away to be Whitlock out on the track, but this was a distraction that provided the opportunity to break cover and make ground. He leapt up and sprinted for the big pine-wood barn with a steep corrugated-iron pitched roof.

The door had been padlocked, but the hasp had been ripped out of the battens with a wrecking bar. He pulled one of the doors open and saw Bailey's Dodge and a Toyota pickup. Checked both of them quickly for weapons, but they were clean. He grabbed an ancient shovel on the way out and headed for the farmhouse. The muscles in his legs were heavy, like running through molasses. He knew it was too late.

A pitted horseshoe hung horns-up over the rear door of the farmhouse, placed there once upon a time to ward off evil spirits. It might have done its job for decades, but not now.

Wickedness was inside. The time for circumspection was over, but Virgo knew his energy reserves were running low. He steeled himself for one last effort and charged into the kitchen, metal edge of the shovel poised to strike out or slash. Empty. Dirty pots piled in the sink. A stench of rotting food and flesh. Blowflies crawling on every surface and blotting out the windows.

He bowled straight on through into the hallway and then the first room on the right. All his military training on how to safely search a building was for nothing. He was past caring. If there'd been a boobytrap, he'd have been blown into oblivion, but there was nothing. A stained mattress on the floor and a pile of men's clothes. Total absence of evidence to indicate it was where Stacy had been held.

What was that? Virgo was about to enter the opposite bedroom, when movement flashed in the corner of his eye. Something in front of the farmhouse. He ran out onto the porch. There it was. A hulking figure dragging a body by the ankles down the last section of driveway. He didn't need to see a face to know the body was Whitlock. What had possessed the kid to leave the track? Guilt or a sudden overwhelming desire to prove himself?

Virgo saw a camping table and chair on the porch, with a pair of binoculars. The lookout post. Also a laptop displaying a grainy black-and-white image. He went to take a closer look, but the hulk had seen him, dropped Whitlock, and lumbered towards the porch. The size of an elephant, in a full paper suit and Redskins cap. Eight-inch revolver made to look like a tiny toy in his hand. Virgo couldn't be sure, but there was something about the pockmarked chin and ridged, simian brow that he'd seen before, an age ago.

Time for a tactical retreat. Virgo backed away towards the fly-screen door. A garden implement was no match for a .357 Magnum cartridge. The giant was closing, but still thirty yards away. Too far to fire accurately with just one hand on the gun and running at a gallop. Something punched Virgo in the shoulder. It spun him round and off balance. As he nose-dived onto the boards, two firecrackers echoed somewhere a million miles away. *Shit.* He'd been hit.

He got onto his knees and went to pull himself up with his right hand, but nothing happened. Total fail. The weight of his body made him topple sideways down onto the boards. Now the pain kicked in. A Jedi had inserted a lightsaber next to his shoulder blade, and plasma was burning into his tissue. He rolled over onto his back. How long did he have?

Think. Standard revolver holds six bullets. He'd heard four shots when he was at the rear of the farmhouse, and now two more. What if Whitlock got one off first? That left one in the cylinder. Or maybe his opponent was old school, and only loaded five, so as to leave the trigger on an empty chamber for safety? Unlikely. No, his best chance was to make it inside. Find a place from where he could launch a counterattack, even though the element of surprise might be lost if he left a trail of blood. Hobson's choice. He used his good arm to get vertical, and lunged for the fly-screen handle.

Whoa. What just happened? Who moved the door? He crashed into the jamb and collapsed in a heap. Grappled himself upright again, like a drunk trying to make it off the floor for a final nightcap brandy. The sky was spinning. His body had gone into shock, and he had to get the circulation firing again. The brain needed oxygen, but it wasn't the right time to lie down and put his feet up in the air. He relaxed his stomach and concentrated on breathing.

The world came back into focus, but it was too late. The barrel of a gun was six feet from his chest. A face he now recognized cracked into a grotesque grin. So this was how he was going to meet his death. Blown away by an oversized child psychopath called Jacob, now grown into an adult one.

Even bigger, but the same deranged kid that Hartman had used as a case study on the initial training course for FBI negotiators. Textbook maniac. Hartman said it showed that you could communicate with the devil if you followed the bureau's Behavioral Change Stairway Model of negotiation. Looked like he and Beelzebub had kept in touch.

Virgo said, 'You're Jacob Hollingworth.'

The textbook maniac looked confused. 'Don't say my name.'

'You don't have to do this. I can help you.'

'Not this time.' Jacob made a barely perceptible shake of his head. 'No more hospital.'

'No more hospital.' Virgo went with the old mirror technique. Rinse and repeat. 'No more hospital.'

Jacob hesitated. Sweat ran down his forehead, and both sets of knuckles whitened on the grip of the revolver.

Virgo said, 'What do you want to do when this is over?'

Jacob's brow puckered into a frown. A guttural, but unintelligible sound escaped from his mouth.

'How can we make it better than last time?' Another question to keep the pressure on.

Jacob said, 'No more hospital.'

Virgo nodded. 'Yes, no more hospital.' The new mantra. He could keep saying it, if it bought time. 'No more hospital.'

Then something flickered behind Jacob's porcine eyes, and he took a step closer. Threatening and agitated. 'You're Virgo.'

It wasn't the moment to do the *actually-I'm-a- Gemini* gag. 'Calm down. I'm here to help you.'

Without any indication, Jacob pulled the trigger. The hammer reared up and snapped down. *Click.* No firecracker went off. Whitlock hadn't managed to get a shot away. Bless him. All six had come from the revolver pointing at his sternum, and now it was empty.

Virgo didn't wait for an invitation. He drove his left fist

into Jacob's nose, rotating the wrist for maximum impact. At the same time, the butt of the gun crashed into the side of his own head and sent him sprawling onto his front. Cheek pressed against the decking boards. Dizzy from blood loss. Spidey-sense kicked in, and he twisted his head back just as the sole of a boot stamped down.

He needed to get up, or he was finished. Now came the toecap of the boot, swinging towards his face. He shot out his left arm and blocked it. Shudders ran through his body. He tried to flip himself out of the way before the next one came, like a salmon on dry land. *Booooof...* A size 14 industrial boot struck him in the ribs. No pain. Something in his brain had stopped registering damage. He rolled and rolled again.

When he stopped, he caught sight of the old shovel. Grabbed the shaft one-handed, and whipped it up and around in one movement. The iron scoop caught Jacob on the side of his neck. Not a clean strike, but enough to break the skin and cause him to stagger backwards. Virgo forced himself up onto his feet. Senses still swimming. Not in peak combat condition, but now he had a weapon.

Jacob pawed at the wound on the side his neck, and the sight of his own blood seemed to enrage him even more. He flared his nostrils and charged. Virgo was ready. This time he jabbed the blade of the shovel forward, like a fencer thrusting out an epee, and Jacob came onto it at speed. The rusty metal edge met Jacob square on the chin and snapped his head backwards. He was dazed. He tried to charge again, but his legs had gone. He tottered in a squiggly arc, then fell down the porch steps into the dirt.

Virgo went after him. He couldn't move fast, but he got there in time. Jacob lay on his back, blinking, as though he couldn't understand why he was looking up at the sky. The opportunity was there to neutralize him forever. Virgo stood with the blade of the shovel resting on the hulk's throat, and blood from his own shoulder dripping crimson patterns onto the white coveralls. He was tempted. One swift guillotine chop and it was over. He had no qualms about playing the roles of judge and executioner. Mad or bad, it's all subjective. But there was something more important.

'Where's Stacy?'

Jacob said, 'Dead.'

'Where is she?'

'Take a fucking hike, pal.' Jacob had trouble moving his jaw. The words were stunted.

'Do you want to go back to the hospital, or a one-way trip to hell?' Virgo lifted the shovel.

Jacob pulled a crooked smile. 'Go on, do it.'

Virgo cursed himself. Never try and bluff a psychopath. 'Where's Agent Bailey?'

'Same as the other one. Dead as shit.'

'Why don't we save time? Tell me where they are.' Virgo looked around for something to tie his prisoner up with. There were cables on the porch, but he didn't want to risk it. Too far away. He tried to think of alternatives, then realized he was swaying. The ground moved. Tiredness washed over him.

Jacob laughed. 'Hey, you're bleeding out, pal.'

Virgo shook himself. He knew he didn't have long before consciousness left him. A last dose of adrenalin squirted itself into his bloodstream, and he went for the steps back up onto the porch. The shovel was too heavy to carry, so he dropped it, and his eyesight came and went. He couldn't think straight. He knew he needed to finish searching the farm. Stacy and Bailey were there somewhere. If there was the slightest chance of saving them, he had to do it.

He'd reached the fly-screen door when he saw a reflection in the glass. Virgo drew on his final reserves of energy to spin and deliver a roundhouse kick into Jacob's thigh. The paralysis was instant, but temporary. He sent an angled front snap-kick into Jacob's kneecap and expected to see the joint give way. It didn't. The strength wasn't there. He tried to land a massive left hook, but when his fist came up against Jacob's cheekbone, the big man didn't flinch. There was no power behind it. Reserve gas tank empty.

The only option left was to get the other side of the door before Jacob regained mobility. He went for it, but a huge hand clamped his shoulder in a vise and stopped him. Everything went fuzzy. He was swiveled round. Couldn't breathe. When his eyes focused, he saw the grinning face of a deranged demon.

Jacob had both giant paws wrapped around Virgo's windpipe, and he was pinned up against the timber wall. Nowhere to go. He used his good hand to try and prize the choking fingers off his throat, but it was no good. He didn't have the strength left or the leverage. Instead, he lashed out with his left fist, but Jacob had him at arm's length, and the blows couldn't reach their target.

Black spots appeared in front of his eyes. He was dying. He kicked upwards as hard as he could into Jacob's groin, but it made no difference. Either the freak was a eunuch, or he had brass balls. He thrashed about with his body, as violently as he could to try and break free, but Jacob had him nailed up on the wall, with no weight on his feet.

More spots clouded his vision. He thought he saw Crystal. She was waving to him. Wearing the pastel-lemon linen dress she always took on holiday. They were on the trip to Europe that they'd spent months planning and saving for. Saint Peter's Square, Rome. He'd lost her in the crowds outside the Basilica and panicked. Gone racing around, bumping into backpackers and tour parties, with a lump the size of a basketball in his chest. His worst nightmare. Then a gap opened up in the sea of bodies, and she was there. Everything in the world was restored to its perfect order, and he could relax. It was over…

The pressure on his neck disappeared. Death had arrived to save him more suffering. Except he could now feel the ground beneath his feet. *What the…* He choked and coughed and rubbed his throat. *What the fuck…* There were no massive hands there anymore. He shook his head and opened his eyes. *What the fuck is that?*

Jacob Hollingworth stood in front of him. Six inches of stiletto steel protruding from the front of his chest. Not the hilt of a knife, the tip. He'd been skewered from behind, by a blade as big as a sword. There was a look of surprise, almost comic amusement on his face. Then there was a hideous squelching sound as the knife was slowly withdrawn, and his face changed. He looked scared and desperate. He opened his mouth to say something, but his legs buckled, and he went down.

Stacy Donovan lifted the oversized blade above her head and screamed like a banshee. Then she brought it down. Her kidnapper was already dead before the second strike harpooned the midline of his torso to the wooden deck and left him stapled there on display, the most grotesque butterfly of any collection.

CHAPTER 49

THE VISTA CAME STRAIGHT from a holiday brochure, or maybe a child's coloring book. Sun glistened on a cobalt Caribbean, and yacht sails tacked on the trade winds coming down from Cartagena. On the horizon, the Rosario Islands sat sprinkled like chunks of cookie dough on blue icing, and by the shore, waves rolled onto a private beach in a languid, hypnotic rhythm. Virgo helped himself to another Scotch and sank back into the leather sofa to try and relax, and admire one of the best views Colombia had to offer.

He sat in an expansive, air conditioned glass atrium. To one side, a massive kitchen with more marble-countertop than Home Depot, and to the other, a paved terrace and infinity pool, with its own swim-up bar. Decadent, but cool. He swirled the ice around in his tumbler to make it melt a little faster, then poured the Scotch down his throat. It was probably some kind of sacrilege to down a Macallan single malt in one hit, but he was tense and restless despite the luxuriant surroundings.

There was a sound of keys jangling and a door being

closed. Nick Hartman walked into the kitchen, carrying a gym bag, and started to press numbers on the alarm pad.

Virgo said, 'Zero, six, nine, three, delta.'

Hartman dropped the duffel, and turned round. The bureau's greatest-ever living ex-negotiator lost for words.

'I still use my old badge number for PIN and passwords as well.' Virgo eased himself up out of the sofa. 'Guess we're both creatures of habit.'

'What do you want?' Hartman had found his voice, but it was cold.

Virgo ignored the question and gestured around the interior of the mansion. 'Nice place.'

'Okay, how much do you want?'

'That depends.' Virgo scratched his chin. 'How much did you make from short-selling the stocks of those companies involved in Babylon Inferno? Did you manipulate both Wall Street and the London markets?'

'I think you already know how much.'

'Not really.' That was true. Virgo had asked the accountants in the bureau's white-collar-crime team, but they couldn't put a figure on it. Hartman had instructed multiple traders to place bets on the value of shares in several companies going down. Bagshaw-AI being the main one. After Daniel Donovan gave his bombshell announcement on primetime TV, the stocks had tumbled as soon as the markets opened Monday morning. A conservative estimate was that he'd cleared $30 million.

Hartman walked over to the kitchen island. 'Come on, give me your account details, and I can transfer it now.'

'If you're going for the pistol that's Gorilla-taped beneath the overhang, I've already emptied the mag.' Virgo pulled a handful of 9mm shells out of his pocket and rattled them. 'It would be really embarrassing for both us if you pointed it at me and the thing just went *click, click, click.*'

Hartman faltered, but recovered well. He picked up a pen and jotter. 'No, I mean it. Give me a number. Think big.'

'The beauty of your scheme was that it didn't rely on Babylon Inferno being actually mothballed for good. All it needed was someone with the senator's profile to say that it wasn't going to get funded.'

'Listen, I'm not going to apologize.' Hartman bristled. 'The bureau fucked me. Thirty years, and for what?'

Virgo turned and looked out the panoramic window. The hubris of the man disgusted him. 'I went to Bailey's funeral. Did you know she had two kids?'

'That shouldn't have happened, or the killing of that intel clerk who wanted to make agent.'

'His name was Mitch Whitlock. I went to his funeral too.' Virgo stared out at the ocean, the sight of its endless journey keeping him calm. 'You can say their deaths were never your intention, but what about Stacy Donovan? Or are you going to blame your pet freak for what he was going to do to her?'

Hartman shook his head and didn't say anything. He still had the pen and jotter in his hands, as though money would always get its own way in the end.

Virgo laughed. 'You sprang him out of hospital, and me out of jail. Two of life's failures sent on a mission to make you a fortune.'

'My bad. I didn't realize what a truly fucked-up crackpot you are. You make him look sane.'

'Is that really why you chose me for the job? Because you thought I was past it? Soft in the head?'

Hartman said nothing.

Virgo huffed to himself. 'Maybe you were right.'

Hartman had overcome his shock of coming home to find an uninvited guest. He dropped the pen and pad and came over to the atrium. The swagger was back. Virgo looked him up and down for any sign of contrition, but there was none.

His old boss had shed a few pounds, but that was probably down to his new lifestyle, not pangs of guilt. The clothes were smarter too. No battered straw trilby and soup-stained tie. He wore pressed shorts and a crisp shirt with a crocodile motif. Maybe the disheveled harebrain had all been an act for the benefit of his work colleagues. Sometimes, people you thought you knew well turn out to have a different side.

Virgo said, 'It's over, Nick.'

'No, no, no. Remember the five key principles of negotiation.' Hartman was animated. Arms flailing, and eyes out on stalks. The magnetism that had once made him a great teacher was still there. 'Always remain adaptable and open-minded. There's times when you have to be flexible and open to new ideas to reach a solution. Things evolve. Life's dynamic. Let's explore the opportunities.'

'What was that other key principle you used to talk about so much?'

'Preparation?'

'Trust.' Virgo shook his head. 'You can't have a constructive discussion with someone who doesn't trust you.'

Hartman looked like he was going to argue the point, but changed his mind. 'Please yourself. Nice work tracking me down, but I came here for a reason.'

'Cocaine?'

'No extradition treaty with the United States.'

'I know.' Virgo scratched the itch in the small of his back, and his hand came back clutching a Glock 19. 'Who said anything about extradition?'

Hartman froze. 'Eddie, let's talk. Remember what happened in Mexico.'

Virgo stared into the panicked eyes. He'd come here for one reason only. Justice. Sometimes it's tempting to put your principles to one side and take an easier route through life, but Virgo couldn't do it. He was bound by an overriding doctrine: never compromise. And that's why Virgo walked up to Hartman, pressed the barrel to the man's perspiring head, and blew out his brains.

CHAPTER 50

ACCARDI TOOK a swig of Corona Light and said, 'I mean, what are you actually going to do?'

'I don't know.' Virgo's bottom lip hung out in an indication of uncertainly. 'Drive up and down the coast. Go for hikes.'

'On the Pacific or back east?'

'I'm sticking as far away from Quantico, Virginia, as I can.'

'But you did get the all clear? The bureau rescinded the arrest order?'

'It was the DOJ. They said it would amount to gross unfairness.'

'Guess it helped that you saved Stacy's life.'

They were sitting in canvas chairs outside Virgo's RV. It was a preloved Winnebago Porto, parked on the boulevard in front of Santa Barbara's east beach. Between the dunes and the palm fronds, you could just see the old oil-drilling platforms in the channel, shimmering in the haze like giant, mechanical arachnids. Turn inland, and the Santa Inez mountains beckoned with boutique wineries and lavender pastures. Not a bad place to do nothing.

Accardi fished a packet of cigarettes out of her bag. Marlboro Red, not Camel. 'Don't vagrants get rousted by the state highway patrol?'

'I don't mind if they move me on. New day, new location. No time to get stale.'

Accardi couldn't find her lighter. She tipped the contents of her bag out and rummaged out a plastic disposable. 'You're fucking weird, you know that?'

'Yes.'

'Still want to meet up at the Edelweiss Inn and Suites in three years?'

Virgo smiled. 'Thought it was five?'

'You don't have to answer.' She jumped in. Lit the Marlboro. 'It's in my diary. That's all I'm saying.'

Virgo stood up and flipped the burgers on the foil barbecue. 'How's Stacy?'

'Back in college. Doing good.'

'She's strong.'

'It took two CSI guys to pull that German knife out of the porch boards.'

'I meant mentally.' Virgo took another beer out of the coolbox and twisted off the cap. He'd not seen Stacy Donovan since she'd visited him in hospital, but the grit in her character had stayed with him. She'd turned up unannounced and unaccompanied at the intensive care unit to thank him for saving her life, and he had reciprocated, because if it weren't for her medical training, he'd have died before assistance arrived at Rosstal farm. A kind of poetic balance.

'She must get it from her mother, because that jerk of a father is weak as piss.' Accardi screwed her face up. 'He screams about privacy and press intrusion, then signs up for an exclusive TV series.'

Virgo was nonplussed. 'I don't have a television or listen to the news.'

'Don't say it as though it's something to be proud of.' Accardi pointed a Marlboro at him. 'You a hermit as well as a vagrant now?'

'What's he done, Senator Donovan?'

'Made a pact with the devil. Stage-managed interviews, where he breaks down and cries with repentance for his historic sins of the flesh, and in others, blames his dead brother for sneaking dirty money into his bank accounts.' One episode is just Stacy's abduction and how the trauma has made him a better person. It's all about him.' Accardi pretended to stick a finger down her throat and vomit.

'He's just thinking about the next election. It's what politicians do.'

Twenty yards down the street, the *thump, thump, thump* started up again. Guy in his twenties outside a campervan, beating the hell out of a full drum kit set up on the edge of the path used by cyclists and joggers. Not busking, just playing to the Pacific Ocean for his own pleasure. A little closer, an old woman with a bow-legged Labrador sat cross-stitching a giant sunflower, powered by regular sips of what looked like sherry.

Virgo knew he was part of a strange, paradoxical community now. People who had opted out of society or changed their relationship with it: the nomads, the beach and bush-dwellers, loners, dreamers and ordinary folk just running away from something life had thrown at them. It kind of suited him. There was no pressure to conform, and the constant sound of waves turning over made the night-times less of an ordeal. But...

There was a loud, exaggerated cough, and when he looked up, something in Accardi's face had changed.

She stubbed out the cigarette. 'Been down to Colombia lately?'

'Okay, now we're getting to the real reason for you coming up the coast to see me.'

'No, really, I was worried about you living in a tin box and burning the crap out of budget beef patties.'

Shit. Virgo saw a grease fire had flared up on the throwaway griddle. He tonged the burgers across to a smoke-free section. 'Hartman killed himself. The coroner had no doubts.'

'Funny thing to do when you've just hit the jackpot on the stock exchange.'

'Remorse is a powerful emotion.'

'Do you think a cold-blooded bastard like Hartman ever felt a moment's contrition for what he did?'

'Everyone's got a breaking point.'

'Bullshit. Some people are so evil they never register the pain they inflict on others. The deluded ones are worse — those who think they're genetically superior.'

Virgo didn't much like the direction the conversation was going. He pointed the barbecue tongs. 'So, what do you think, Detective?'

'The report said Hartman shot himself in the head with his FBI service weapon.'

'Did you think he'd have handed it in? Maybe he was in a bit of a rush to flee the country, after he'd kidnapped a senator's daughter and got three fellow agents killed.'

'I was just wondering if it was the same Glock 19 that was in your possession when you were arrested at La Souris nightclub.'

Virgo stayed schtum and tried to decipher the spangle that had just appeared in her eye. Either it was mischief or a zeal to enforce the law without fear or favor.

She said, 'Remember? In the interview room? You said it was Hartman's personal issue.'

'Did I?' A tingle of ice ran down Virgo's spine. 'Whatever happened to that gun?'

'Yes, in fact, I made a note of the serial number and tried to call Hartman to verify it was his.'

'A record of the serial number? Should be easy to check against the one found next to Hartman's body.' Virgo managed to squeeze out a weak smile of resignation. Looked like his days as a nomad were over. Ironic, because he thought he'd been smart covering his tracks this time. In Mexico, he'd acted in a rage in front of witnesses; in Colombia, he'd gone to great lengths to make sure his cold revenge was concealed. Maybe he just wasn't cut out to be a killer in the civilian world.

'I brought the note with me.' Accardi picked up a folded sheet of paper from amongst the strewn contents of her bag. 'Thought we might phone the coroner and check to see if the serial numbers match.' She stood up, eyes laughing now, and held the edge of the paper over the grill. 'Oops, how did that happen?' A flame from one of the cremated patties caught the sheet, and she held it until the fire had consumed all but one corner, which she then dropped onto the barbecue.

Virgo watched the final piece of incriminating evidence turn into ash. It can be a fine line between freedom and incarceration, but this time he was on the right side of it.

Midnight, he lay in the bed of his Winnebago and listened to the ocean. Its infinite cadence resonated and eased the dog-whistle blare in his left ear, but did nothing to fill the gap next to him, where Crystal should have been. In his soul, it was hard to imagine a day when her loss didn't overshadow his own mundane existence, but he knew it would come. Time heals, even if you don't want the prescription.

He rolled onto his back, hands behind his head, and gazed up at the stars through the uncovered skylight. It was still difficult to dwell too long on the future. To him, it was an unwritten chapter, and he wasn't sure what he was going to type next or what ending to plan. The responsibility scared him, and he wished he could flick back through the pages to an earlier time, when it wasn't just him. The only thing he'd ever known how to do was fight or work, and now both were gone for good. There would come a day when he needed motivation to get out of bed in the morning, but who'd want to hire a convicted murderer that NBC News had labeled, *the crazy guy*? Of course, there'd been loads of TV coverage on his role in the Donovan case, and some of the media outlets had gone to town on his FBI past and what had happened down in Guerreo state. Water off a duck's back. Hiking and meandering up the beauty spots of Highway 1 would have to do, and it was better than jail.

Virgo didn't know what time he'd fallen asleep, but it was 03:47 when a notification on his phone pinged to wake him up. He unlocked the screen and squinted at the brightness of the message:

> My name is Rosalind Palmer. I'm the CEO of a multinational corporation based in the US, and one of our senior managers in Brazil has been taken hostage. Call me on this number if you want the job.

He rolled out of bed, found a quarter in his pants' pocket, and flipped it. Not a classic decision-making model in the world of professional law enforcement, but it was the best he could come up with. Sometimes, the only thing you can trust is fate.

ABOUT THE AUTHOR

Did you enjoy *Zero Hour*? Please consider leaving a review on Amazon to help other readers discover the book.

———

Growing up, Steve Sheffield always wanted to be a writer and went to university where he managed to gain a bachelor's degree in English Literature. However, due to spending too much money on drink, he was forced to abandon his literary ambitions and get a job in the police, where the pay was more reliable. He became a detective and worked multiple homicide inquiries and investigations into organized crime, while also completing a master's degree in Criminology. The final seven years of his service in the force, he was head of a specialized crime department responsible for intelligence, surveillance, drugs and undercover operations. These days he writes books about a different kind of investigation and justice — quicker, unorthodox, brutal and generally more satisfying. He still spends too much on drink.

Printed in Great Britain
by Amazon

56027482R00158